blurred lines

Originally Titled When the Stars Align

The West Side Series
Book One

isabel jolie

ISABEL JOLIE

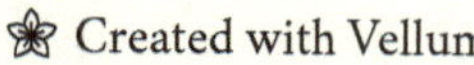 Created with Vellum

one

ANNA

The snow-white pigeon swoops up and down, flirting with the reflection within the sliding doors. A sign of things to come, Al would say. My Australian labradoodle quivers at my side, ready to charge. The glass door slides open, and the pigeon flies sky high out of sight.

"Chewbacca, how was your Sunday morning walk girl?" My big curly beast wags her tail so hard her whole body wiggles and weaves. She leaps onto Al, completely oblivious to her human on the other end of the leash. Both paws land right above Al's protruding, bulbous belly. He laughs and gives her a treat. A *treat*.

"Al, you can't give her a treat when she jumps on you." A good dog owner would scold her sixty-five-pound canine and tell her to get down, but these two have a sort of odd love thing going on.

Al ignores me. Normal. "Did you see the pigeon circling the glass?"

"Yes! Have you ever seen a pigeon do that?"

"Nope. Must be a sign. Good things coming."

I smirk. Al and his signs. I'd estimate Al is in his mid-fifties. He's wearing the building doorman uniform of black pants and white button-down shirt. His shirt's never starched. Al and I share an aversion to ironing. We don't share a belief in random signs directing our destiny.

When Al sees Chewie, he always steps out to greet her. He scratches behind her ears, and she licks his chin, making him laugh. Because, yes, she's *still* standing on her hind legs with both paws planted on his chest. Crumbs from the treat she inhaled litter his wrinkled shirt.

"Is someone moving in today? I noticed the curtains are hanging in the elevator." The building hangs quilts to protect the sides of the elevator from gashes during a move. My apartment building, The Wimbledon, features twenty-six floors and four elevator shafts. This one building houses as many people as some suburban neighborhoods. Weekend moves are the norm.

"Yeah, two units. One on your floor, actually."

"Nice." There are six apartments on my floor, but my neighbors are relative strangers. I have one mean, grumpy neighbor who complains any time Chewie barks. "Any chance Sixteen-C moved out?"

Al grins and in baby talk answers my question to Chewie's bushy face. "No. Mr. Truman's still there, so Chewie here has to be quiet. You have to be quiet, don't you, girl? No barking, right, girl? Gotta be quiet. Yeah, that's a good girl. Such a good girl. Such a good, good girl."

Chewie responds by wagging her tail and licking him from the bottom of his chin up to his nose. He laughs, her front paws fall to the floor.

"How's the weather out there today? Looks like it's a good one."

"It's gorgeous. You should definitely take your lunch outside. Blue skies. Not a cloud anywhere. The high's gonna be sixty-eight.

Couldn't ask for a better September day. Next week, we've got a cold front heading in. But by the end of the week, warm weather will be back."

I nod as he shares the forecast. Al's a walking, talking weather report. "We did the full loop around Central Park today. Some of the leaves have started changing color."

I peer out the glass doors of the lobby at the street and the facing brick building. Cars whiz by, and a faint horn sounds every now and then. You can't see the sky from where I'm standing, but the blue sky and fall-scented air lurk in my mind. A stunning weekend day, yet work calls. It's fine. I have a good view from my home office. "I'm gonna head on up. I'll see you later. You here until six?"

"You know it," Al responds with his signature wink and gunshot finger point.

"See ya later."

Chewie and I only have to wait a minute for the elevator. We walk in, and I hum a bit as I scratch the top of her head. The stainless steel elevator door slides to close. A hand shoots through the gap to force the door open. Chewie lunges, and I tighten my grip on the leash. "Chewie!" I scold.

Once I have my shaggy girl under control, I lift my gaze from my dog and take in the man standing on the threshold of the elevator. My mouth drops open. My lungs contract.

Hazel eyes I haven't seen in four years stare back at me. The blue-gray suit offsets those chameleon eyes, casting a bluer hue. The short, trimmed beard makes him appear older and more distinguished. The dark, curly, college student hair, now cut in a shorter, controlled, professional style, says business.

My skin tingles. From shock or from being in his presence again, I'm not sure.

Jackson's eyes flick between me and my rambunctious, shaggy brown beast. "Anna?"

"Jackson?" Chewie attempts to jump on him, and I give a quick pull on the leash and command, "Sit." I close my mouth, but I'm still gaping. How could I not be? Jackson lives in Atlanta. I never thought I'd see him again.

Through my peripheral vision, I notice Jackson's hands flexing, as if he's stretching his fingers. He blinks his eyes in rapid succession. I imagine he's as shocked as I am. He half shakes his head and exits the elevator. My stomach freefalls. A second later, he wheels in two large black suitcases.

My heart's beating a million beats per minute, and I stare at the panel of floor buttons. The door slides closed, and the elevator lurches upward. Proper elevator etiquette reflex compels me to ask, "What floor?"

He doesn't answer but leans over to the panel with his index finger extended. Then he slowly pulls back. "You've already pushed it. Sixteen."

I blink. My heartrate speeds as I scratch Chewie's ears, trying to collect my scattered self. The moment is surreal. I fold an arm against my stomach and focus on breathing until the elevator doors open and we both exit.

The silver door slides closed behind him, leaving us standing in the hall facing each other.

"So, are you visiting someone?" Judging from the two oversized suitcases, either he's the worst packer on the planet or he's staying a while. Or maybe he's not alone?

His Adam's apple shifts as he swallows. His gaze wanders over the length of my body, sending chills through my core. This man has intimate knowledge of me, of us. My cheeks burn with the thought, or perhaps it's simply his presence. I cross my arms, defensive. What on earth is he doing here?

His chest heaves, and I hear his exhale. "I'm moving in." He peers down the beige hall lined with dark green painted doors.

Dull brass numbers hang on the front of each door. I'm Sixteen-B, and we're standing in front of Sixteen-C.

He points to the end of the hall. "I'm Sixteen-D."

I point in the opposite direction. "Sixteen-B."

Our voices mingle and crash over each other as we speak at the same time.

"Ah, you're moving here?" My voice comes out squeaky and high-pitched. *Get it together. He's just a guy you used to know.*

He stares ahead at the elevator door. "Good job opportunity."

"What are you doing?"

"Law."

"Are short answers your thing now?" It comes out bitchier than intended.

He narrows his eyes into slits. "I'm at a new firm. M&A. What are you doing these days?" His gruff tone is oddly appealing, although completely undeserved.

"I'm a creative director. At an agency called Evolve." It's on the tip of my tongue to say more, to tell him I work on the Heineken, Greenpeace, and National Geographic accounts. But I stop myself. His dark gaze radiates an unfriendliness I'm not sure how to navigate. Chewie stands beside me, tail still, watching, a sign she's picked up on the tension. She's unsure of Jackson, and so am I.

Jackson angles his head in the direction of my apartment door. "Do you live alone?"

"Yes. I had a roommate up until two months ago. She moved to Prague." I could rattle on but don't. My gaze falls to his chest. His hand rests on the handle of one of the suitcases. Beneath his jacket, he's wearing a form-fitting starched shirt. Subtle muscular lines lead to a firm, narrow waist. His clothes fit so well I suspect they are custom. I also imagine he still flaunts a six-pack, because, well, he did in college.

I flush, visualizing his pectoral and ab muscles. The hardness of those muscles beneath my roaming fingers. Over the years, I've thought about him often. Most often when playing with my favorite vibrator. The stuffy hall is far too warm, and I hope the burning sensation on my cheeks doesn't mean I'm blushing.

We stand there staring at each other. I have so much to ask him, but then again, I don't. Things didn't exactly end well with us. But he's new to the city. *Be kind.* "Do you need help getting unpacked?"

The muscles in his jaw flex as if he's grinding his teeth. "No, thank you. Take care." He heads down the hall, pulling his two suitcases behind him. He stands in front of the door and flips through keys on a ring. He looks up from his keys and catches me staring. Now my cheeks are most definitely bright red. With a shaky hand, I unlock my door and rush inside.

Stunned, I flop down on my futon, a relic from my first post-college days. The stained, beaten-up piece could stand an upgrade, but sofa shopping doesn't interest me.

I pull out my phone and press my best friend's name. She may live in another country, but she's still my BFF. My first call.

She picks up. It's evening, her time. Before she gets a word in, I blurt, "You are not going to believe who moved into the building. On our floor!"

two

. . .

JACKSON

Wandering into the sports bar with Chase, my gaze floats to the ceiling where men's neckties hang. A thick layer of spider web-like dust clings to most of them. The bar has a tradition of cutting men's ties off and nailing them to the ceiling. College teams and associated paraphernalia litter the walls and shelves. My shoes grip the sticky floor, and the place reeks of spilled alcohol and what might be vomit doused in Clorox. No surprise Chase Maitlin would choose a shithole like this to watch the game.

Nodding at the bartender, I order a Michelob Ultra and claim the stool next to Chase. The LSU and Tulane game runs on all seven screens scattered around the sports bar. A game I couldn't care less about.

After my early morning flight, and after getting an unwelcome shock, I changed clothes and couldn't sit still. My furnished apartment requires no effort. Still, I headed out and purchased some things I'd need. Toilet paper, paper towels, coffee. Then I explored my new neighborhood before meeting Chase. Checked out the nearby delis, shops, and restaurants. I couldn't sit still and had no desire to return to the apartment.

Sitting, after pounding hard sidewalks all day, feels good. Pain radiates from the balls of my feet. "Man, I spent hours today walking around. My feet are killing me."

Chase leans over and glances at my feet then sort of chuckles. "You'll get used to it. We walk here way more than you probably did in Hotlanta."

"You're probably right," I agree, shaking my head. "Anyway, I can't get over how expensive this city is. Rent here costs the same as a mortgage on a four-bedroom home in Atlanta."

"How's your new place?" Chase asks, grinning.

I reach over and slap the side of his head. "About that. What the fuck, Chase? You set me up in Anna Daughtridge's apartment building?"

He smirks as he takes a long swallow of his draft beer. I roll my eyes. Chase lived with me my last two years of law school, along with two other guys from my class. Chase and one of my room-mates, Brandon, went to undergrad together. When Chase got into business school at Carolina, he moved in with us. Three law school students and one b-school student. There was no question which degree required more effort.

"Do you like the place or not?" he finally responds.

"It's fine. But you couldn't give me a heads up?"

He shrugs. "You guys dated a long time ago. And for, like, a New York minute. Does it matter?"

I angle my head and glare at him. Fucker. Yeah, it matters. Dickwad.

Before I respond, he continues, "Anna's friendly with her building manager. Tenants are moving in and out of The Wimbledon all the time. For some reason, the building manager allows subleases. I figured you'd have a good chance of finding something there. It's hard to find places in the city. And, presto. You got a sublease. How long's it for?"

I grit my teeth. There's no point in letting Chase have it. It'd go over his head. "It's month to month. I will say I lucked out with a furnished sublet. Tracey, the manager, she hooked me up by putting me in touch with this guy. He has six more months on his lease, but if I want, I can take it over when his lease is up." I pause as I sip my beer. "So, did you tell Anna you were asking for her building manager's contact info for me?"

Chase scratches the side of his head, and I can tell he's trying to remember the conversation. "No."

Fucker. Clueless as ever. But I shouldn't have asked him. The shock plastered on Anna's face when we ran into each other made that much clear.

"Look, man, you'll never see your neighbors. It's different here. And aren't you still looking for another place?"

"Yeah," I sigh, frustrated. "I had to readjust my criteria with the realtor. I have a few more places I'm going to check out. I had planned to buy pretty quickly, but I'm gonna need to take some time to research the market. Prices here are insane."

Chase taps his beer glass against mine. "Welcome to New York." And then he laughs. "What finally drew you here, anyway? I was shell-shocked when I got your email saying you were moving here. I seem to recall 'never New York' coming out of your mouth."

"I had a good offer. And things change," I say, tapping my fingers along my beer bottle to release frustration. The guy loves to push it.

"Yeah, things change. Doesn't mean I don't get a kick out of feeling your pain as you adjust to a real city. I remember visiting you in your palatial townhome." He grins.

"Yeah, well, you won't enjoy visiting me anymore." Thinking about what kind of apartment I'll likely end up buying makes me grimace. "I moved because it was a good offer. Junior partner now, senior partner within five years. Hopefully, I'll be name partner by the time I'm forty. The timeline here is way better than my old firm."

"Work, work, work. You know, there is more to life than just work, right?" Chase asks, eyebrows raised.

I study him. He's wearing khaki shorts, sneakers, and a faded t-shirt that reads, "I deliver all night long." The words surround an image of Santa's face. It is the weekend. But still, he's approaching thirty. He looks like a frat boy. Back in Chapel Hill, he partied hard. He'd been in business school when I was in law school. We'd had two different Chapel Hill experiences. And his attire and general demeanor tell me not much has changed over the last four years.

"More to life than work, says the almost married man?" I raise my eyebrows and tap his glass again, smiling. I doubt he's anywhere close to proposing, but I like to yank his chain.

He bites his lip and angles his eyes. "Where'd you get that idea from? Have you been talking to my mom?"

"Well, you have a serious girlfriend. I'm waiting for the announcement." A serious girlfriend is new for Chase. He always hooked up with random girls in grad school. A certain dark-haired girl I really liked comes to mind, and I grind my teeth.

"Yeah? Hold your breath while you wait," he says, a light smile on his face.

He watches the game, completely oblivious to how dark my thoughts dive. Years have passed, and I'm still pissed at him.

We drink our beers and watch the game for a while. During a commercial break, Chase pipes up, "I'll make sure you like it here. I'll introduce you around. If you decide you're okay with it, Anna can help too. She's a good friend of mine. She has a lot of friends around the city she can introduce you to."

Running into Anna had been beyond unexpected. At first, I wasn't sure if it was her. In some ways, she hasn't changed. But now she's even sexier than she was in college. It defies logic. Her Lycra leggings highlighted the muscular lines of those long legs. She'd had on this open zip-up hoodie over a workout tank top that shouldn't have been sexy, but I couldn't stop stealing glances at the soft lines of her cleavage and the flat stomach hugged by the form-fitting top. Her dark, wavy hair had been pulled back in a ponytail. Still long. No make-up. Fresh and natural. Just like back in college.

"I didn't know you two still kept in touch." I discreetly ball my left hand into a fist as my right circles my beer.

"Oh, yeah," he responds, focusing on the game.

That's it? My fist raps the table in frustration. *Come on, man. Give me more.*

"How long did you guys date?" I probe. If they're good friends four years later, the breakup must have been amicable.

Chase looks at me, squinting in thought, as if he's not sure he remembers the answer. "We didn't date."

"Well, you definitely hooked up. I seem to recall some great 'stories' you chose to share." I'd been so angry I avoided him the last few weeks of school.

Chase gives me his signature I'm-a-badass-frat-boy smirk. I suppress the urge to reach out and strangle him. He sighs. "You remember that, huh? Well, we decided to just be friends. And she's good friends with Angela, so don't mention it, okay?"

For some reason, that bothers the fuck out of me. I haven't met Angela yet. But it seems wrong she's hanging out with a girl who slept with her boyfriend and she has no idea. Isn't that girl code or something?

"Jackson?"

"Yeah. Of course." I shake my head, more at myself than Chase. What these guys do is not my business. "What's Anna up to these days?" And yeah, she's not my business, but I'm still curious about what she's like now. I'd never date her again, but still, I'm curious.

Standing in the hall earlier today, when she pointed at her

apartment door, I wondered if she lived with someone. At the very least, she's probably seeing someone.

There's something about Anna. A glow. A warmth. She's natural. Down-to-earth. A brown-eyed girl you wish had been your neighbor growing up. Faint freckles you can really only see when she doesn't have on any make-up at all. I close my eyes, trying to remember if I'd seen those freckles today.

Chase breaks into my thoughts. "She's a workaholic. Like you." He adds the "like you" with emphasis as if it disgusts him. I roll my eyes and take a gulp of beer.

"She dating anyone?"

I ask the question as nonchalantly as possible while feigning watching the game, but it still draws his attention. He jerks his head and grins. "You into her?"

"Dude. Just making conversation. Even if I was interested in Anna, and I'm not, I don't have time for a relationship. These next few years will be crunch time."

"You set your own priorities. But, yeah, the Jackson I remember had no reason to date. Girls made it way easy for you."

I don't argue. Let him think what he wants. Guys like Chase Maitlin always love to believe every guy is getting tons of random sex. Back in the day, Chase loved to gloat about his own adventures. That's never been me nor will it be.

"Well, times are changing. You've got a girlfriend," I say, tapping his drink in a soft salute.

He responds with a broad smile. "Yeah, you'll meet Angela soon. We'll be sure to invite you out so you can meet folks, expand your network." He rolls his shoulders, eyes to the game. "I'll take you out. Show you the New York singles scene. It blows Chapel Hill out of the water. Atlanta too."

"Thanks. But I need to get my bearings at my new firm. I won't have much free time."

"Yeah, right. You'll still find time to go out and get laid. And I want to hear all about it. Now that I've got a ball and chain I've got to live vicariously through my single friends."

I rub the back of my neck to ease my frustration. "Man, I'm not the guy you want to be living vicariously through. Trust me. Even back then. I think you've built me up in your head." I fall into my stern lawyer voice to convince him I'm speaking the truth.

He gives me a shit-eating grin. "Oh, fuck. Don't try to deny it. You hooked up with a different girl almost every time you went out. I couldn't believe how lucky you got. All. The. Time."

I laugh. Maitlin's still such a frat boy. "First, I studied until almost eleven. Then on the random nights I would meet you guys out, I'd show up completely sober. Everyone else would be tanked. It was like low-lying fruit all around. And you know Chapel Hill… like, seventy percent female. If you had come out with me later at night, sober, you too would have had girls clinging to you. They don't cling if you're hammered."

Chase laughs. "Yeah, right. That's what my problem was."

We sit there, watching the game, and have another round. I pull out my phone and check apartment listings. Pop questions to Chase about neighborhoods when I come across something interesting. Text back and forth with a few agents to set up some more appointments.

As the game ends, Chase downs the last of his beer and levels his gaze at me. "So, next weekend. Angela and I are going to meet some friends at Central Park. Supposed to be a nice fall day. Throw some Frisbee. Picnic. Take advantage of the nice weather before winter. You in?"

"Sure. Text me the deets, and if I can, I'll make it."

"Great. Angela definitely wants to meet you."

I hesitate, but there's no harm in asking. "Will Anna be there?"

He sticks his lower lip out before answering. "Maybe? Not sure. Probably. She hangs with us. Is it gonna be a problem?"

My eyes go to the ties hanging on the ceiling. A symbol of men rebelling against the institution. "Nah, it'll be fine." Four years have passed. It's fine.

We toss some bills on the bar for the tip and head out. Chase pauses by the door. "Man, about Anna. She's actually become a good friend. Like, a *good* friend of mine. So, don't treat her like the others, okay? We're in NYC. You can get plenty without having to muddy the waters with friends. *My* friends." He taps his chest to emphasize my.

Oh. Is that the way you want to play it? You short little fuck.

I glare at him as he continues talking. "I'm telling you, she's good people. You'll see. Don't fuck with her, man." He sighs. Then, as if remembering he and I are actually friends too, he adds, "Good to see ya', man. Glad you're here."

I scratch my jaw, incredulous, as we leave the bar. Chase is worried about Anna. Meanwhile, she crushed me. Still don't understand why, but I gave up trying to figure our situation out a long time ago. Pretty much gave up the same day Chase described her as "the best lay of his life."

Chase doesn't need to worry about Anna and me. No way am I going after that for a second round. Nope, never again.

three

ANNA

Music drifts through my office, an upbeat Jack Johnson tune. Some would think a raise would be the best thing about a promotion. Nope. My recent promotion to creative director means a private office and music courtesy of Alexa.

I had my choice of art from the agency's archive, and decided on a vintage Heineken life-size subway ad for one wall. The far wall showcases my favorite print ads for my clients. Brightly-colored throw pillows dot my off-white sofa, and fresh flowers sit in a vase on my desk, a Monday morning pick-me-up ritual and love note from me to me. Something I especially appreciate this morning, after my blast with the past.

This morning, I felt like the *Pink Panther* music should be playing on stereo as I stealthily opened my apartment door and carefully peeked out. After verifying a vacant hallway, I headed out for my morning walk. When we exited the building, I saw an athletic man who looked a bit like Jackson stretching. It might not have been him; it's hard to see in the low morning light. But I turned right and headed to the river. Silly, really. I'll run into him from time to time. Today, though, avoidance struck me as the best plan. Of course, four years ago, I chose avoidance, and then he stopped talking to me.

My office door pops open, and a blonde messy bun faces me, muttering as she searches the ground.

Grabbing my purse and standing, I laugh. "Delilah, what are you doing?"

"My earring popped out right as I was opening your door. Ah, here it is!" She retrieves a long orange plastic feather and stands, looking up at me. "I forgot to put the thingies on the back, and these keep falling out everywhere I go. They're too light."

I grin at my friend, walking toward her to head out of my office. "Wardrobe issues. Bummer."

"Yeah. Hey, where are you going? I was coming by to see if you wanted to grab lunch."

"Sure."

A large shadow steps up behind her. Delilah glimpses Nick, then spins around to face me. Her back to Nick, she scrunches her face up and tilts her finger into her mouth to mimic a vomit face.

I bite my lip to keep from laughing.

Oblivious, Nick taps the door frame and asks, "Do you have some time, Anna?"

I grin and say, "Yeah," as Delilah whirls out of the office.

Nick Norwood, the group account director and a senior executive in our agency, isn't stopping by my office for business reasons. He's not my friend. He shifts a few throw pillows and settles into the sofa, acting as if he's stopping by for a lengthy chat.

At first glance, some might say he's attractive. With an expansive wardrobe of tight-fitting designer clothes that would fit in at most high-end trendy clubs, he's easily the best dressed executive at our agency. Even so, his hulking demeanor and willingness to forego personal space creeps out most of the women, myself included. Year-round, he rocks a fake tan, styled blond hair, and too-white teeth. At the very least, it's fair to say he's not my type.

About six months ago, I went to one of Nick's notorious apartment parties with my team and had way too much to drink. I didn't eat before arriving, and after a couple of drinks, I blacked out. The whole night is a complete black hole. The last time I drank so much I blacked out was in college, and even then, nothing so extreme.

I woke up in his bed and could tell by the absence of my panties I was fucked, both literally and figuratively. I grabbed my clothes and left his apartment as quietly as possible, hoping against hope he'd remember as much, or as little, as I did. My luck was shit. Since our sexcapade, Nick has hovered around my office like a hunter seeking prey.

When it was clear he remembered the night's events, I gave him my best "it really should have never happened" speech and "holy cow, I had way too much to drink" explanation. Smiling, he leaned down to my ear and said, "Don't worry. We'll keep us under wraps," then smirked, ran his finger up and down my arm, and swaggered away. Gross.

Last month, he asked me to hang out after work, and I said I had plans. He glared at me, eyes roving up and down my body. I summoned my Jedi powers and stayed strong. I'd thought the Force had been with me, but an hour later he barged in with an urgent project, and my whole weekend became a whirlwind because of a last-minute request from his client. It seemed a stretch he'd concocted said emergency because he was pissed at me, but still.

"Not sure if you saw, but the Giants are playing the Packers this weekend. The Giants are going to have a pretty kick-ass season…" Nick continues, as I sit half-listening. Nick spends his weekends with our agency's founders and has been here since it opened. If it weren't for his senior executive status, I'd let my inner bitch out. But I like working here. I love my accounts. So, I try to play nice. Nice enough. I still make it clear at every opportunity I am not interested in him. At all.

A blonde with a messy bun bouncing outside my door catches my eye.

I jump out of my chair and shout, "Delilah! Wait, I forgot, we still need to review the Greenpeace concepts." I give a timid smile to Nick as I grab a paper and pad from my desk. "Sorry, Nick, but I need to meet with Delilah. Can I catch ya' later?" The man has wasted thirty minutes of my time, rambling at first about a new business pitch, and then nothing else to do with work came out of his mouth. He has to have some work of his own to do.

Nick stands, looking Delilah up and down in his own special, skeevy way.

What's that about? Why does he always do that?

"Yeah, just come on down to my office later," he says, and he reaches out and slides my hair behind my ear. I jerk back instinctively.

Seeming unmoved by my reaction, he gives a polite nod to Delilah on his way out.

Delilah walks in and softly closes the door, plopping down onto Nick's vacated spot on my sofa, a knowing grin plastered on her face.

"We don't have any creative to go over, do we?"

I let out a deep sigh. "We do, but we don't have to go over it right now. Thanks for saving me from Mr. Touchy. Just hang out for a minute. I don't want him popping back in."

"Does he still ask you out?" Delilah asks, eyes narrowed and focused on me.

"Sometimes. He doesn't seem to be getting the hint. And I swear his 'urgent' requests are timed to coincide with when I say no to him. It's making me paranoid." I crumple the piece of paper in my hand, frustration seeping out.

"Anna, you should totally go to HR."

"Have you lost your mind? I don't want to be *that* girl. I just want him to leave me alone." I hadn't told anyone about *the* night. Not even Delilah. It's just too mortifying. But I'm certain my story to HR would be tremendously weakened if they knew what had happened between us. And Nick would certainly tell them. Other than creeping me out with his suggestive looks and touches, he hasn't really done anything. The timing of his emergencies could totally be in my head. No, HR isn't the solution.

Besides, filing a sexual harassment claim, even if they decided in my favor, would probably mean I wouldn't move further here, and it would definitely make me less attractive if I tried to move to another agency. My dad owned his own business, and I grew up hearing stories. Women who spoke up weren't viewed favorably, or at least weren't as preferable as job candidates without a sexual harassment suit in the past.

Delilah pulls her legs up and stares at me, the bun on top of her head shaking slightly as she shifts on the sofa. Wearing an old gray sweatshirt, black leggings, and Converse sneakers, she could easily be mistaken for a college student.

I sit back down at my desk and spin in my chair, suppressing the urge to give out a little "wheee" to relieve some of the tension in the room. Large brown eyes continue to study me intently.

"What?"

"You know you're hot, right? Long, dark, glossy hair, athletic body to kill for, smart, successful. You've got it going on, girl. Nick is a creep, but most of the people here are in their twenties, and reality is it's kind of like a fraternity mixer here half the time." She tilts her head and looks thoughtful. "You are constantly turning guys down. If you refuse to partake in the goodness, why don't you just fake a boyfriend?"

"What?"

"I mean, you don't seem interested in the guys here, so what's the harm? You know Clarissa in accounting? She had the same issue with Nick until she got a boyfriend. Once she became unavailable, he started sending his underlings to deal with her. Nick is a group account director. Maybe if you get a boyfriend, he'll lose interest, and you can start dealing directly with Darren." Darren is an account director, and he's in an equivalent position to me. From an organizational structure, he should be my day-to-day account side contact. "It could mean a better life for all of us," she says, emphasizing *all of us*. Delilah raises her eyebrows, clearly insinuating Nick's questionably-timed client emergencies are cutting into her life too. She's on my team, so she's not wrong.

"Fake a boyfriend? Really? That's your answer to the creepy account guy who's a little slow to accept I'm not interested?" I huff.

She huffs right back. "No. My answer is HR. But if you aren't willing to do that..." She lets her sentence hang in the air for a dramatic second. "A boyfriend is an idea," she mutters while twisting the friendship bracelets lining her wrist.

"I think faking a girlfriend would be more fun." I grin, joking around.

Delilah rolls her eyes. "So, how was your Sunday?"

I rub my hands up and down my face, trying to joggle Nick Norwood from my thoughts. It's Monday morning. The weekend flashes before me. Delilah and I saw a band together Saturday night. Then, Sunday. Hazel eyes.

"Small world story. An ex from college moved into my apartment building."

"Is that good or bad?" She's twirling a loose piece of hair that escaped from her messy bun.

I play with the pad on my laptop to pull up my email. Good or bad? What a good question. When I don't respond, she stops searching for split ends and watches me, waiting for an answer. I doodle on the corner of the desk calendar with a pencil as I explain. "It's not good or bad. Things didn't end well with us. I get the feeling he can't stand me, which doesn't really make sense."

"What happened with you guys?"

"Nothing. And, I don't know. Everything. We met my last semester of school. I was interviewing, working. He was preparing for the bar, interviewing. But, for a few months there, it was like, well, it was pretty amazing." Since hanging up with Olivia yesterday, I've spent a lot of time strolling down Memory Lane, and remembered more questions than answers.

Delilah bites her lip, smiling. "Amazing, huh?"

"Yeah. And then, I guess reality hit. Tough talks. He wanted me to move to Atlanta. But he didn't ask. He pissed me off, is what he did. I didn't return his calls for a few days. Then suddenly he wouldn't even talk to me. Look at me. College age maturity at its finest." An email about a project catches my attention, and I skim through it.

"And then what happened?"

I return my attention to Delilah. "That's it. Graduation happened. I moved to New York. He moved to Atlanta. Yesterday was the first time I'd seen him in four years."

"And what was it like?"

Shocking as hell. My stomach still flutters around him. Of course he's as attractive as ever. Maybe more so. I bite the inside of my lip and remember his short answers. How he seemed to want to get away from me as quickly as possible. "He's still an asshole."

Delilah sighs and drops her head back against the wall. Then she throws the back of her hand across her forehead, all drama. "Why must they all be assholes?" she singsongs.

Yes, indeed. Why, oh, why?

four

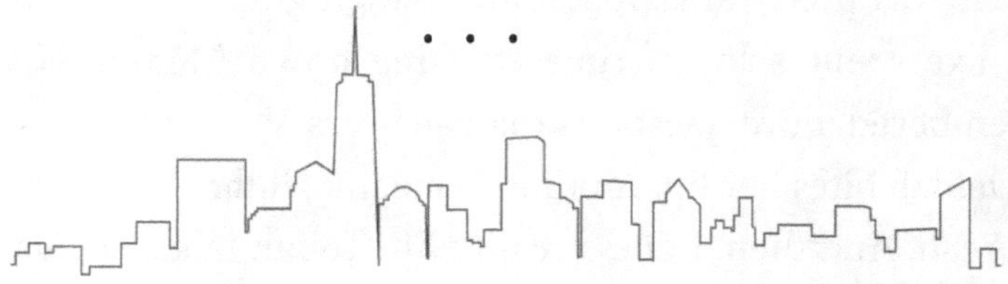

ANNA

The week flew by. The *Pink Panther* soundtrack played in my head each morning of my stealth routine. It turns out I could've had a career in the CIA. I'm good at tiptoeing around. I'd catch glimpses of him on the sidewalk and whip around to head the opposite direction. Completely mature behavior.

Now it's Saturday morning. A whole week spent in avoidance mode. Yet here I am, heading to the park to meet Chase and Angela. I never asked, but my gut tells me Jackson will be joining us. I just kind of know.

My hair in a ponytail, I'm sporting my favorite Saturday ripped jeans and a faded old Hard Rock Cafe guitar tank. My stomach flips and flops. Which is silly. There's absolutely no reason to be nervous about seeing him.

Chewie stops and starts the whole way, alternating between lunging and halting. She's all about the smells. One day, I'm going to train her to be a well-behaved dog.

My outfit isn't a match for the frat boy image I remember Jackson cultivating in law school. And it definitely isn't a match for the corporate executive I'd seen Sunday. Why was he wearing a suit on the weekend?

Yeah, my twenty-six-year-old self won't appeal to Legal Eagle Jackson at all. Four years ago, we were college students. Pseudo-adulting. I thought I'd never see him again. I stalked him on Facebook once or twice after drinking too much, but he has a private page. All I could see was a single photo of him on a mountaintop somewhere. Thank god I'd never been on FB drunk and sent a friend request.

Over the years, I thought about asking Chase for Jackson updates. They had been roommates, and when we stopped seeing each other, I made it a point to not bring Chase into the middle of it. Although I had wanted to. So many times. I'd wanted to ask Chase if Jackson was mad at me. Ask him what was going on. Did he not want anything to do with me because we were moving to different cities? Or did he stop responding to me because I wouldn't change my plans to accommodate his?

That period of time at school was over in a flash. The last manic few weeks of school. Then, in New York, it never made sense to bring it up. Why dwell on a fling? Even if at the time I would have never used the word *fling* to describe Jackson and me. But do flings ever feel like just a fling when they're happening?

"Anna!" rings out near the upcoming 77th Street entrance. Al and the weatherman nailed it with their predictions of a blue sky, brisk fall day. Pedestrians crowd the sidewalk. A concrete wall borders the park and lines the right side, a barrier between the street and the park. Yellow and red have replaced the green leaves on the maple trees dotting the street. I search along the wall, past the vendors lined up along it to sell jewelry and caricatures, looking for the source of the shouts until I locate Angela. She's jumping up and down to get my attention, her blown-out, flat black hair barely moving with each jump.

I wave my greeting and quicken my stride, giving her a warm hug when I get to her. I don't see Jackson, but I'm pretty sure he's nearby. My skin tingles, sensing his presence. The same as in college. The same as last weekend.

I follow Angela, and as we round the corner, I spot Jackson and Chase standing inside the park entrance.

Jackson's wearing a faded gray UVA t-shirt, ripped jeans, a baseball cap, and Asics. In this outfit, he doesn't look like a high-powered attorney. No, lucky me, today, he looks like the guy I knew four years ago.

His brown hair sticks out from the sides of his baseball cap, curling up along the rim. He's gonna need a haircut soon. I wonder if it's long enough for him to mess it up when he runs his hand through it, an old habit I used to love. His hazel eyes are dark, at least from a distance with the sun behind him.

Damn, he's still crazy attractive.

He doesn't wave, just watches me as I approach. He gives a slight nod in greeting, but those lips remain in a straight line.

I'm aware I'm staring at him, but I can't stop myself. He checks out my dog and bends to pet her. "What's her name?"

"Chewbacca. I call her Chewie."

"You named a girl Chewbacca?" he asks, squinting up at me, somewhat amused. Finally, his lips leave flat line mode.

"Yeah. She has long, brown, curly-ish hair. Don't you see it? I'd always said if I got a chocolate shaggy dog, I'd name it Chewbacca. When I found her, and she was a girl, I figured the name still fits. She's kind of a beast. She grew into her name. The pet shop told me she'd only be about thirty pounds."

"You went to a pet shop to buy your dog?" Disdain lines his words. I understand the condescension. Guilt wracked me when I first picked her up. But I was passing by, and this pet shop had the puppies out in a fenced-in area. She looked up at me, wagged a fluffball tail, tripped over her giant paws, and that was all she wrote. My mom had passed away. My emotions were sky-high. Done. I walked out with her.

"Hey, guys," Chase interrupts our exchange, "let's head this way. We can find somewhere to sit on the grass over here. Angela has blankets, and I have the Frisbee. You girls can hang out while we're playing."

Following the three of them, Chewie and I bring up the rear. Only Chewie keeps trying to catch up with them, and I keep pulling her back. Chewie requires a chest harness because I'd break her neck otherwise.

When we get to the grassy area Chase has picked out, Jackson turns and bends down to pet Chewie again. She raises her head to him with adoring eyes and wags her tail like crazy. Jackson laughs.

Angela watches the two of them as she smooths out an enormous blanket. "Well, Jackson, she seems to like you. Guess that gives you the all-clear."

He grins then wrinkles his brow as if thinking about her comment. "Did someone give you a reason to doubt me?" he asks Angela but scowls at me.

Angela laughs. "Don't get defensive. I meant dogs are great judges of character. And she likes you."

I play with the grass near my hand, weeding through the clovers for one with four leaves, choosing to ignore his questioning expression. I haven't said word one to Angela about him, so he might as well drop it. His unspoken criticism of me buying a dog from a pet shop still hangs in my mind. "I would have adopted from a shelter," I say, clearly being the defensive one. "But she was sitting there, furry with big, giant paws. It was love at first sight. I couldn't leave her."

He's still scratching behind Chewie's ears. "I'm not judging."

Right.

"Although I can't see how such an enormous dog makes sense in an apartment."

I get the sense he'd like to argue more, but instead drops it and grabs a Frisbee. Good thing, too. What does he expect me to do? Exchange my dog because he doesn't approve?

Once the guys start playing, Chewie pulls on her leash to join them. I have to sit up and clutch her harness to keep her by me. "Stay" isn't a word she's mastered yet.

Jackson calls, "Hey, let her go. We'll throw with her."

Choosing to relax on the blanket rather than berate my child, I leave her leash on but let her go. She sprints straight toward Jackson. *Traitor.*

Angela leans back, face to the sun. Central Park in fall. There's no better place when the weather's right. And today, it's stellar. Manhattanites are out in full force. We've claimed a nice area in a grass-covered field, quite a distance from the jogging path. The field is surrounded by trees, and in the distance, skyscrapers hover. Above, the sun shines warm, and the blue sky envelops us.

My heart races, and a light sweat beads on my forehead. I lean back like Angela, playing it cool. I inhale, filling my lungs to capacity, breathing in the crisp fall air.

Without opening her eyes, Angela asks, "So, what's the story with Jackson? Chase hasn't said much about him."

Their Frisbee game has evolved into more about the dog fetching than any kind of true Frisbee game. "Hmmm. They were roommates both years of b-school for Chase, and for Jackson's last two years of law."

She opens her eyes. "Did you know Jackson well?"

"Kind of. We dated. Briefly." I leave it at that. There's no need to share more.

"Chase said he was a player. Did things not go well with you guys? Chase was a little worried he may have been a jerk to you."

"No, actually, things were good. But we met our last semester.

Bad timing, I guess. We had jobs in different cities." Things didn't end well, but I've never understood why. He asked me to move to Atlanta. No, he told me to move to Atlanta. That pissed me off. But then, from there, I'm not sure what happened. And if it didn't make sense then to try to figure it out, it doesn't make sense now.

"Well, now you both live in the same city. Same apartments. Any chance now? He keeps looking over here."

I glance over at Jackson, but his back is to me as he jumps to catch a Frisbee. He almost gets knocked out by Chewie flying through the air in pursuit of the same flying disc.

"No. No chance." She raises her eyebrows, silently asking for more. "He kind of reminds me of my ex. When I started seeing the controlling side of Jackson, I pushed away. Of course, the timing wasn't right, and nothing would have happened with us, anyway. But, no, I have no desire to repeat my mistakes. And now, he's kind of an ass. No, no chance." I shake my head, firm in my answer.

Angela rolls on her side and holds her head in her hand. "Tell me about this ex. Was it serious?"

"Four years."

Her eyes pop open, and her eyebrows raise. "High school boyfriend?"

Yes, too many years. I sigh. "Junior and senior year of high school. Then freshman and sophomore years of college."

"What was his name?"

"Evan."

"First love, first everything?" she asks with a cute, teasing, tell-me-more smile.

"Yeah."

"Didn't go well?" she prods.

I sip my coffee before responding. "You could say that." Saying it didn't go well felt like an understatement. My first relationship had been a lonely prison. Escaping didn't tear my family apart, but it created a divide. No part of me felt like dwelling on the painful piece of my past. Not on a beautiful day like this. Not when it was so far behind me. And not with Jackson within hearing distance.

I change the subject to her upcoming birthday party. Her parents are renting out a small Italian restaurant in the West Village.

"I've been asking Chase, but he's been such a guy. What should I wear?"

Angela smiles, closing her eyes again as she basks in the sun. "Wear a cocktail dress." Then she frowns. "No jeans, okay?" She opens her eyes and stares at me, wanting to ensure sure she has my attention.

I snort. "Fine. Fine. No jeans. Message received. That's why I asked." I widen my eyes at her in mock irritation. "I'm allowed to wear jeans to work. I love jeans. But I do get dressed up from time to time."

"Yeah, well, I'll believe it when I see it. You could wear jeans, I guess. But it's dressy. My parents are going all-out for this party. It's my twenty-fifth birthday. They like to make a big deal of the fives and zeroes. We have the whole restaurant to ourselves, so you'll be around my family and friends. I guess it doesn't really matter what you wear."

"I own some dresses. I'll look presentable, promise."

"My cousin David is going to be there."

She's mentioned this cousin before. "What's on the menu?" I continue watching the guys toss the Frisbee, avoiding her gaze. I couldn't care less what she's serving, but I'm not interested in being set up on a date with her cousin. Jackson's back is to me, and I can't help but notice his strong calves and his nicely shaped ass. Judging from his biceps and the shape of his shoulders, he's gained muscle since grad school.

Angela ignores my menu question. "You're gonna like David. You two will hit it off."

"Please, no…" I trail off as Jackson and Chase walk up and join us on the blanket.

Chase grins. "Angela, give it up. You and the matchmaking."

Angela groans, throwing up her hands in exasperation. "She and David are gonna hit it off. And if not him, I have others on my list. Anna never dates, and she should. She's like the bloody Virgin Mary over here."

"I'm not that bad," I protest as Jackson mutters, "I doubt that's true."

What the hell?

Jackson tenses a bit as Angela glares at him. Seeming to catch himself, he rushes to cover his gaffe. "Yeah, I don't blame you on the blind date thing. I'm not a fan either."

Angela's eyes narrow further.

Man, I love this girl. She packs an unexpected punch. Chase definitely found a good one.

"What do you mean by you doubt that's true?" Angela sits straight up. Her posture is aggressive, as if she might pull a weapon out from underneath the blanket and charge.

Oh, boy. Here goes. I love how Angela jumps in for her friends with a take-no-prisoners New York attitude. But Jackson's a lawyer. Fighting with him is beyond exhausting. She has no idea what she's getting into. And something tells me I'd be the subject getting battered in this fight. A fight I don't understand.

"Sorry, wrong thing to say." Jackson holds his hands up in surrender.

"Jeez! And it's not a blind date if I'm just introducing them," Angela snaps. Catching Chase's warning eye, she changes the subject. "So, Jackson, are you getting settled now?"

Before Jackson can respond, Chase jumps in. "Anna, I've told Jackson you have lots of people you can introduce him to. Between us both, we can help him branch out and get settled here."

I nod, trying to think of who I know in the corporate executive world. I can't really see the suit from yesterday blending in with any of my advertising friends. Other than Chase and a few other UNC alumni I hang out with, contrary to what Chase seems to believe, I don't have a great many friends. I mean, I love dancing and bars and am familiar with bartenders and folks at the places I frequent. But I can't see lawyer Jackson blending in at any of my haunts. He seems more of a fancy dinner sort of guy. Like a younger Harvey Specter from *Suits*.

Jackson seems to read my mind. "I appreciate the thought, but I'm not going to have a lot of time. I work long days and have a lot of client lunches and dinners. Not much time to meet a lot of new people and go out. If I had a lot of free time, I doubt I would have agreed to move to this city."

The last part of his sentence is stated with tons of disdain. I do recall him saying something along the lines of, "No way in hell would I live in New York."

"Give it time. It will grow on you. You've just got to find your favorite escape places," I tell him.

His forehead wrinkles. "Escape?"

"Yeah, you know. Central Park. Along the river. Places to get off the streets. Jogging trails. The High Line. A bit of nature."

He tilts his head. "Are you a runner now? You didn't used to run. Or at least you refused to go running with me."

"I didn't refuse. I was just busy."

"If I remember correctly, you rode your bike to intramural soccer practice. And you point-blank told me you found running boring. At least, I think boring was the word you used. Do you run now?"

"Noooo. But I walk Chewie. A lot. She's a big girl." And she is. She may weigh only sixty-five pounds, but add in her hair, and she's the size of a miniature horse. Barely a year old, she's still a puppy. Boundless energy.

Jackson nods, seemingly pleased to be right about me not

running. Angela leans back into Chase's chest, using him as an armrest.

Jackson and I have our own corners of the oversized blanket, and Chewie comes and sits between us, bridging the divide. His focus is squarely on my dog, and I stare at his forearms and the flex of muscle as he scratches her. She rolls over on her back, asking for a tummy rub in the most unladylike way, legs spread wide. I roll my eyes at my shameless dog as Jackson obliges.

After a while, Jackson stands and stretches. "It's good to see you guys, but I need to head out. I've got a few apartments to check out today."

This is news. "Oh, where you're staying is temporary?"

"It's month-to-month. I want to buy but need to do research first."

Disappointment fills me. Which makes no sense at all. I've been full *Pink Panther* trying to avoid him all week. This is good news.

Chase rests back on the blanket and thrusts his chin to Jackson. "You want to hang out with us tonight? Or are you going to hit the bars alone? Nothing beats being single in New York," he says, wiggling his eyebrows up and down suggestively.

Angela smacks Chase on his chest, and he gives her his goofy grin. "What? I'm taken. Gonna live vicariously through this big guy."

Jackson starts backing away. "I'll give you a call about tonight, Chase. Later, guys."

He tosses a hand up in the air to wave goodbye without sparing a glance my way. If he was interested back in the day, he's definitely not now. Whatever. He's just a guy I used to know. He'll buy a place and years will go by before our paths cross again, if they ever do.

five

. . .

ANNA

The week passed by without a single Jackson sighting, but then again, work had been nonstop. My team presented campaigns to two different clients plus we got pulled into an impromptu dinner with the Heineken team. The manic week meant I dropped the *Pink Panther* routine and came and went without any precautions. And, as it turns out, precautions weren't necessary.

Now it's Saturday evening, a week after my park outing, and I'm heading out in gorgeous black stiletto heels and a little black cocktail dress. The form-fitting classic dress is my go-to for evening business events or any kind of evening adulting. It hugs my curves in a sexy but appropriate way and falls about five inches north of my knees. Sexy but still suitable for meeting parents. The shoes are Olivia's Christian Louboutin stilettos she left behind because she "couldn't pack everything." She told me to enjoy them. So, on rare occasions, I do.

I hail a cab because, well, heels. Those *Sex and the City* sirens were so full of Hollywood BS when they waltzed around sidewalks in Manolos. No woman in her right mind with the ability to hail a cab would ever prance around like those women. Concrete sidewalks are hard. And stilettos aren't known for soft padding.

As I head to Angela's birthday dinner, I pull out my phone, deciding to reach out to my BFF on the ride over. Olivia moved to Prague after she split with her boyfriend. She claims she wasn't running from him and just had a good job offer, but I'm not sure I believe her. Selfishly, it all worked out for me because I ended up with my own apartment. Her move was timed extraordinarily well with my promotion and raise. Still, I worry about her and try to check in often. I click on WhatsApp, the cheap way she picked to communicate while she's abroad.

Me:
No. Jackson will prob be there.

Olivia:
Have you seen him much?

Me:
No

Olivia:
? Do u not want to see him?

Me:
No

Olivia:
Keep an open mind. You never know. You guys could reunite.

Me:
Ha! He hates me.

Olivia:
LMK how party goes.

Me:
Will do.

Olivia:
BTW no one hates you. Everyone loves Anna. :-)

The cab pulls up to the restaurant. It's on a nondescript street in the Village. Small restaurants, hip boutiques, and art galleries line the lane.

As I pull the heavy wood door open, Angela's mom wraps me in a warm hug and offers a glass of wine. Middle-aged men and women I don't recognize are milling around, holding cocktails or wine glasses. All the men are in jackets and ties. Angela did not lie. Folks are dressed up to celebrate her most recent journey around the sun.

Across the room, I spot Angela and Chase in a corner, surrounded by two older couples, presumably family. Angela's mom guides me over to a thin, dark-haired man around my age wearing spectacles. His black hair is the exact color as Angela's and I immediately notice family resemblance in the facial structure. "Let me introduce you to Angela's cousin, David Bergen. His father is my husband's brother."

I give a polite smile and extend my hand.

David takes my hand in a cordial, loose hold and responds to Angela's mom. "No, I haven't had the pleasure of meeting Anna yet, but I've heard a lot about her." His slightly clammy hand presses into mine. When he releases my hand, I reflexively wipe my palm on my dress. His eyes follow my hand, and I stop mid-wipe. I give him an awkward, timid smile.

Mrs. Bergen excuses herself to greet another guest. David clutches my elbow to guide me to a more private corner near the bar. "I've heard a lot about you. Angela told me she's been trying to get you to agree to a blind date for a while."

I sort of chuckle. "Yeah, I don't like blind dates."

He smiles. "Well, I'm hoping after tonight, it won't be a blind date."

Oh, my. He seems nice, but not my type. "Yeah, I don't..." I pause. "I'm super busy with work." I truly suck at the blow off. Graceful maneuvering of the conversation has always been a skill beyond my reach.

My comment must intrigue him. He steps closer to me then rubs his finger along my elbow and asks, "Why? A beautiful girl like you. Angela said you don't date much, but now I've seen you, it doesn't add up."

I back up a few steps to create some needed space between the two of us. To delay responding, I sip my wine. I'm waffling between telling him I'm fresh out of a bad relationship or telling him it's an extremely stressful time at work when my skin tingles. Without seeing him, I know. Jackson is here.

I scan the room and there he is. Jackson, in a dark suit, crisp shirt, and plum tie. My breath catches. He's moving toward us, glancing between David and me, with a glass of what appears to be scotch or bourbon in his hand.

"Hello," he says with a polite nod.

I attempt to steady my voice and quell my nerves as I introduce the two men. "Hi. Jackson, this is David, Angela's cousin. He works in finance. Jackson lived with Chase in grad school, and he's recently moved here to New York."

They nod at each other. David swallows back the rest of the wine from his glass. "Can I get you both another drink? I'm gonna head to the bar."

"Thanks, but I'm good." I hold up my almost full glass so he can see.

Jackson does the same, responding with a brief, "I'm good."

After David walks away, Jackson stirs the ice in his tumbler with a bored expression. "You're the only person I know here. I expected a younger crowd." He looks around the room and mutters, "Not that I'd know anyone, anyway."

"Yeah, I suspect it's mainly family. Maybe some colleagues? It's nice of her parents to want to do this for her, but it is a little odd with the mix of family and friends."

Jackson's eyes drift over me. As his gaze roves up and down, I start to fidget and shift on my feet. I stand taller under his gaze. Goosebumps rise on my arms. There's no physical contact, but the heat of his perusal makes me hyperaware of my own body. I become aware of the sensation of my nipples against the lace of my bra, and I press my thighs tightly together. I watch two couples standing against the far wall, aiming to look anywhere but at Jackson.

"Is David your date?" he asks. I turn to him. He's no longer looking at me. He's observing two men talking near one of the tables.

"No, no, he's not. But Angela seems to be playing matchmaker. He's the guy she mentioned at the park."

He nods. "So, you haven't explained to her you're not really a relationship girl. You'd prefer to just fuck?"

My eyes widen. Did I hear him correctly? "Excuse me?"

Dark eyes glare at me. Definitely a serious, I-don't-like-you-at-all kind of look.

David returns holding three glasses of wine. Jackson and I still have our drinks, so it appears David is expecting us to double fist. We had declined his offer. Reeling from Jackson's statement, I take the glass David offers me and set it down on a nearby table. David sets one glass on the nearby cocktail table and chugs the one in his hand.

What a shit show. David hovers by my side, as if I'm his date. I'm flustered and want distance from him but have nowhere to go. Jackson remains where he was standing before David walked up, scowling at me.

David breeches the uncomfortable silence by telling us it's time to get seated. "I checked, and we're all sitting at the same table."

Fabulous.

I'm seated between Jackson and David. There are nine others at our round table. Everyone else seems familiar with each other. The large table size requires smaller conversations on the perimeter.

David's leg keeps bumping up against mine under the table. The man Jackson's been talking to turns back to his wife. With no other option, Jackson shifts to angle his body to me.

"What have you been up to the last four years?" he mutters, resigned to making small talk with me.

Well, both my parents died, I finally have my own apartment, and I've met the love of my life in dog form. And why the hell would I tell you anything after what you said to me?

"Not much. Work. You?"

He gives me a slight grin. "Work, huh? Yeah, me too. And a move to a new state," he adds, almost as an afterthought.

Are we really doing this? Chit chat? "How are you liking it so far?"

"It's fine. I'll be spending a lot of time at the office. Depending on the client, I sometimes travel a lot. It doesn't matter where I live."

"Is that any way to live?" I ask and immediately regret it. I sound too derogatory. Too judgemental.

"Doesn't sound like you're one to talk." he snaps back.

Fantastic. I put the asshole lawyer on the defensive. That should make for a lovely evening.

Right about then, David's hand caresses my thigh.

Really? Could this night get any worse?

I remove David's wandering hand from my thigh and place it back on his leg. I glare at him in an attempt to communicate a silent "keep your hands off me." He grins, looking sheepish but also a bit like an errant teenager.

The man on the other side of Jackson asks him a question. The two of them resume their prior conversation. It sounds like a discussion about New York financial advisors.

I stare straight ahead, stuck between handsy David and Jackson's back. Four empty wine glasses sit in front of David's place setting. He leans into me and pats my hair. I inch away from him. One more inch, and I'll merge into Jackson's back.

David snorts and sort of giggles. "You're trying to get away from me."

I attempt a gracious smile then announce to the table, "Excuse me. I'm going to the restroom." No one glances my way. Out of the corner of my eye, I see David snatch my glass of wine and drink from it.

I take my time in the restroom, hoping by the time I exit, our plates will be clear. Then I can graciously make my excuses and leave. I do wonder if Chase will be popping the question tonight. The whole party has an engagement dinner kind of feel. Chase and Angela have been making the rounds visiting with the guests together. Well, if he's going to propose, I'll have to miss it. Hanging with drunk David all night isn't gonna happen.

I exit the restroom and stop. Jackson's leaning against the wall. Glaring at me. He steps forward and guides me to the back of the hall away from the restrooms.

"What are you playing at?" He sounds angry.

"What?" I ask, floored. What the hell is going on?

"David. Is he your end goal tonight?"

I tilt my head in confusion, trying to figure out what he could be angry about. I'm missing something here. "What? In case you haven't noticed, David is drunk. I don't know what to do. I'm not playing at anything. I'm trying to be polite and not cause a scene."

He looks me up and down as if he's judging the veracity of my response. "So, you aren't planning on banging her cousin?"

I open my mouth, shocked and pissed off. "What? No! I just met the guy. He's drunk. Like, crazy drunk. Have you not been sitting there for the whole dinner? And thanks for helping me out, by the way."

I push past him, but he grabs my elbow, spinning me around.

"I figured you do roommates, why not cousins?"

What the fuck?

"What. Are. You. Talking. About?" I whisper-screech.

He puts his hands up in a defensive gesture. "Look, you and Angela seem like good friends. Chase hasn't told her you two fucked in college, and now she's setting you up with her cousin. It seems to me you'd realize if she knew the truth, she wouldn't want you with her family."

I stand, stunned for a minute. Then anger rips through me. Index finger held out and swinging like a sword, I let the mother-fucker have it. "First, I don't want to date her family. Second, I never fucked, banged, or whatever with Chase. Ever!" My finger bounces around, and I suppress the urge to stab him in the eye with it.

He stands before me, rubbing his chin. Not saying a word. Fucking lawyer.

I throw my hands up, frustration mounting, about to blow. "Where are you getting this?" I hiss. "You are such a hypocritical fuck. You were a huge player in school. And. According to Chase. You still are! You think you know me? Well, you don't, you fuck!" I want to punch a wall. "I don't know where you get off." I pause, forcing myself to calm down. "I don't know what you've heard, but you are wrong."

"What I've heard?" He stalks toward me, crowding me against the wall, glaring down at me with stormy, dark green eyes. "I was there. Do you not remember?"

I pause, a dizzy sensation coming over me. I have no idea what he's talking about, but I know one thing. "You. Are. Wrong."

I tear down the hallway and hear him call after me, taunting. "Running away?"

When I exit the hall, I see a few women casting curious glances in my direction. My whisper-shout may not have been so whispery.

Shoulders back, I storm out, charging for the subway station. What the hell? What does he think he saw? It was four years ago. There's no telling what he thinks he saw. Fucking asshole.

six

· · ·

ANNA

Knock. Knock. Knock.

The rapping noise outside my door sends Chewie into a barking frenzy. Loud barking will have Lester from unit C at my door in minutes.

I leap up to open the door.

Jackson stands in the hallway. He's still wearing his suit. Before I can tell him to fuck off, Chewie bounds past me and plants both paws on his chest. Damnit.

Chewie's tail thumps the wall with each frantic wag. I grab her collar and pull her down.

I peer down the hall in search of Lester, fully expecting a scolding. My grouchy neighbor does not like dogs. But thankfully, Lester hasn't opened his door. One good thing for the day.

I grip Chewie's collar and glare at Jackson.

He bows his head. "I may have been out of line."

"You think?"

"Can I come in?"

"Why?"

Apologetic green eyes peer down at me. "Please?"

I glance down the hall again and step back, swinging the door wide. "Only because I don't want Lester coming out yelling at us for talking in the doorway." And because I don't like to hold in anger. The new me strives to let things go. I learned the hard way life's too short not to.

He steps inside then bends down to greet Chewie with a warm hello. Clearly, Jackson likes dogs. So, not drenched with evil. Just an asshole—not an evil asshole. I stand with my arms crossed, waiting. I'm tired, and I've had a shit night. Whatever he wants to say, he needs to say it and get out.

Finally, he rises. "I was out of line tonight. I had a couple of glasses of bourbon." He shrugs. "I didn't like seeing you with David. I saw his hand on your thigh during dinner and..." His right hand balls into a fist, and he exhales. "I know. Out of line. It's been years since we dated." His gaze lifts from the ground, and he looks directly in my eyes. "It won't happen again."

His sincerity cools the boiling anger.

He turns to leave, and I reach out and tug his sleeve. "No. You've got to give me more than that. You didn't make any sense tonight. What was that about me sleeping with Chase?"

He squints, and his expression says I'm out of my mind. "I was there when you and Chase got home from your date."

"Chase and I never went on a date."

Jackson takes off his coat and loops it around one of his arms. "Do you remember when you went out for sushi?"

Chewie decides Jackson's done with her, jumps up on the futon, and spreads herself out.

"Vaguely. Right before we moved here. Jackson, what's this about?"

"It was about a week after we broke up. You know what." He

stops and rubs a hand through his hair. "You're saying you never slept with him."

I stare at him.

"You never slept with Chase?" he asks.

"No," I answer in an angry, annoyed tone, because I'm freshly angry and annoyed.

He nods. "Hmmm. Chase said you were the best lay he's ever had."

"He *what*? When?"

"About a week after we broke up."

I kind of laugh. There are so many things I want to say to him —I need to say to him. We've got a lot of stuff we need to get straight. I'm in flannel pajama pants, a white tank top, and yellow polka dotted socks. But fuck it. "Would you like to sit? Have a glass of water?"

Confusion crosses his face.

"I have a few things I want to say. Before you leave."

He sits in a chair. I sit on one of the barstools. "First, Chase and I never. We never went out on a date. He's a good friend. I don't have any idea why he would say we hooked up. But I will find out." Jackson studies me, judging. I'm sure he's doing his lawyer lie detector bit. *Lie detect away, buddy.* "Second, you can't say we broke up. We had a rather heated discussion. Then I never heard from you again."

"Never heard from me again? I texted you. I called. You never called me back. I went to your apartment and left messages with your roommates."

"Ahm, really, Jackson? Do you not remember all of my texts to you? Asking you if everything was okay? Asking what was going on?"

"Before those texts, I texted you." He pulls on his chin, rubs the skin back and forth like the great thinker. I get the sense he wants to continue arguing, but he's also come to the realization that I'm right. We never broke up. We stopped talking to each other.

He abruptly stands and walks out of the den and into my home office.

My den is small and dark, without windows. My apartment is a two-bedroom convertible, meaning a wall cuts the living area in half to create a second bedroom. The configuration leaves a small den without windows and then a room with windows that can be used as a second bedroom or office. There's no room for a kitchen table. A short bar long enough for two stools divides the den from the galley kitchen.

My home office, or studio, is the second bedroom half, and windows line the far wall. I have a desk with two large Mac monitors set up against the back wall. I like to work on graphic design projects with a view of the north end of the city. I also have my painting easel set up so I can stand and paint.

All three walls of the studio hold a smorgasbord of paintings and photographs. Interspersed with my work are ads and magazine pull-outs for inspiration.

I follow him into my office. He takes slow steps around the room, studying each item hanging on my wall. The city lights twinkle through the curtainless window.

Finally, he talks to me. "I'm sorry. I mean, to be clear, I'm going to kill Chase."

I understand the sentiment.

"But I'm sorry. About tonight. About…" His lips contort into a frown.

He points to a black and white photo on my wall. It's an angled shot of Franklin Street. He'd stood patiently beside me while I tested different positions, angling the camera to capture the geometric lines of the doors. I liked the symmetry the angle captured. I converted it to black and white and framed it as an homage to the past. He taps the photograph but doesn't say anything. I know what's going through his mind. He remembers the day. A rare afternoon we skipped our classes to hang out together. Shared blue cups at He's Not Here. One of the last lazy warm spring days before the manic rush of the end of school descended.

He heads back into the den and points at my futon with an amused smirk on his face. "Haven't seen one of those in a while."

I can't help but grin. My apartment furniture could definitely stand an upgrade. "It's from college. Most everything else is my old roommate's. She left the furniture behind. Furniture shopping's not my thing." I glance around my apartment. "Guess it wasn't hers either. Most of this is the furniture she moved in from her college apartment."

"Nice art. I like it." He points to the canvas piece in vibrant colors hanging over the futon. It's not anything special, but it works to brighten the space. I painted it a while back. It's a suitable Ikea poster replacement.

Jackson turns to me, an earnest expression on his face. "Any interest in being friends?"

I bite my lip. "So, let me get this straight. Now that you know I never slept with Chase, we can be friends?"

He rubs a hand through his hair. It's too short for the movement to rough it up. "You have no idea how angry I was."

"That's why you were so cold to me, huh?"

"Yep."

I'm tired and emotionally exhausted. "Sure. Friends." I take a deep breath. "Do you want to talk about what happened? I mean, back in Chapel Hill?" The last real conversation we had together ended with my crying and running away as he called after me.

"No need. It's behind us."

I stand there, unsure of what to say. I'm torn. I kind of do want to rehash what went wrong, and part of me wants to keep it all buried.

"You know, even though we live on the same floor, you'll probably never see me. I live at the office. But the next time we do see each other…friends." He extends his hand for a contractual handshake.

I force a smile and take his hand. "Friends. You've got it. Although you may see my dog walker more than me. You're not the only one who spends a lot of time at the office."

"You have a dog walker?"

"Yeah. With how much I work, I shouldn't even have a dog. And as you pointed out, she's big. The dog walker helps get her energy out so she won't destroy things or bark." I hesitate, unsure about how much he wants to stand and chitchat. "The neighbor between us, well, he complains any time she barks."

Jackson scratches Chewie's ear, and she rolls over, exposing her belly. "A dog walker must cost a pretty penny here."

"It's not cheap. I wake up early to take Chewie for a solid walk each morning, but by the time I get home, I'm usually too tired to do much more than make a lap around the block. She does better if she gets out in the middle of the day."

"Where do you go walking?"

"Mostly just up or down the avenue, but if I'm going to do a long walk, I'll head to the park or over by the river."

"I run each morning. What time do you go?"

"Around five-thirty."

"Maybe I'll see you one morning." He taps his hand on the door before leaving, and, as if it's an afterthought, asks, "What's the deal with the complaining neighbor? Anything I should be aware of?"

"Well, his name is Lester Johnson Truman."

Jackson's eyes widen and he grins. "Seriously?"

I rock back and forth on my feet, smiling. "Yep. I figure with a birth name like his, he's entitled to be a grumpy bitch."

Jackson laughs. It's a great sound to hear. He doesn't laugh often. When he does laugh, I can't help but smile.

"He's not such a bad neighbor once you get to know him. Because his door is right in front of the elevator, he's aware of everyone coming and going. He'll yell at anyone who's loud in the hall. Don't think about playing your music too loud either. He calls down to complain to the doormen, who then have to report to building management. I've received two warnings from them. But, on the whole, he's fine. I look at him as our floor's private security."

Jackson nods, absorbing the information on our mutual neighbor. "Got it. Well, see you around." As the door closes, I hear him add in a low voice, "Neighbor."

I close the door and lock it then grab my phone from the kitchen counter. My thoughts spin. *Chase, what the hell?*

She won't be up, but I shoot off a text. A sort of SOS.

Me:
So, Jackson and I are friends now.

seven

ANNA

Monday morning, I head out the glass apartment doors with Chewie. Streetlights illuminate the sidewalk. At 5:30 a.m., it's still dark. The sun flirts with the new day off on the horizon. But sunrise won't happen for a while. There's a chill in the air. New York City never sleeps, but this early in the morning, there is a noticeable lull in activity.

Jackson stretches near a bench. Before, I would've turned right out of the building to avoid him. But now we're friends, and I prefer the park, so I turn left. Chewie lunges forward, nearly ripping my arm out of its socket when she recognizes her new friend.

I pull back hard on the leash and in my most commanding voice shout, "Stop!"

Hearing my command, Jackson stops stretching and smiles. A big smile. "Hey, there. So, you really do get up this early?"

Walking the dog, coffee in hand, is my morning ritual. I've been an early riser for as long as I can remember. Now, I like to be the first in the office in the morning. I also prefer to exercise before work, if one considers walking the dog to be exercise. "It's kind of my thing. Surprised?"

He rubs Chewie's head and in a low deep voice responds, "Yeah, I am."

I let his comment slide. Most people assume creative types are sleeping late kind of people. "Where are you off to run?"

"Park. Where're you headed?"

"Same as you. But I'm walking. So, I'll watch you run ahead of me." I can definitely think of worse views than Jackson's backside.

"Ever think about running?"

I snort. "No." I hold up my reusable Starbucks cup of steaming joe with a lid on it. "Coffee. Two birds, one stone. Coffee plus workout."

"Walking is a workout?"

"According to my Apple watch it is. I meet my exercise goal each morning on my walk."

He gives me a you-can't-be-serious look. "A run would be better for Chewie. She's a big dog in a small apartment."

Truth. But while I'm pretty athletic and love sports like tennis and soccer, running without someone chasing me has never had great appeal. I nod in agreement with Jackson. I won't argue with him. When he's right.

"Tomorrow morning, meet me at the same time and go for a run with me. I'll drop off a strong cup of coffee outside your door after I shower. You can drink it on the way to the office. You'll still kill two birds with one stone, and you won't have to make coffee."

Like making coffee is a time suck. I have that machine scheduled with a start time. And I already drink coffee on the way to the office. I'm more of a multi-cup kind of gal. But he's not wrong about my beast.

"Think about it. If you want to head out tomorrow, be here, same time."

Chewie and I follow down the street, my gaze trained on his ass until he blends into the handful of people out this early in the morning.

After I walk Chewie, I shower and head to my office, the whole time thinking about Jackson. Running with him appeals to me. I've never been a runner, but if he coaches me, maybe I'll grow to love it. I'm slipping into the shady side of my twenties, and my jeans are a tad tighter in my upper thighs. And it'd be time with Jackson.

My phone rings as I push my office door open and flip the light switch.

"Friends, huh?" No hello. Oliva picks right up where I left off.

"Turns out he was pissed at me. Chase told him I slept with him."

"What? When?"

"I do not know. Sometime back in college. I'm a little fuzzy on the details. I'm going to have a chat with Chase."

"No shit. What a jerk." Olivia's been friends with Chase almost as long as I have.

"Yeah. I'm meeting him for lunch this week. He's got some explaining to do."

"No shit. But now you and Jackson have cleared it all up. Can't you be more than friends now?"

An image of Jackson's powerful, commanding business suit persona comes to mind. "I don't think so. We're different now, you know? He's, like, Mr. Corporate. And the thing is, nothing has changed for me. I still remember our last fight. Jackson has it in him to be controlling. I've dated controlling. Once was enough."

"I hear ya," Olivia intones. Then she proceeds to tell me all about a Ukrainian wearing extremely tight high-rise jeans who tried to pick her up at a bar last night.

eight

. . .

ANNA

The next morning, I head out at the same time, sans coffee. Jackson's doing a calf stretch beside the same bench as yesterday, and the second he sees me, he grins. It's a familiar, relaxed, happy, kid-like grin that sends my stomach into fluttery somersaults.

"No coffee. Have you decided to give running a try?"

Chewie lunges toward Jackson and jumps right up on him, planting both paws on his chest. I laugh, both at Chewie's eager greeting and at Jackson's surprise.

I'd been hesitant to run with Jackson. A part of me felt like he was so cocky he'd assume I would come. But he hadn't assumed. Or at least, his eager smile feels like he'd hoped. My smile spreads so wide my mouth muscles hurt.

"Yeah. I decided you're right. Both Chewie and I could use some cardio."

"Wait. I need for you to repeat your statement while I record it."

"Record?" Then it hits me. "That you're right. Ha. Ha. You want to record me saying you're right. Got it."

And yes, he's still grinning and my stomach is still fluttering.

"I've been running for years. You're in good hands. We'll start off easy and build up. 'Kay?" he asks, taking Chewie's leash from my hand.

"Sounds like a plan. You going to take my dog?"

"You'll have enough to focus on without having to worry about her. Plus, she needs to get used to it too, right? She wasn't trained to run with someone?"

I scratch her ear. "She's barely trained in general."

"You don't say?"

Yes, he's still cocky.

We head off together in the direction of the park. He places himself and Chewie on the side near the road with me near the building. Then we start running. He keeps Chewie on a short leash by his side. She learns fast, staying close, responding to the short jerks he makes on the leash.

Ten minutes later, a burn in my lungs and a side cramp force me to slow to a walk. We're barely inside the park. Sweat runs in beads from my face and down my neck. My chest is so sweaty areas of my t-shirt are now wet and a darker color than the rest, especially over my boobs. Lovely. I'm gasping for air and sound like a locomotive after ten minutes running.

"Hey, good start. We can do more tomorrow. I can set your watch up with a run-walk pattern too. I like the run-walk to get you in shape." He puts his hand up to give me a high-five.

Great. He thinks I'm a lard ass. Maybe I am. He takes off to finish his run, because ten minutes running doesn't equal a workout for Mr. Fitness.

When I leave my apartment to head to the office, I find a recyclable Starbucks cup, filled with hot coffee and a yellow Post-it note. "Great job today. Don't forget to stretch." I smile the entire way to the office.

An hour later, I'm retouching an image when I hear a soft tap on my door. "You look different today." Delilah leans against the door, coffee in hand, studying me. Can it be that obvious? One workout?

My lungs still burn. But it's a good burn. It reminds me of the burn I used to get when I swam laps for the middle school swim team. It feels good. I'm energized. I've already answered emails, and I'm putting some finishing touches on some graphics for a print ad. It's 8:45 a.m. On a normal day, I'd be wrapping up email and news stories at this time, yet to start real work.

"I went for a run."

She enters my office and sits on the edge of the sofa, facing me. "Damn, I'd hoped it was a morning sex glow."

I roll my eyes. My office phone rings, and I glance over to see the number. I immediately recognize the 540 area code. Mrs. Hart. My mom's best friend. My ex's mom.

She's been calling me. I scrunch my nose and say, "I've gotta get this." Delilah nods and pulls the door closed, leaving me to my call. "Mrs. Hart. Hi. How are you?"

"I'm fine, darling. How are you? I've been thinking about you."

I wish you wouldn't. "I'm good, Mrs. Hart." I pause because I'm not sure what else to say. Before my mom passed away, Beverly Hart would never have called me. Now she calls about once a month, and it is sweet. If she wasn't my ex-boyfriend's mom, I might want to foster this relationship.

"Well, honey, I know you're at work, and I don't want to keep you, but I wanted to see if you've given any thought to your Thanksgiving plans." Oh, yes. She wants my brother and me to join their family this year for Thanksgiving since we don't have parents to come home to. Again, it's sweet and thoughtful. It's also not happening.

"Bobby'll have to work. Residents always have to work holidays. And I'm going to stay here and celebrate with friends."

"Are you sure, dear? We'd love to have you. I know things didn't work out with you and Evan, but you'll always be like a daughter to us." There's an awkward pause. "You'll always be family."

"I know. Thank you, Mrs. Hart. You'll always be like family to me too."

As I hang up the phone, it occurs to me I should make some Thanksgiving plans. If I don't, I'll end up at the hospital cafeteria hoping Bobby has time to meet me over a ten-minute break or at Chase's family's home without Bobby. I pick up my phone and call Olivia.

nine

ANNA

"Hey, you!" At five feet seven inches tall or so, Chase is almost my exact height. Sometimes I have wondered if our similarity in height helped keep us in the friend zone. It's not like I focus on a guy's height, but I do like to wear heels without towering over my date. But even if he'd been taller, there'd never been any spark.

Chase wraps his arms around me and lifts me into the air. It's the signature Chase hug. His boisterous embrace fills me with such happiness. All the warm feelings temper my desire to strangle him.

After four years in New York, I've come to appreciate my true friendships. New York can be like an ocean for the shipwrecked—water everywhere, but none you can drink. Yes, people are a constant. But New Yorkers often seem to roam around with blinders, avoiding eye contact and interaction. It's hard at times to make a real connection. I have plenty of acquaintances, but not many people I'd consider close friends.

Chase was more of an acquaintance at Carolina, but given he

was the only person I knew moving to New York, we stayed in touch. We fell into a ritual of texting funny jokes to each other and meeting up for lunch on the regular. When something's out of whack—career-wise or dating-wise—we chat it out at lunch. It's also nice to hang out with someone not in your industry. Chase works in finance as an accountant. There's never any danger of either of us talking shop when we get together.

I work in Midtown, not too far from where Chase works. The proximity has also helped us stay in touch. Had his office been Downtown, we probably would have dropped the lunches ages ago.

Chase guides us to our table, and we sit. I study him, mentally running through ways to address the giant elephant in the restaurant. There's no way I can *not* ask him why the hell he lied to Jackson. It's the *how* I'm struggling with.

After the waitress walks away with our lunch orders, Chase leans back in his chair and asks, "How's ad-land?"

"Groovy. Working on a whole new batch of Heineken subway ads. Maybe if you're nice, I'll give you a frameable copy."

I watch as he dips bread into the olive oil, coating it with so much oil it glistens. I notice his phone lights up. He glances at the incoming text and flips his phone over without responding.

"How're you doing? How's Angela?"

Chase grunts. "Everything's good. Did you know her parents were hoping I'd propose at her birthday bash?"

I smile. "It did cross my mind. Not so much her parents hoping, but it had a big announcement kind of feel to it. All her family around, you guys working the crowd together as a couple."

Chase stuffs bread into his mouth and taps his fist against the table as he chews. After swallowing, he continues. "Well, never crossed my mind. Angela's not so happy. I'm not sure if it's because I didn't propose or because it didn't cross my mind."

"Probably both," I answer. On a normal day, I'd be more than happy to dissect the Angela-Chase relationship. Today, though, other items are on my agenda.

He nods as he continues to stuff his face with bread.

"Jackson and I've been running together. Did he tell you?"

Chase wipes his mouth with a napkin and takes a swallow of water. I have his attention. "No. I haven't seen him. A few texts here and there."

I'm not surprised.

Chase asks, "Are you two getting to be friends?" A smirk plays across his face, but the expression swiftly shifts to serious. "Be careful with him, okay, Anna? I don't know what he's like now, but he used to be quite the player."

The waitress delivers our lunches. A Venetian salad for me and an enormous steaming plate of lasagna for Chase. We like to come to this place because they have lightning-fast service.

I wait until the waitress hustles away, then ask, "Is that why you told him I slept with you?" I ask, studying his reaction.

He holds his fork mid-air, and his eyes pop open a bit. His mouth opens slightly then closes. He places the fork down on the table and rests both hands on his thighs. "Anna." He bows his head and exhales loudly. "God that was a long time ago. It was stupid. I only said it once."

"Why say it?" I have my own theories, but I need to hear his answer.

He runs his hand across his buzz-cut hair. "I don't know. We came back from sushi, and all the guys were sitting around. One of them asked if I'd been tapping that." He stops, looking both shameful and guilty. Good. He should be. He is. He raises his head and tilts it to the side. "If it helps, I told them you were the best lay of my life."

My mouth drops open then I bite my lip to suppress a laugh. "No, Chase. That doesn't help." I sigh. For some reason, maybe because it was four years ago and college strikes me as being a different era, I'm not angry. More puzzled. Flabbergasted. "Why? Why do it?"

"Those guys, Anna. They always scored. Always had undergrads coming back, staying the night. We should've put in a rotating door. I mean, here I am, this kind of short Jewish kid. I don't know. It's the way guys are with each other." He picks up his fork but doesn't start eating. "Can you forgive me? Are you mad?"

I roll my eyes in exasperation. "Eat, Chase. Before it gets cold. And yes, I've already forgiven you. I mean, I'm pissed. But it's done. Did you know Jackson has been mad at me for four years because of it? He didn't speak to me after you told him your bullshit story."

Chase's mouth is full of lasagna. He's squinting while chewing, as if thinking. Once he swallows, he says, "No. I didn't know. But now that I think about it, he didn't really talk to me leading up to graduation either. It was months after graduation before we started texting. I chalked it up to new jobs and new cities." His tone changes to mild incredulity. "Were you guys actually dating?"

"Yes! How did you not know?"

He opens his mouth. Closes it. Repeats the action a few times. I dig my fork into his lasagna. I always order the salad with good intentions, then eat Chase's lasagna. The lunch lasagna here could be a family size dinner portion.

He watches me dig into his lasagna. "Shit, Anna. I'm sorry. I guess I had it in my head Jackson wasn't a one-girl kind of guy. I wasn't paying attention. And you and I weren't really friends yet. I mean, remember? We grabbed food a few times once we realized we were both moving to New York."

I wave my fork in the air. "Yeah, I remember. We started talking more when Jackson told us we were both moving to New York. That's why we ate sushi together that night. We were comparing notes since we were both apartment hunting."

Chase stares at the condensation on his glass, thoughtful.

"Yeah. I guess that's another reason I didn't think of you guys as dating. He'd already accepted a position in Atlanta. You had a job in New York."

"It was a sore point for us, for sure." I toy with the pepper shaker as I reflect on the one fact that shadowed us back then. Our eventual move to two different states.

"You guys were serious enough you were debating changing your plans?" He sounds stunned.

As I dig into his lasagna, I answer, "Debating might not be the right word. Arguing. Fighting. It's kind of exhausting dating a lawyer."

We are silent for a bit while we both eat.

Once we're done, he leans back. "So, let me guess. The timing of my little tale hit after you guys had had an argument, and then you never heard from Jackson again."

"Something like that." Something just like that. Complicated by the fact I'd dissed him for a few days. But back then, he was pissing me off. His whole attitude that my career didn't matter as much as his. Yeah, Chase didn't help matters, but Jackson and I weren't exactly on a road to happily ever after.

Chase balls his napkin up and puts it on the table. He places his credit card in the bill folder and tells me, "Lunch is on me." Today, I will let him pay. "I guess I owe Jackson an apology too."

I nod in agreement.

"How angry is he?"

"Well, he's not going to punch you. He won't do anything that might result in a lawsuit."

Chase taps the table, thoughtful. "He's not going to say anything until he can confront us together."

I snort. "Why do you say that?"

"Because I know the fucker. It's classic prosecution tactic. He's gonna want to see how we react to his questions when we're in the same room."

"You don't think he believes me?"

"Oh, he wants to believe you. But he's gonna have to see for himself. Watch our facial expressions when he asks about it." Then Chase rubs his hand through his hair and utters a long, drawn-out, "Fuck." There's a lengthy pause before he asks, "But we're still friends, right?"

I smile. "Yeah, Chase. We're still friends."

ten

JACKSON

"Morning, Brandon."

When the door opens, cold air slaps my face. I jump back inside to zip up my running jacket.

A deep chuckle rolls behind me. "Yeah, man, it's chilly out there."

I brace myself for the cold.

"Enjoy your run, Mr. Hendricks."

I head to the empty bench I use for stretching. Chilly doesn't cut it. It's freaking cold. The early morning sky is darker than normal. It's going to be a cloudy day with rain coming in by afternoon. I count off jumping jacks and high knees before attempting to stretch. What if Anna won't want to run through winter? I can take Chewie for her, but damn. I'd miss running with her. It's the only time of my day I spend with someone not from work.

I stretch my neck from side to side then move to hamstrings and quads. While I don't like the thought of running without

Anna, she'll either run or she won't. There's nothing I can do to change her mind.

She doesn't run with me on the weekends. I do a longer run on Saturdays, seven miles, so it's just as well. Friday and Saturday nights, she goes out. Hence no running on Saturday and Sunday for her. On the weekend, she prefers long walks later in the morning.

Chewie greets me first as always, lunging and looking like she's about to drag Anna down the sidewalk. I bend to pet the dog and glance up at Anna. "You ready?" Today's the big day. She's agreed to run three miles with me. She's been working up to this.

"Hell, yeah!" She's beaming. She likes to see herself as this laid-back creative type, but the girl has a competitive Type A streak running through her too. She starts stretching beside me, doing the moves I've taught her. Without saying a word, I take Chewie's leash. We've got a system. While she stretches, I sit back and watch. She's just a friend, but I am a guy.

Her black Lycra leggings show every muscular curve in her legs and hug the shape of her ass. Her breasts bounce in her tight tank tops as she runs. Today, her long-sleeve running shirt molds tightly to her curves. Any guy would like to look at that each morning. Her brown hair is pulled into a high ponytail, and it swings as she moves. No make-up. She probably brushed her teeth, got dressed, and came straight out here. So different from the women I typically date. Or the women I meet at bars and whose numbers I never keep.

Her bright smile and warm eyes catch me off guard. Sometimes I feel a little overwhelmed by her. She's so damn beautiful. Natural. Sometimes I stare at her and remember her nipples, remember her moans, her smooth, bare pussy. I remember all the little noises she makes when she comes. But, no.

I've thought about her, now that I know she didn't sleep with my roommate. But one thing Chase was right about. Anna's not the kind of girl you date casually. And I don't have time for more right now. I didn't move to a city I don't like to jump on the slow road in a law firm.

"You ready?" She's rubbing her hands together to keep them warm. We need to get moving.

"Remember. Focus on your breathing and rhythm. Breathe through your nose."

We all three take off. Chewie and I are close to the road, tucking her safely on the side of the sidewalk next to the building.

She keeps pace, smiling. "It's like you're training me for a marathon."

I raise my eyebrows. That would be fun to do together. "Maybe I am." As if I'd have the time.

In her husky I'm-trying-to-talk-while-running voice, she says, "You might need another running buddy. This one's good with three miles a day."

I laugh out loud. "On good weather days, right?"

"Hey, I went running with you last week in the rain. Did you forget about that, Coach?"

"You complained the whole way. Did you forget about that?"

We round the corner into Central Park, and all hell breaks loose. Another dog catches Chewie's attention. I shout and yank the leash, but it's too late. Chewie rushes in front of Anna, and she goes flailing forward, right over her dog, hands first onto the pavement, her legs a mangled mess below her. I haul Chewie back with one angry pull on the leash and glare at the dog.

With Chewie under control, I bend to Anna's side. I trail my hands down her legs. Her foot twists in an unnatural angle. Blood covers her palms. Small rocks line the torn skin. A gaping hole exposes a bloody knee, also littered with tiny rocks and what looks like slivers of glass. Basically, her body mopped up the gunk of a city sidewalk. "Are you okay? Do you think you can stand?"

She kind of nods, and I place her arm around my shoulder as I help her up. She starts to put weight on the twisted ankle. She buckles immediately.

"Ow," she gasps. She's staring at her bloody palms, grimacing. Her skinned palms aren't what I'm concerned about. I've been running since I was twelve years old. In a best-case scenario, she has a sprained ankle.

"Are you okay?" I ask again. She doesn't respond. She's bent over, studying her bloody knees and hands, her hurt ankle hanging in the air with no weight on it. My hands brush over her, searching for any immediate swelling. Any sign I should rush her to an ER, even with a dog in tow. "Anna? Answer me."

"Yeah. But I don't think I'm making three miles today."

No shit. "Yeah, I'd agree with you."

I don't see any bones protruding. Nothing warranting an ambulance. I lean down and scoop her up.

"Whoa!"

I head back to our building. Chewie at least has the good manners to follow along on the leash without pulling or making it more difficult.

"You don't need to carry me. I'll be okay."

"No, you won't be. We need to get you back and get some ice. See why you can't put weight on your foot. When we're back at your apartment, we'll see how it is and decide if we need to take you to a doctor."

"Seriously, Jackson. You're going to hurt your back. At the very least, stop and we'll grab a cab."

"You aren't heavy. And I don't have any cash for a cab. Do you?"

She doesn't respond. Just stares straight ahead. Her hand on my shoulder fluctuates between a firm grip and a looser clasp. As if I would drop her. I hold her close to me and focus on getting home.

My concern for her outweighs any discomfort from the strain of carrying her for several blocks. My skin tingles along my neck where her bare arm touches me. A heady awareness of her body being so close fills me, and the arousal drives me to half-mast. Focus.

Brandon sees me through the glass doors and rushes to open them. I trudge in, Anna in my arms, Chewie still right by my side.

"Anna, are you okay?" Brandon asks.

"Yes, but can you push the elevator button for us, please?" I answer, winded.

Brandon runs to the elevator bank ahead of us and asks someone else to stand aside as he prepares a private elevator for us. I make a mental note to give him a good holiday bonus. He rides up in the elevator with us and opens Anna's door.

I settle her down on her futon and thank Brandon. He shakes my hand and says, "No problem, Mr. Hendricks. Anna, you ring downstairs if you need anything, okay?"

Anna wheezes out, "Thank you, Brandon," as she grimaces, clearly in pain.

I gently feel from her knees down, watching carefully for any signs of pain. I run my hands down her right leg, all the way to the end, and not seeing her react, I remove her shoe. Then I cradle her left leg. When I touch her left ankle, she immediately pulls it back and cries out in pain. I untie her left shoe. I want to rip it off like a Band-Aid, but I force myself to ease it off. The entire time, Anna's face contorts in pain.

Her ankle is now visibly swollen. She needs an x-ray. I tell her so, and she disagrees. Typical.

"It's okay. I'm okay. You can stop, Dr. Hendricks," she says, sounding annoyed.

I stand, irritated with her. She needs to see a doctor. "Do you have a first aid kit?"

"Yeah, there's one under the sink." She points toward her bathroom.

There's no need to lose my cool with her. I go to grab the kit so I can clean up her open wounds. If she has a wrap, I can wrap her ankle and try one more time to convince her she needs to visit a doctor.

I reach into the overstuffed cabinet below her sink. The back of the cabinet is jam-packed with random stuff. The front of the cabinet has two sets of stacked baskets. I glance through the baskets, looking for something resembling a first aid kit.

Tampons. Make-up. Nail polish. Maybe twenty things of nail polish in one basket. Who needs so much nail polish? Does she even wear nail polish? Moisturizer.

I tilt a different basket to me and pull out a long rubber piece. I hold it up and close my eyes. Holy shit. Her vibrator. I smirk. I grab the basket and look through it. Anna's added to her collection over the last four years. I kind of like thinking she's needed sex substitutes. I toss the dildo I had in my hand back in, then I see the small, flat vibrator. The We-Vibe vibrator. I bought her this one. It's purple. There's a flat vibrating piece that lies above her clit and then curves around inside. Holy shit. I still remember how those vibrations felt against my dick. I'm fairly certain it's the same one I bought her. On a total whim. We wandered into an Adam and Eve store, giggling like teenagers. I saw it in the case and was intrigued. We had a lot of fun with it.

I step out of the bathroom and hold it up. "Is this the same one I gave you?"

Anna squeals and grabs the throw pillow she's lying on and places it over her head. "Oh. My. God. Jackson. Get out of my bathroom."

Um, no. I need to at least clean up the blood. Laughing, I put the vibrator basket away and continue my search. She's so damn adorable. And now I've got a hard-on.

Okay. Enough of that. I'm never finding anything underneath her sink. I reach for a washcloth from the rack and run it through warm water. This will have to do.

I approach her, ready to clean up her wounds and confirm they are all indeed minor scratches. The bleeding has stopped. The fall mangled her skin, but she'll be okay. Except for her ankle. I frown, skeptical. "Are you going to be okay getting to work?"

"Yes, I'll be fine. I promise. Go to work! You already missed your run because of me. No need to be late to work too."

She has a point. I don't want to be late. But if she needs me, work can wait. I don't have a client until midmorning. "Be careful. Let me know if you need anything. And do you have an extra apartment key?"

"Yeah, why?"

"In case I need to stop by and take Chewie out for a walk. Or I need to bring something to you."

Her hands massage her injured leg, and she grimaces. "Yeah, there's an extra key on the hook. You can grab it. I'm gonna be fine. But good for you to have a key, in case I lose mine. Backup."

"Yeah, backup. I'll leave you one of my keys too."

Every part of me tells me I should be there to help her get to work. Find a doctor then get her to work. Based on the swelling, it looks like a sprained ankle.

I head back to my apartment. She'll be okay. I know this. Still, I schedule an Uber and leave a yellow Post-it note with her coffee by her door. Then I speak to Brandon and ask him to go out and talk to the Uber driver when he arrives in five minutes. I tell him to offer the driver fifty dollars cash to wait for Anna and drive her to work. I order the Uber on my account.

I look Brandon in the eye as I hand him a hundred-dollar bill. "Make sure she gets in the Uber. I don't want her taking the subway today. And if you switch shifts with Al before she comes down, tell Al."

Brandon looks me in the eye and not at the bill. Good man.

"Yes, sir."

As I'm headed out the door, Brandon calls, "Do you think she's going to need crutches?"

"Yes. I told her she needs to go to the doctor. Not sure she will." That girl is stubborn.

"We may have some extra crutches in a closet. Pretty sure we do. I'll bring them out in case she wants to borrow them."

"Thanks. Appreciate it." I make a point of looking him in the eyes the way my dad taught me so he gets my sincerity. It's good to know I can trust him to look out for Anna if I can't be here to do it myself.

eleven

ANNA

I never realized how hard it is to get ready on one leg. By the time I hobble out of my apartment, my right thigh—the leg not sporting a softball sized ankle—burns from all the one-legged hopping and my quads are on fire.

A coffee cup and yellow Post-it note sit to the right of my apartment door when I head out to the office. The note says "Do not put weight on your ankle. Go to the doctor. Let me know what he says."

Yes, sir, boss man. His thoughtfulness brings a smile to my face, but I can do without the domineering attitude. I roll my eyes. Southern men. They can be so overbearing. It's the kind of note I'd have expected from my dad. Or from Evan. I cringe.

As I approach the door of the building to head out, Brandon charges toward me holding crutches. "Anna. Here, I have these for you."

"Thanks so much. Where'd you get these?"

"They were in the hall closet. Mr. Hendricks scheduled an Uber for you. It's waiting outside."

"What? He did?"

"He seemed pretty concerned. And he told me I have to make sure you get in the Uber, so you have to. Don't get me in trouble, Anna." He sounds like he's almost begging, and I suppress a laugh.

Jeez. Is he scared of Jackson? He does refer to him as Mr. Hendricks, which strikes me as weird, but I've never said anything. All the doormen refer to him as Mr. Hendricks.

Thinking back, the first time any one of them called me Ms., I'd shut it down. No, thank you.

"Don't worry. I'll take the Uber. Thank you for the crutches. Whose are they?"

"I don't know. They've been in the back closet since I started working here. They won't be missed. When you don't need them anymore, I'll put them back."

Brandon helps me out to the waiting white Prius. "Anna?"

"Yeah?"

"You really should go to the doctor."

My swollen ankle and foot throb. I couldn't tie my tennis shoe closed. I'm wearing a loose skirt because jeans or anything tight were a no-go. "Yeah, you might be right."

He taps the top of the car twice to alert the driver to drive on, a big smile on his face.

I pull out my phone and snap a picture, then forward it to my brother.

Me:
Think I need to go to the doctor?

Bobby:
Where are you?

Me:
In Uber headed to work.

Bobby:
Come to ER at St. Vincent's. I'm working today.

What did you do?

Me:
Fell when running.

Bobby:
Come now. Probably a sprain but I can wrap it for you. Can you put weight on it?

Me:
No. I'll stop by the office. Then head 2U.

Bobby:
It's not busy. Come now.

I lean over to the Uber driver. "Can you change my destination? Can you take me to St. Vincent's?"

With a perplexed expression on his face, he stares at the screen in front of him like he's not sure what to push to change the destination address en route. Then he glances back at my crutches laying in the passenger seat next to him. He never tackles touching the screen, but mutters, "No problem."

I text Bobby.

Me:
See you in a few.

. . .

Then I realize I'd better alert the team at work about the situation.
I set up a group text to Delilah, John, and Margaret Weisner.

Me:
Hi. I'm going to be a little late this morning.
Fell running and have a swollen ankle.
Headed to doctor and will be in after.

Delilah:
Holy shit. U okay?

Me (private text to Delilah):
It's a group text!

Delilah:
Sorry about that, everyone. Didn't see the
distribution.

Margaret:
Let us know if you need anything, Anna.
Delilah, please inform Anna's team.

Delilah (private text to me):
No group texting so early!

The driver pulls up to the hospital. Bobby's standing outside the
ER doors in his scrubs waiting for me. Like a good big brother,
he's at the car door before I can open it.

Bobby forces me to sit in a wheelchair. I'm wheeled to x-ray
then to a private room in the ER. The x-ray doesn't show any frac-
tures or breaks. Bobby sits on a stool, ACE bandage in hand, and
with a firm but careful touch wraps my ankle.

"This guy you were running with, he couldn't help you get to the hospital?"

"Nah, he had to get to work. At the time, I didn't think I'd need to see a doctor."

"Who is this guy?"

I roll my eyes. Ever since Dad passed away, Bobby's tried to step into some sort of protective dad role. "He's a friend."

"A friend you were out running with before work?" He's done with the ankle wrap now and has my hands flipped over to study my scratched skin.

"He lives in my building. He's been acting kind of like a running coach."

He opens a bottle of clear liquid while repeating, "Running coach."

Then he squirts the liquid on my hands, and I shriek. "Ow! What the…?"

He snatches my hand back and continues squirting the liquid goo. "Keep still. I want to clean this out. It looks like dirt's still in there."

I hide my hands behind my back and glare at him. He glares right back at me. "Anna Elizabeth, stop." Bobby's eyes meet mine, and we sit there glowering at each other until I burst out laughing. Jerk off.

A nurse walks in, and Bobby gives her the bottle. "Would you mind cleaning up my sister's hands and knees?" His hand hovers near my waist, a sure sign he wants to tickle me or maybe give me a wedgie. I shift closer to the nurse for protection, smirking at him. He grins and removes his plastic gloves. "As a general rule of thumb, when your foot is so swollen you can't tie your sneaker, you need to go to the doctor."

I laugh. "Thanks, brother dearest."

I came in wearing a Birkenstock on my healthy foot and a sort of tied sneaker on my swollen foot. I pull the matching Birk out of my bag and test it on my foot. With the wrap, it should stay on.

"So, you're not dating this guy?" Bobby asks while watching me play around with my footwear.

"Nah. We're just friends."

"Are you dating anyone?"

"No. Are you?"

"Touché. But I'm a resident. Unless I meet someone at the hospital, with the same hours I have, dating's tough. But you aren't a resident."

The nurse glances my brother's way. She's an older woman. I get the sense she wants to enter our conversation, but instead she finishes cleaning up my knee.

"Why this interest in my love life?" I ask my brother.

"I wouldn't call it an interest." He stands at the end of the bed, overseeing the nurse's work. "We had a rough go of it, losing both of our parents in two years. I need for you to be happy. You're my little sister. I want to watch out for you. Evan's the last guy I remember you dating. Ages ago."

"I'm fine." I reach out to grab his hand and squeeze. The fresh wounds burn a little, but I don't let go. "Really. I'm fine. I just haven't had much interest in dating. Having a serious relationship so young kind of made relationships a low priority for me."

The nurse finishes up on my knee, gives me a kind smile, and strolls out.

"I get that. I do. It felt like you and Evan were basically married." He sits on the end of the bed. "It had to hurt when Mom and Dad sided with him."

"Yeah. It did. And I hate I never really set things straight with them. I always thought I had more time. Even after Dad died. But I'm okay. I have regrets. A lot of regrets. But I'm okay."

Bobby pulls me in for a hug. "I'm here if you ever need me. You know that, right?"

"Yeah. I do. And I'm super proud of you. Don't worry about me, okay? You focus on becoming the awesome doctor you are destined to be."

He grabs my ponytail and tugs. "Hey, you're all I have. Don't forget. If you need me, I'm here. You may have to wait if there's been a fire or a shooting and I'm on ER rotation. But as soon as the crisis is under control, I'm yours, and I'm here for you."

I pull him in for another hug. I hardly ever get to see him. Might as well make the most of it. "I love you. And do not worry. I'm good."

He clasps my chin and forces my head up. "You've had one relationship. Try again. They won't all be bad."

"What about you?"

He heads to the nearby sink to wash his hands. "You think I want two dudes as roommates? If I could find a hot chick to date and live with while I'm a resident...well, it would be fucking awesome. Did you notice any of the ladies in this hospital when you came in?"

I actually hadn't noticed anyone, but I crack up at his insinuation. "You're saying the ladies in this hospital aren't hot enough for my sexy bro?"

He lifts me and places me back in the wheelchair. "Time for you to get to work."

"That's it, isn't it?" I tease.

"Look around. I'm not at a televised hospital in Seattle, am I?"

"Yeah, but I bet you're Dr. McDreamy to quite a few of the ladies here."

Before he can respond, a different middle-aged nurse named Sharon walks in. She tells Bobby he's needed in another room.

After he leaves, she leans in and in a conspiratorial whisper says, "Trust me. If your brother wants to date, he can get a date."

Interesting. Seems neither of the Daughtridge kids is eager to get trapped in a relationship.

———————

I'm hobbling down the hall when a hand rests on my shoulder. Nick. I cringe. "Anna, babe, what'd you do?"

I arch my shoulders in a get-your-hand-off-me kind of movement. He lifts his hand. I answer him as I continue down the hall. "I fell."

I can feel his eyes on me as I venture away. My skin crawls.

Once I'm in my office, I close my door and pull out my phone. There's a text from Jackson. In an instant, I'm smiling.

> **Jackson:**
> How's the patient?

> **Me:**
> Good. Will need to take a couple of days off running, but all good. ;-)

> **Jackson:**
> I'll walk Chu.

> **Me:**
> Thx. UR the best.

> Seriously, thx for today. And an Uber.
> Really? I can take care of myself. But thx.

Three dots appear and disappear on my phone. Repeatedly. I sit there staring at the phone screen. Waiting.

> **Jackson:**
> Did you go to the doctor?

> **Me:**
> Yes. My brother did x-rays. Nothing broken.

> **Jackson:**
> Do you have dinner plans? Want me to pick something up after work?

So tempting. My ankle throbs. But I've got plans to go out after work with Delilah and Stacy. Back in high school, I canceled plans on friends so often they stopped asking me to do stuff. By senior year, it was pretty much the Evan and Anna Show. For years, if I went out, it was with Evan. I promised myself I'd never be that girl again. Never cancel plans for a guy.

This time, my throbbing ankle justifies a cancellation. And Jackson's just a friend. But a promise to myself is an important one. I can't break it. I don't cancel plans. And canceling for a good-looking guy who somersaults my insides? It's too slippery of a slope. Too much of a repeat. Not again. But I do have an idea.

> **Me:**
> Actually have plans with work folks. Want to join us?

> **Jackson:**
> Sure. You need to stay off your ankle. Don't forget.

I did not expect that response. I expected him to say no. That's what I'd expected.

Butterflies rumble in my stomach. Happy and nervous emotions whirl and collide. Some girls love the so-called butterflies, but I've never been a fan. I don't like being out of control or my body reacting against my will. It's borderline nausea.

I tell myself it's all ridiculous. I'm being ridiculous. Jackson's just a friend. A running buddy. He has no interest in a relationship. I have no interest in a relationship. We went down the dating path. Been there. Done that. So, stomach, calm the F down.

twelve

JACKSON

I head out for lunch and toss my hand up in a quick wave at Celeste, our receptionist, then stop when a shorter guy in khakis catches my eye. He's hunched over reading his phone, his pants hem high so high colorful socks are on full display. *Chase?*

I step forward and kick his leg. The phone clatters across the floor, colliding with the wall, and the noise reverberates through the quiet of our lobby.

Anger flits across his face for the briefest of seconds before Chase jumps up and retrieves his phone. When he turns, head down, there's a definite fear to his stance.

"Hey, man. Wanted to see if you could grab lunch."

My mouth opens a bit. Is he out of his mind? "You thought I'd have time to grab lunch? On a random day? When it's not in my calendar?" I shake my head in disbelief as I charge toward the elevator. The fucking prick.

He follows close on my heels. The elevator is packed with

people headed out to lunch. We don't speak until we make it outside.

"Hey, I'm sorry, man. This is the third day I've stopped by."

I spin around to face him. "What? Is scheduling lunch beyond your skill set?"

"No! You won't return my calls. Or my texts. I need to apologize."

That does it. I grip his blazer and shove him against the closest wall. Out of the corner of my eye, I notice the action garners a couple of spectators. I don't give a damn. "Yes, you do owe me an apology. Best lay of your life, huh?"

"Fuck, man. I'm sorry. I'm so sorry. I didn't know you were dating her. I swear. I didn't realize. I didn't realize you'd give a shit."

I push him hard, grunt, and break away. I head toward the deli across the street.

At the counter I order a tuna salad, grab a coconut water, pay and bump right into the lying prick.

I want to punch him, but he sticks his hands up in a defensive measure and begs. "Man, please. I don't have a good excuse. It was a shit move. The only thing I need you to know is I didn't know. I didn't know it would hurt you. I didn't know it would hurt Anna. I swear to god. If I'd known, I would've never. Never would I have done it. Ever."

I stare at him. I'm a lawyer. As a lawyer, you develop a sixth sense for liars. For pieces of shit. What he did was shit. But, Chase, he's not a piece of shit. He's a friend. And he's been a good friend to Anna. A good friend when she moved here and didn't know anyone. And it was four years ago. If Anna can forgive him, so can I.

I grab him by his neck and take my fist and ruffle his hair, then stick my finger at him like I'm going to poke his eye out. "You ever do that fucking shit again…" I give him the look I hope communicates I'll kill him. I hope it silently conveys my threat, because I'm a lawyer. No need to have that shit come back and bite me in the ass.

"Where's your lunch?"

"I haven't ordered yet."

"Go get it. I've got, like, five minutes."

As he's ordering, I ask him to lift his pants leg. He squints like he's not sure he heard me correctly, and I wave my hand upward. He lifts his leg. Superman and Wonder Woman are flying all over his socks. And I think I see a Yoda. A Yoda. His socks are a random collage of superheroes from various universes.

I roll my eyes and lead him to my favorite park bench.

thirteen

JACKSON

Heading out of the office, I see the digital clock on my assistant's desk and halt for a moment, staring in disbelief. Six-thirty on a Friday.

Guilt riddles my insides, inwardly cringing as I wave goodbye to people on the way out. All the first-years are still at work in the cubicle farm. At least two partners type away on laptops as I head out. As a matter of course, I prefer to be the last to leave.

Images of Anna putting weight on her swollen ankle have been going through my head on repeat. She won't take her injury seriously. Won't use the crutches. By meeting her, I can insist we take a cab home and prevent her from navigating the subway.

I imagine Anna sitting on a barstool. Single men prowling around. An injured girl, plenty of openings for men to pick up a conversation. A sitting duck for any asshole to come up and play Prince Charming. Fuck that.

As I open the door into Sullivan's to meet Anna, my muscles

immediately tense. My right hand balls into a fist. A tall, muscular, blond man leans into Anna, his entire body pressed against her side. One hand is holding a beer, and the other lies possessively around her back.

I stand frozen to the ground, trying to decipher what's going on. *What the fuck?* Is she with this guy? If yes, I'll leave. No way am I hanging around her and the guy she's bringing home tonight.

As I stare, Anna leans farther away, almost turning her back to him. She looks like she's trying to catch the attention of another woman standing by the dartboard. She looks uncomfortable, and that's all I need to know.

As I head her way, Anna sees me, and her entire face breaks into a warm smile. "Jackson!" she shouts. Is she happy to see me or thankful for an escape?

I tread forward. She leaps off the barstool and hops toward me with one-legged jumps. She flings her arms around my neck when she reaches me. My breath catches as her breasts press against my chest and her arms slide from my neck to my shoulders. I run my fingers through her dark, soft, loose waves. My arms circle her in a hug, and her light lavender fragrance surrounds me. Like magic, my tense muscles relax.

I watch the douchebag who had been crowding her. He remains at the bar with his beer in hand and a snide expression.

She reaches up to angle my head down so she can whisper in my ear. "Will you do me a favor?"

I pull back a bit so I can see her honey brown eyes, my arms still around her shoulders. "Yeah," I whisper back. I'll do anything for her. Protect her. Care for her.

"You see the guy who was standing by me at the bar?"

"Yeah." I glance over. He's watching us.

"He's a colleague, and he's a bit overbearing. Can you pretend we're dating?"

She couldn't possibly know how happy her request makes me. I grin. "Abso-fucking-lutely." She hasn't mentioned this guy before, but I don't like him. And if he's a colleague, it's definitely not okay. If he'll treat her like that while out with others, I can't help but wonder if he also comes on to her at the office when they're alone. I'll have to remember to ask.

I wrap my arm around Anna's shoulder. She tilts her face up, and I lean down closer. Something deep inside urges me to take possession, and I brush my lips against hers. Yes, we're pretending, but she asked to send a message to the jerk.

Her lips are soft. Her eyes widen with surprise. I press my lips against hers again, and she shocks me by rubbing her hand along my face and opening up to deepen the kiss. My tongue slips into her mouth and dances with hers. Goosebumps spring up along my arms, and blood rushes to my cock. It's a fake kiss. An act. Damn if I don't enjoy it, though.

Her cheeks flush pink. I'm out of breath and have no desire to address the guy standing near us, or anyone else, for that matter. Her kiss drives me crazy. I want to carry her out of here and find a private place to kiss her until she begs for more, but I refrain. She's here with colleagues. We're pretending. Then I see her wrapped ankle.

"Have you been walking on your ankle much? You should be sitting."

The fondness in her warm brown eyes cuts me to the quick. She seems grateful I'm concerned for her. We're friends. Of course, I'm concerned.

I guide her back to her stool. Anna introduces me to Nick, the asshole, and Delilah and Stacey, her colleagues.

Nick and I exchange hard looks as we shake hands. *That's right, asshole. Hands off. I'm a lawyer, and a sexual harassment lawsuit has your name on it, free of charge, motherfucker.*

Nick holds his beer, his eyes assessing. His scowl zeroes in on my arm wrapped around Anna's shoulder.

Anna snuggles into my side as she carries on a conversation with Delilah. She feels good, her soft, full breast pressed against me. This is a game I enjoy playing. Maybe a little too much.

With an almost angry tone, Nick interrupts. "Anna, you haven't mentioned a boyfriend."

"Yeah, well, I just moved to New York a few weeks ago," I offer. *Look at me, asshole, not her.*

She adds, "We knew each other at Carolina."

He watches us—no, glares at us—and he continues drinking his beer, his face radiating anger.

Nick and I continue eyeing each other as I politely answer questions from Delilah and Stacey. Both are art directors on Anna's team and seem particularly interested in meeting their boss's "boyfriend." Delilah, in particular, flips her hands around and bops up and down as she talks. The mass of hair on top of her head bounces in tandem.

Nick finishes his beer, sets it down, and says, "Well, I'm going to call it a night. Need to prepare for my party tomorrow." He directs his attention to the three women. "You ladies are coming, right?"

Delilah and Stacy, with big smiles, assure him they'll be there. Delilah adds, "Yeah, it sounds like a pretty big crew is gonna make it. Should I bring my Jell-O shots?"

"Please do. Love those." Directing his gaze to Anna, he asks, "Are you coming?"

Anna's unease is evident. She snuggles into my side and caresses my chest. *Hell, yes.* My pride grows, and a feeling of protectiveness surges. That's not the only part of my anatomy surging. Damn Anna.

"No, I'm not gonna be able to make it. Jackson and I have plans."

I nod along with her. *Take that, asshole. And anything you want, Anna, I'm game.*

After he leaves, Anna shifts away from me on her stool. Delilah jumps up and down in front of us, a huge grin plastered on her face. "Holy shit! You took my advice and got a fake boyfriend."

Anna grins over her beer. "Hey, how do you know he's fake?"

I can't help but wonder the same thing.

Delilah smiles. "Because you never date. And you'd tell me if you actually went out on a date. I've worked with you for, what, three years now, and you avoid dates like I've never seen anyone avoid dates."

Now, this is interesting information. Unexpected. At Carolina, I'd seen her many nights out dancing with different guys, shaking her ass to a variety of bands. And she went on dates with me.

Anna appears a bit uncomfortable at Delilah's assessment, but she doesn't argue. She goes for a conversation turner instead and asks Delilah about some guy named Josh. The conversation then pivots and focuses completely on Delilah's love interest.

As Anna interacts with her colleagues, I can't stop watching her. Her long, dark hair falls in loose waves midway down her back. Her loose, flowing skirt drapes over her lean, muscular legs. Legs I admire running in shorts or tight leggings each morning. Her oversized gray sweater has one large hole near the bottom. She dressed for comfort today, but even in loose and casual, she oozes sexy. I can't help but think about what's hidden beneath her clothes. Those large, dark nipples, her flat stomach, and her perfect, curvy ass.

She's beautiful, but she isn't my type. My type is more suits, sexy, form-fitting pencil skirts, and heels. Corporate sexy. Boardroom sharp. No, she's not my type. And it would be the height of stupidity to hook up with someone living on my floor. And I don't plan to be in a relationship again for another five years, at the earliest. The kind of hours I have to put in is not conducive to a relationship.

Back at Carolina? Yeah, I had wanted a relationship with her then. I'd wanted to rearrange our plans to be together. She didn't. And now, the timing doesn't work. Maybe in another four years.

But I need a date for a work event coming up. After I played along with this, she owes me.

On the cab ride home, I deliberate the facts. We're just friends. Doing each other favors. I'm going to be running her dog for her until her ankle strengthens.

Almost as if she's a mind reader, she says, "Thank you for hanging out this evening. And for pretending to be my boyfriend."

"Yeah, about that. Does that guy treat you like that at the office?"

She looks out the window, away from me. A slight pink blush colors her cheeks. "Sometimes. I've got it under control, though."

That wasn't really what it looked like to me, but Anna doesn't respond well when I argue with her. "Well, if you need me to play along as your boyfriend, I'm happy to do so anytime."

"I should take a selfie of us and frame it to put on my desk. It seems like a crazy thing to do, but it would drive home the point." She sounds proud for coming up with the idea.

"What point? That you aren't interested?" Has she lost her mind? She should tell the guy she's not interested. If that doesn't solve it, there are legal ways to handle him.

"Yeah." She smiles and nods. Does she not realize there is something seriously wrong if she needs to fake a boyfriend to deflect someone's attention at work? Since her focus has returned to the window, away from me, and she's fidgeting, I decide to drop it. For now.

Instead, I go for the question I want to ask. "Since I helped you out, can you help me? Return the favor?"

She gives me her full attention. "Sure. You need to deflect attention?"

"Yeah, but of the partners' wives variety."

"They're hitting on you?" she practically squeals with a huge smile.

"No. Not at all. But I've been warned they are like piranhas if they sense a single guy around. They have a reputation of being aggressive matchmakers. Blind dates. Even worse, blind dates with daughters and friends' daughters." I shiver dramatically and widen my eyes in mock fear to drive home the point. She giggles. "There's a work function coming up. I could use a fake date."

"Sure, I'd love to be your fake date."

When she giggles, it makes me feel ten feet tall. I'd forgotten what that felt like. Yes, she's the perfect date to bring. Gorgeous, fun, and doesn't want a boyfriend. Doesn't want me so there's no misplaced expectations. Perfect. She's perfect.

fourteen

ANNA

Early Saturday evening, the knocking on my door sends Chewie into a manic round of vicious barking. Her tail wags frantically behind her as she charges. Both front paws pound on the door as she jumps at it, as if there's a chance she can defy the laws of physics and pass through it.

I leap up, ignoring the jabbing pain in my ankle, and hobble to the door as quickly as a one-legged injured person can. If possible, I'd like to avoid a third warning from building management.

I scold Chewie, telling her to hush, as I open the door. As soon as the door opens, Chewie stops barking, which is good. She lunges forward, paws landing square on Jackson's chest, which is bad. Jackson kind of laughs and scratches beneath her ears. He's wearing a form-fitting black V-neck, faded jeans, and running shoes. He looks absolutely delectable. Casual Jackson is my favorite Jackson.

"I probably should have texted. Wanted to see if you wanted to order dinner in. I think you said you're staying in tonight, right?"

Rain has splattered across my windows all day. A cold, miserable rain that's doubly miserable on windy city streets. Bobby stopped by early this morning to take Chewie for a long walk. He left with strict instructions for my dog walker to do the afternoon walk. I've been a lump all day, alternating between reading and Netflix.

"Yeah. It's rainy. Great night to stay in." I point at my ankle and grin. "No dancing tonight. That's for sure."

Jackson follows me inside to the futon. My menu basket sits on the coffee table. We claim opposite ends of the lumpy futon. I'm in loose flannel pajama bottoms and a gray ribbed tank top with thick fluffy socks. My hair's kind of a wavy mess. It did occur to me he might come over, but I thought it would be a little later.

He flicks through the menus and picks up the one from Peng's Noodle Folk. One of my favorites. "Ramen and dumplings sound good?"

"A man after my own heart." I stand and hobble over to the kitchen. "Do you want red or white?" Before I reach the kitchen, he's behind me. He scoops me up and delivers me back to the futon.

He grumbles, "Stay off the ankle." He opens the door and flips the lock so the door can't close on him and calls, "I'll be right back."

Chewie stands by the propped-open door. The black tip of her nose fits inside the gaping crack, and she stands sentry.

Within minutes, Jackson returns with two bottles of wine and two wine glasses. "Red okay? I didn't ask, but it goes best with what we ordered."

"That's fine. I love good wine. I really love those glasses." The wine glasses are enormous, and there's an artistic indention in the curve of the bulb on one side.

He holds one up. "I bought a dozen of these on a trip to Napa last year. Handblown glass. The large glass allows the wine to breathe. Also holds a lot of wine." He wiggles his eyebrows in a playful, exaggerated way.

He picks up my phone from the coffee table and thumbs through playlists, finally selecting one of my more random lists with funky melodies. Phosphorescent's song, *New Birth in New England*, drifts from my wireless speakers through my apartment.

It's one of my favorite songs. As the singer sings about having another beer, I sit back, swirling the wine in my glass and ponder how many glasses of wine I'm going to allow myself to drink.

"You've been on your ankle too much. Sit back." He grabs some throw pillows to position behind my back then sets another pillow down and props both my legs on it. Then he ventures into my bedroom and comes back with one of my throws. He cocoons me in the soft throw then plops down at the end of the futon.

His bossy, commanding side normally irks me, but the wine and relaxing music has me feeling mellow. And it's kind of nice to be taken care of. I can't remember the last time anyone treated me with so much care.

Our food arrives, and Jackson handles everything. Pays the delivery guy, sets out the plates, and cleans up when we're done. Four years have passed, but it's like no time has passed at all. We're good friends, hanging out like we used to. We talk about music, about food, good restaurants, and my favorite places in the city.

My phone pings, and I read the text.

Delilah:
Still not coming tonight?

Me:
No

> **Delilah:**
> Hanging with the Todd Snyder man?

> **Me:**
> Who?

Jackson leans over to read my text. "Todd Snyder?"

I tap the back of my phone as I await her response. "No idea."

> **Delilah:**
> The guy from the bar last night.

> **Me:**
> Jackson?

> **Delilah:**
> He was wearing Todd Snyder.

"Were you wearing a brand called Todd Snyder last night?"

He raises one eyebrow, a contemplative expression on his face. "Yeah, I guess. Maybe. I use a personal shopper. Your friend knows her brands."

> **Me:**
> Why do you know men's brands?

> **Delilah:**
> Girlfriend, why don't you?

I toss my phone onto the table. It's rude to be texting in front of Jackson, anyway.

Jackson picks up my sore leg and rotates my foot, checking for tenderness. I lean back, sipping my wine, and enjoy watching him. My loose pajama pants allow his hand to roam, and as we talk, his strong hands massage my calf muscles. My whole body relaxes into his touch.

"Is Delilah a good friend?"

"Probably too good of a friend, considering she works for me. An opening is coming up in another group, and I'm going to recommend she take it. My agency isn't huge, and we all hang out together, but she's become one of my best friends. It'll be better for her if she switches groups, you know?"

He nods in agreement. "I can see that. My firm in Atlanta was enormous. Cutthroat competitive. I don't have a frame of refer-ence. But I can see how it would be tough to manage a good friend." He shifts, adjusting himself on the futon, and adds, "I'm glad you didn't go to Nick's party tonight."

He has no idea about the history there. But he did meet Nick.

"There was no way I was going to the party. I don't like him. He's a strange guy. But he's a group account director, a level up from me. He's close friends with the founders of the agency. I have to play nice to some degree. He was one of the first five employees."

"Well, I don't know what he's like in your office, but I can tell you that what I saw in the bar was not acceptable behavior for a colleague, especially a senior colleague."

He sounds like such a lawyer. Or maybe a dad. Yes, what he's saying is true. But I can't explain the entire situation to him. "I know. I promise I've got it under control. Thanks again for being my fake boyfriend." I smile, and a warmth spreads as I remember our kiss. Our kisses. "The kiss surprised me," I whisper. "It was nice."

His eyes widen. I notice his eyes have a dark green hue tonight. That's one thing I used to love about Jackson. His chameleon eyes. And personality. He can flip from boyish to serious in a nanosecond. I loved knowing all his sides. And that he has sides he doesn't share with others, but he shared only with me.

He lifts my healthy leg onto his lap and presses the sole of my foot, using his strong fingers to knead and press. I shift to allow him greater access. If I were a cat, I would be purring loudly. Man, foot massages might be my favorite. Evan, my ex, used to do this when we were watching movies at his house in the basement, when our relationship was new. Such a long time ago.

Jackson studies my feet, as if examining my navy nail color. Minutes pass, and I hear a quiet, "Yeah, I agree. About the kiss." He's quiet after his admission, and so am I. I'm about to suggest we pick a movie when he asks, "Have you ever thought about what would have happened if we'd taken jobs in the same city?"

His question surprises me. "Hmmm. If we'd planned to move to the same city, we wouldn't have fought."

He nods, silent, contemplative.

"But, Jackson, I'm glad we went to different cities."

He drops my foot. "You are?"

"Yeah. I wanted to make it on my own. I needed to. I think."

He studies me and reaches out to grab the remote, then pauses. "Right now, that's what I need. To be on my own. Work has to be my top priority."

I get it. I do. Jackson has a lot to prove to his dad. To his family. His dad wanted him to join his company, and he chose law. No one gets it more than I do. I nod to show him I understand.

"But if things were different, if dating made sense for me, there's no one I'd rather date than you."

Swoon. Right there. Swoon. "Right back at you."

He frowns. "Why exactly is dating not in the cards for you right now?"

I heave out a sigh and run my hand through my hair. "I'm kind of in the same boat, work-wise, I guess? I'm a creative director. I have a team of people, almost all older than I am, reporting to me. I'm doing work on three accounts plus helping out on new business when I get the chance. It's a lot." Green eyes study me. "My parents never wanted me to have a career. They wanted me to get married. It was…I don't know. Both my parents aren't here now, so maybe it's ridiculous. But I feel like I have something to prove. If not to them, to myself. Does that sound crazy?"

He raps his foot on the floor several times in quick succession. "No. Not at all. Doesn't answer why you can't date, though."

"Why is work a satisfactory answer for you and not for me?"

He chuckles and leans over to tap his finger on the tip of my nose. "Good point."

We both sip our wine.

"Over the last four years, have you dated?"

I shake my head. He raises an eyebrow, questioning. "You've got to understand. My last four years have been intense, to say the least."

"How so?"

"Less than a year after graduation, my dad was diagnosed with lung cancer. It was a tough time. Lots of trips back home. He passed away two years ago. Then, about a year later, my mom passed away. Suddenly. Heart attack."

"I'm sorry. I can't even imagine how difficult it would be. Losing both your parents so close together."

"We had a lot of stuff between us. Things we never worked through. The fact we never buried the hatchet, so to speak, made it more difficult."

"What things did you never work through?"

"Things. Stuff with my ex." I tilt my head and study the wine in my glass. "Do you mind if we don't talk about it?"

"Sure."

"Can we just watch the movie?"

We pick *Voyeur*. It's a documentary about a guy who bought a motel in Colorado in the sixties and watched the guests from a secret room he built above the hotel. He watched for decades and chronicled everything he saw in notebooks. It's disturbing but also weirdly sexy at times.

About midway through, it loses appeal. Jackson's fascinated by potential legal ramifications, and he's researching legal statutes. My heart goes out to the old men seeking fame this one last time in their lives. Both the voyeur and the journalist covering the story are, at the end of the day, seeking one last moment in the limelight.

"What do you do for sex?" Jackson's deep timbre breaks me out of my forlorn thoughts about the two elderly men.

The direct question surprises me, and fail to smother my laugh. The buzz of the wine makes me bold and open. "You saw my basket in the bathroom. I have more in my bedside table."

His face breaks into a huge, boyish smile.

"What?" I ask, grinning, knowing exactly what he's thinking about.

"That's quite a collection."

My cheeks burn with embarrassment. "Yeah. I'd hoped you'd miss those." Awkward. "But they serve a purpose. To answer your question." I lift my eyebrows and smirk. It's hard to have a serious conversation about masturbation toys.

Jackson grins. "So, vibrators in lieu of sex. Do you go on casual dates?"

I swirl the wine in my glass as I answer. "No. There's no point. I don't want a relationship. I was in a relationship for four years. It's not what I want. Not right now. I want to focus and concentrate on me. Living my life, for myself. That's what I want."

"Women tend to say they don't want a relationship when they want to have sex with all kinds of different people and want to justify it." I study Jackson as I finish off the wine. His bare feet are kicked out on the coffee table. The man has sexy feet. What man has sexy feet? The worn jeans have a frayed hem ending near his ankle, where a few black hairs curl.

"That's not it. Not for me. Promise. And besides, what about you? You don't want a relationship either." He's being pretty judgmental for someone standing in my shoes.

He shrugs in a noncommittal way, but it's obvious he's fighting a smile. "I'm not against relationships. I just don't have time for one." He reaches over and pinches my leg. "You didn't really answer my question."

I open my mouth, torn between jumping on him for a somewhat chauvinistic attitude or joking around. "You mean about sex? You saw my collection. Stop asking!" I take a throw pillow and toss it at him, laughing. "What about you?"

He smirks. Shoulders back, arms crossed, he communicates an odd combination of both proud and defensive. "I have sex. I don't date."

Now I'm curious. "Where do you find willing women?"

He runs his hands through his hair. "Bars. Around town. There are women who want the same thing." Perhaps his earlier comment about women is based on experience.

"Doesn't it get exhausting?"

"What?"

"Finding random people to hook up with."

His forehead wrinkles as his eyebrows raise slightly. "Yeah, it does. I don't do it all the time. Only when I need a release."

"I guess I don't know how to do casual sex. I'm not a 'meet them at a bar, bang them in the bathroom, and say goodbye' kind of girl. That's never appealed to me. I feel like after the first date, expectations are set. I'd expect that's even more true after sex. Titles are applied. Girlfriend. Boyfriend. I can't begin to imagine how the casual dating scene works."

"Speaking from experience?" He squints, taking me in.

"Yeah."

"Not from us, though, right? Did you think I—"

"No," I jump in. "No, not you. Not us. Back then. My first boyfriend. Let's just say it was a lot. With you, at Carolina, since we were already going different places and we were both so busy, I never felt pressured." I pause and pull a throw around me. "At least, until you told me to get a different job and move to Atlanta."

He jerks back. "I did not tell you any such thing."

"Yes, you did."

"No, I didn't. You are wrong."

"Yes, you did!"

Without any warning, he lunges over me, and I squeal. He's all hands, grabbing my waist and tickling. I screech and wiggle, and we're both laughing.

I squeal, "I give. I give. Stop. Stop."

"You admit I didn't tell you to do anything?"

"Yes." *No.* I pull back, and we're both breathless. "Do you do this to everyone you interrogate?"

He bites his lip and grins. "Only stubborn ones. Only you." Jackson jumps off the sofa and heads into the kitchen. He comes back with a second bottle of wine and fills our glasses. He sits down, and his eyes sparkle. "I have an idea. A proposal of sorts. Something that might work for both of us."

"A proposal?"

He nods, a big grin on his face. He reminds me of an errant boy up to no good. "Yeah, we're friends. Right?"

"Yeah."

"We're good friends. Known each other for years. Comfortable with each other. Well, as you are aware, I'm not looking for a relationship at all. As a matter of fact, with my work hours, no one in her right mind would want a relationship with me." His speech picks up tempo, faster and faster.

"Yeah?" My head swirls with a slight buzz, and I find myself focusing on his biceps and forearms. He's wearing a braided leather bracelet with silver endings. Dark hair covers his arms, and I have an urge to reach over and rub my fingers through it. He's stopped talking. I lift my eyes to his dark, green, hungry gaze.

"What about friends with benefits?"

I snort. "*What*?"

He holds up a hand and attempts a serious, firm expression. "No decision tonight. Think about it. Neither of us wants a relationship. If I'm being honest, I actually don't like dating. I find it to be time-consuming. I do occasionally hook up with women I meet out at bars, but I'd rather not have to make the effort."

"The effort? Really? You mean talking to a woman?" I remember him in college. Girls surrounded him. Now that he sports suits and has a powerful air, I imagine the only difference between college and now is he's surrounded by women of all pedigrees.

"No, I mean going to bars. Playing the game, flirting, trying to get them home with clear expectations for no follow-up."

Grinning, I gaze at him, amused at his explanation.

"Don't knock me on this. To some degree, you feel the same way I do. You don't like dating, or at least you don't seem to. Casual hookups aren't necessarily the best."

I roll my eyes. The two of us are similar, but he's being ridiculous. Friends with benefits never works.

"You and I, we already know we're sexually compatible." He's right, there. If a girl had a spank bank, I'd say our two months together in Chapel Hill fills a large percentage of mine. "You won't feel like you are at risk of slipping into a relationship, because it's not an option with us. It's not something either of us wants. I'm not going to try to apply the girlfriend title. Casual can work because we'll agree to it before anything starts. And we'll still be friends. We'll be intimate with someone we care about. Which, I suspect, Anna, is the only kind of intimacy you want."

Right again. After the one night with Nick, there aren't enough words to describe how dirty and ashamed I felt. Embarrassed. Wrong. I'm still dealing with the aftermath of my drunken mistake.

My skin tingles. My heart beats faster. He slides closer. Temptation. He's gorgeous. Maybe more so now. My body thrums with anticipation. I swallow. Damn the wine. Is the wine making this whole crazy idea seem reasonable?

He doesn't want a girlfriend. I don't want a boyfriend. But we both like sex. He's not going to tell me what to wear, or who I can be friends with, or how to spend my time.

"Would you want to do that with me? I mean, are you attracted to me?" Without doubt, I'm attracted to him. My body reacts when he's near with tingling or goosebumps. My heart races when I see him. But he's the picture of calm. When we're running or talking, he never shows any signs he's into me. He's buttoned up, a consummate professional. I can't imagine I'm his type.

In answer to my question, Jackson takes my hand and places it on his crotch. My fingers curl around the curve of his hard-on. Without thinking, I circle my hand over the bulge, rubbing and stroking. He grunts.

"Do you feel this? How hard you make me? That's what you do to me. I wouldn't have suggested this if I didn't want it."

I squeeze my legs together, my muscles tingling with anticipation. Heat floods my center. Without a shadow of a doubt, I'm dripping, ready. It's been so long—so long since I've had something other than my own fingers or a battery-operated toy.

"Okay," I agree, butterflies in my stomach. This could work. No slipping. An agreement to be casual.

He crawls over me, pushing me back and pressing his weight between my thighs. We're eye to eye. He rotates his hips, rubbing his crotch against mine, eliciting a moan. From me. From him. I'm not certain. "We'll take it slow. We won't have sex tonight, but we'll take our time leading up to it. Make sure you're still on board with our plan tomorrow. Sound good?"

I lift his t-shirt and run my hands over the smooth, firm skin of his back. *Oh. My.* My fingers explore the dips and valleys of the strong, toned muscles on his torso. The curve of his pecs. My throat tightens, making it harder to swallow. "Okay."

He drops his mouth to mine, and our tongues dance back and forth. Soft, testing at first, and then our kiss becomes heated. Ravaging. His body rubs against my clit, the sensation bringing me close to climax. We're dry fucking like teenagers. The rubbing against my swollen labia stokes my libido. I lift my hips, begging for more, and he picks up his pace. I grip his shirt, and we separate long enough for me to tug it off, tossing it on the floor.

He grabs the hem of my tank and slides it over my head. He sits back on his heels, his gaze devouring me. "You are gorgeous. Your breasts are even better than I remember. Perfect." He bends down and presses his lips to my breast softly at first, then circles my erect nipple with his tongue before sucking it. His tongue twirls as he sucks, and I arch my back. Sensations ripple through my body as he plucks and nips, his hands caressing and kneading. I scream out in ecstasy, the mixture of pain and pleasure bordering on too much.

"Shh," he whispers. "We can't have Lester lodging a complaint."

Funny. But as soon as his mouth returns to lavish attention on my other nipple, the humor escapes me. My hips grind against him. His erection rubs between my legs, lighting up my bundle of nerves, but it's not enough. I want more. I need him. Inside. "Please," I gasp. "More." I reach between us, fumbling with his jeans.

"Yeah?" He grunts out the question.

"Yeah." *Oh, god. Yes!*

He shifts downward, and I miss his weight and the friction. He presses soft kisses down my stomach until he reaches the waist of my pajama pants. Lying to my side, he grabs my pants and panties and pulls them down below my knees, using his foot to push them all the way down. He sits up to gently maneuver around my injured ankle and then throws them on the floor.

I'm lying there naked before him.

He pauses, taking me in. "So gorgeous."

I want him. He said we won't tonight, but I'm too excited. Too turned on. \ I want to seduce him. Entice him to say yes. I palm my wet channel, one finger teasing along the crease, sliding in and out, spreading my juices. My other hand twists my nipple and fondles my breast. My sensations are heightened, knowing he's watching. I'm dripping. I rub harder, faster, reveling in the feeling of the heel of my hand applying pressure to my sensitive clit. He watches me, eyes dark. He pushes his jeans down and kicks them off. His hand wraps around his hard cock and strokes.

I'm not sure what possesses me, but I lick then suck my juices off my fingers. We're taunting each other. Teasing. Apparently, sucking my fingers was all I had to do to get him moving again.

He growls and falls onto me. His erection lies flat against my naked stomach. He plunders my mouth with a hunger and need that leave me breathless and wanting. He's familiar, yet new. I want to acquaint myself with every inch of his delectable body.

I wrap my legs around his waist, attempting to situate his cock near my throbbing entrance. His tip teases and dips into my wetness. He pauses, watching, shifting his hips back and forth. His tip slides in. Then out. We both watch, and I shudder. He sits back, placing distance between us, and kisses me, repeating his path around my breasts, sucking and softly biting my nipples, before continuing down. Hovering over my pussy, he looks up at me, eyes questioning and asking permission.

"Please," I pant.

His tongue licks between my folds, teasing, then dives deeper. My back arches in ecstasy. Magic. His tongue. I lift up on my elbows, so I can watch as he hungrily laps up my wetness. His tongue finds my button, and he sucks then nips. He slips two fingers inside, and I ignite. My heart pounds, and my muscles tense so much my toes curl. "Oh, Jack!" The orgasm unfurls through my body with ripples of pleasure. Slippery wetness drips from between my legs.

He climbs up my body and lies beside me, our naked chests against one another. He gives me a slow, tender kiss, and I drink him in, tasting myself, mixed with him. His firm, thick cock presses against my belly. I wrap my hand around him and squeeze then stroke.

He pulls back and rubs a hand along my face and growls, "If you keep doing that, do you think I'll have the willpower to hold back from sinking into you?"

But that's exactly what I want. I want him inside me. I don't stop. I stroke and rotate my hips. He rubs against me, teasing me, making me want nothing more than his cock inside me, filling me. He nips at my earlobe and hisses, "Not a chance."

His movements elicit a flood of sensations, the pressure on my engorged clit building me toward a second orgasm. "I want that. I want your cock inside me."

He closes his eyes, growling as he rubs against me harder. His tip, firm and hard, teases my entrance. I swivel my hips to capture him, to pull him inside to satiate the burning need.

He grips my hips. I look up, questioning. Does he not want this?

He swallows and presses a firm kiss on my lips, his hands firmly holding my hips in place. "I said we would go slow. Let's go slow." He shifts, and his throbbing cock presses against my belly, just above my wet, swollen entrance.

"This is slow?"

"Yes, no sex tonight."

"But what about you? I want to make you feel good."

"Well, I didn't say I'd object to seeing your lips take me," he says with a wolfish grin.

I smile. Now, *that,* I can do. Suddenly, I crave his cock in my mouth. I want to give him pleasure. I want to take him deep in my throat. I straddle him and rain kisses down his neck and chest. I move lower, sliding off the futon to my knees.

I stop to admire him. His chest is muscular. Six-pack abs. And his cock. He's large and thick. His erection aims upward with a nice curve, begging to be ridden. I remember his body from a long time ago. Reality trumps memory. I bend to lick his head, tasting the precum. He grasps the edge of the futon as if he's bracing himself. Turned on by his reaction, I grip him at the base with one hand and take him deep in my mouth. My hand on the base of his cock covers what I can't take in my mouth and moves in tandem with my head. I'm on my knees, but I'm powerful. Right now, I'm all he's thinking about.

"Oh, fuck, Anna. Yes." He utters random words and nonsense as I fuck him with my mouth. His cock widens, and I know he's close. He places a hand on the back of my head, urging me to go deeper. I take a breath and go down as deep as I can until he hits the back of my throat. I pull back and lick, swallowing my saliva and his juices.

"Do you like fucking my mouth?" I ask, wetness dripping down my chin.

He chokes out, "Fuck, yes."

I grin and go back to sucking him off. He places a hand on the back of my head, pushing me deeper. His cock pulses in my mouth. "I'm going to come. God, if you don't want me to…"

I work harder, sucking deeper, hollowing out my cheeks. I massage his testicles, and they tighten before he explodes in my mouth, the taste warm and salty. I swallow every last bit.

He closes his eyes and leans his head back. "Wow."

He holds my hand and helps me up off the floor. We hold each other, our naked bodies pressed together. He gives me a slow, tender kiss. The kiss deepens as I run my hand through his hair. This feels good. That thought snaps me back to reality.

I jerk back. I need space. I've never done friends with benefits before, but something tells me cuddling after isn't going to keep us relationship-free.

I search the floor and reach for my tank top and bottoms. An awkwardness fills the room as I pull them on. Once clothed, I'm more comfortable, but he's sitting on the futon watching me. Naked.

I grab his t-shirt from the floor then locate his jeans across the room where they landed when he kicked them off and toss them both onto his lap.

Jackson's voice rings with caution. "Are you okay? Is everything okay?"

His question stops me. Yes, I'm a little embarrassed. It's a little awkward now. But I'm okay. I enjoyed everything we did. I want to do it again.

I give him what I hope is a reassuring smile. "No. I mean, I feel a little awkward, but I'm good." I tilt my head, uncertain but wanting to give him more. "I enjoyed that."

Jackson sits up and pulls on his jeans. Then his t-shirt. He grabs my waist and pulls me down on top of him and kisses me. His kiss calms me, and I rub my hands along his chest then start toying with his hair. I breathe him in. He smells like pine, clean and fresh. He smells like Jackson. And arousal. And sex.

He exhales and shifts, putting some distance between us. "Good. Tomorrow afternoon, you doing anything?"

My brain's foggy. The orgasm and the wine blend together to slow my thoughts and responses. "No, I don't have plans for tomorrow. Doing some work. I won't be running tomorrow, but maybe sometime next week."

He stands up, decisive. "I'll stop by in the morning to bring

Chewie with me on my run. Tomorrow afternoon, let's plan to hang out."

He heads toward the door.

"Jackson, wait. Are we okay? I mean, this was intense. I'm not sure I totally buy into the whole friends with benefits thing."

Grinning, he saunters back to me and rests his hands on my shoulders. "We're in a great place for friends with benefits. We're both workaholics. Neither of us wants a serious relationship at this time in our lives. But we both like sex. And we are really conveniently located near each other." He grins and bites his lip in the sexy way he has, then leans down and presses a soft, sweet kiss to my forehead.

"If you change your mind, just let me know. We'll play it by ear. Day by day." He brushes his lips against mine. "See you tomorrow."

The brush of lips leaves me wanting more, needy. My intense arousal alone tells me this is not a risk-free plan. But, damn, I really am horny. I'd started watching pornos in my bedroom recently while I masturbated.

Friendship with benefits, as strange and probably unwise as it is, could be the right solution for this time in our lives. There's no risk of slipping into a relationship. Not with Jackson now. Maybe four years ago he wanted a relationship, but today he's a different person. And me. This isn't going to develop into the kind of relationship that derails my future. There's no risk of blinking and becoming my mom. Or finding myself in some controlling relationship without any say in my life. Maybe this isn't the worst idea. Friends with benefits lays the parameters out clearly. No emotion, no demands.

fifteen

JACKSON

Sunday morning, I wake with a raging hard-on. And I jerk off thinking about eating her salty-sweet pussy and sliding into her later today.

Our arrangement will be good for her. Whether she admits it or not, she loves sex. There's no reason for a healthy woman in her twenties to forego sex simply because she doesn't want a relationship. Now that she didn't go and bang my roommate, I can buy she's not a casual sex kind of girl. Friends with benefits will allow her to have sex with someone she's comfortable with. Casual but not random.

I wasn't lying when I told her I'm not crazy about the whole trolling the bar scene for a sexual release. That's never been my jam. I've considered escort services. Visions of a police raid and getting caught with my pants down—*literally*—kept me from ever pursuing the sex for hire avenue. Sex with Anna on a regular basis is something I can do. My cock responds the moment she's near.

She's my wet dream and has been for years. And now I can have her. Without any pressure to buy flowers, get off work early for dates, or spend weekends playing house. There's no stress. Friends with benefits means work remains my highest priority, sans guilt. This solution falls in a huge win-win bucket. No doubt about it.

After having my coffee, I knock on Anna's door to take Chewie for a walk along the East River. She answers the door like normal. This is gonna work. We're friends. Friends with a little extra on the side.

Sunday's my off day, the day I don't run or lift. As I walk Chewie, I initiate the dog's training. Anna loves her dog, but she's soft. It's not okay to have a sixty-five-pound dog jumping on everyone she greets and lunging toward any smell or person. I've never asked, but I'd bet Anna's had many skinned knees thanks to that dog.

Chewie's a fast learner. She responds to a stern voice and quick snaps on the leash. I picked up a book on dog training, and test out the techniques touted by this supposed dog whisperer. She's a smart dog.

When I return Chewie, Anna opens the door, and Chewie wags her body frantically in her signature I'm-so-happy-to-see-you dance. She rears back to lunge forward, and I pull on the leash with one quick snap and say, "No." The brown mound of fur tilts her head up at me. I hold my hand up and she sits. I pet her and pull a small treat out of my pocket. Small treats for good behavior are a dog whisperer secret.

Anna's jaw drops. She falls to her knees and greets Chewie, hugging her and running her hands all around the dog's back. She's going nuts over this dog, acting as if I hurt her. Eyes searching the dog, she asks, "What did you do to her?"

"I'm working with her. She needs training."

Anna removes the leash and opens the door wide. Chewie trots inside, her tail wagging. Anna stands and squints. A wrinkle forms between her eyebrows. She says, "Thank you," but it sounds much more like a question. That's okay. She'll thank me once her giant beast stops dragging her around the city.

"Your ankle looks much better."

She holds it out into the air for me to see. "Yeah, it's not as sore."

"You'll be back to running with me soon. I'd say in maybe two weeks." By the time those two weeks are up, Chewie's gonna be a new dog.

Anna's cheeks are flushed pink as if she's been working out. *What have you been up to, Anna?*

"Well, I've got some work I need to get to. Still up for hanging out later?"

A beautiful smile lights up her face. I stifle the urge to pull her into my arms and kiss her. I'll hold her later. And I'll be doing a lot more than just kissing her.

In my apartment, I jam through revisions on two contracts. Then I read some of the research on Esprit Transactions, a potential new client we're trying to win.

By two o'clock in the afternoon, I have nothing else to do. Someone cleans my apartment. I have groceries delivered. I had planned to wait until four o'clock, but I have nothing left to do.

I rap lightly on her door. Vicious barking booms from the other side, and it sounds like someone's pounding on the door. You'd think a trained-to-kill German shepherd is on the other side attempting to crash through. Yeah, no one's going to attempt to break into Anna's place. Good. It's a double layer of protection. First layer, a doorman. Second, loud, scary, vicious-sounding dog.

The door swings open. Chewie stops barking and wiggles her body in happy greeting. I hold my hand out with the sit signal before she can launch herself onto me. She obeys, and I bend down to her level, pet her, and slip her a few treats.

"I'm not sure what to think about this whole change in her

behavior." Anna twirls two fingers around a section of hair, her eyes seductive.

Is she as excited to do this as I am?

She's wearing a fitted, thin, gray t-shirt and no bra, tight, ripped jeans, and no shoes. I can see the entire outline of her erect nipples beneath the thin cotton. This braless weekend look rocks.

I had planned on hanging out first, doing the friend bit, but I can't wait any longer.

I stalk toward her, kicking the door closed behind me while maintaining eye contact. Her dark brown eyes draw me in.

I reach for her, wrapping her soft, long hair through my fingers, and pull her to me. I kiss her, slowly at first, and then when I don't sense any hesitation, I devour her. She presses her body to me and grinds against me, showing she wants this as much as I do.

Still kissing her, running my hands down her back, I guide her to the bedroom.

Her legs hit the side of the mattress, and I grab her perfect, tempting ass and lift her onto the bed. I stand between her legs, pressing my hard erection against her crotch, her bed the perfect height.

I break our kiss, panting. "Did you decide? Are we doing this?"

She runs her hands down my back, her golden-brown eyes taking me in. Damn. Everything about her says she wants this. A devious grin flashes across her face, and she licks her bottom lip before she bites. *Fuck.*

"Yeah," she murmurs in a sultry way, the sexiest tone I've ever heard.

Facing me, she crawls backward on her hands until she reaches the headboard, her eyes never leaving mine. I stand, staring at her, my brain cut off from the equation. All I want is to fuck her. Now. We need to be on the same page, though.

"Friends with benefits. We're going to do this?"

Please don't change your mind on this.

In response to my question, she bites her bottom lip again, slowly releases it, and nods. Then she lifts her hand and signals for me to come to her. A teasing temptress.

I crawl up the bed to her. Kiss her.

Her hands wander down my back, and she grabs my ass as I settle myself between her legs and press against her, swiveling my hips into the apex of her thighs.

Her hands drift and pull my t-shirt up and over my head. *Hell, yes.*

I follow her lead and toss her t-shirt to the side. She's braless. I groan. "Fuck. So gorgeous." Those nipples. I dream of these breasts.

I lower my head, kissing and sucking on one nipple, then moving to pay attention to the other one. She whimpers as I suck her and apply pressure to her center, rubbing her core. I'm on the verge of coming just from sucking her tits and rubbing it out. Christ, how long has it been since I've had sex?

I lean back on my knees to slow this down. As I unbutton her jeans, she gives me a soft smile and lifts her hips, giving me permission to remove them. I pull off both her jeans and panties and throw them behind me. She lowers her legs, one resting on each side of me. Her pussy is wet and spread open, waiting for me.

"Fuck. Look at you."

I kiss along her thighs. I spread her open and dip my tongue into her juices. She's so wet. She tastes so good. She grips my hair and whimpers. She loves when I go down on her. I want to make her come with my mouth just like yesterday. I set to work, licking and sucking on her clit, toying with her button as she squirms and whimpers. She gasps, "Oh, yes. Oh, yes." I place two fingers inside her and move as my tongue circles her clit. Her back arches off the bed.

"Oh, god, yes. Right there!"

Her tight canal squeezes my fingers as I pump them into her. Then I lean down and blow softly on her center as my fingers milk the remains of her climax. She breathes heavily. The sunlight coming through the transparent shade reflects on a hint of sweat on her brow.

"How are you feeling?" I ask, pretty sure I know.

She runs a hand over her forehead and smiles. "Amazing. God, so amazing." One hand rubs against the side of my face, the other on my chest. Hungry eyes search mine. "I want you now. Inside me."

Oh, fuck.

She slides forward and unbuttons my jeans. I roll onto my back and lift to help her pull them down my legs. She pulls my boxers off with my jeans, leaving me completely naked, my cock throbbing.

She straddles my legs, placing her warm, wet pussy over my cock. She presses her breasts against my chest and leans in for a kiss. Our kiss sets me on fire as she soaks my cock with her wetness.

"Oh, my god. Yeah. Right there. Keep doing that."

"Do you have a condom?"

I reach over to the bedside table where I tossed a condom when we'd first come in. I rip the package open and offer it to her as her hands firmly stroke my cock.

She shakes her head, timid. "No, you."

Not a problem. I slip it on and flip her on her back, situating myself between her legs, flirting with her entrance. I press in slowly, watching her. I could stop now, but soon I won't be able to. I kiss her then nip at her delectable lip. "You sure?"

"Fuck, yes. I want you. Inside. Now."

She's so tight, I pause to let her adjust to me and to slow this down. I don't want to come before we get started. She grips my forearms and gasps, her nails digging into my skin. She lifts her hips, showing me she wants to move.

And then I start thrusting, fucking her hard, deep, and fast. Her hips meet mine, and our rhythm feels fucking spectacular. Her legs wrap around me, and I slam into her over and over. I lower my hand and rub her clit, just like she did to herself yesterday.

She groans, arching into me, and screams out, "Oh, god! Yes, right there."

It's all I can do not to explode right then. But I want to give her one more orgasm.

I lift her leg, adjusting my angle so I can go deeper. I slam into her.

"Oh, my god! Fuck. Yes. Jack. Yes!"

Her muscles contract around my cock, and my release explodes inside her. My body surrenders as I climax. Nirvana. Oblivion.

I fall on top of her, my breathing heavy. "That was amazing." *You are amazing.* I lie down beside her and run a hand over her flat stomach and up to her breasts, caressing her soft skin. My thumb lightly circles her nipple. "You okay?"

She rolls her body onto mine and kisses me, a slow, deep kiss as her hand rubs the growth along my jaw.

I could definitely get used to this.

We hold each other as our breathing calms.

My eyes close. Her naked, sweaty body pressed to mine feels like heaven. I could hold her like this for hours. Cold air flushes against my body, and I open my eyes. She's sitting straight up. She glances at me, jumps off the bed and gathers our clothes. I study her. Suspicious.

"Anna. What's going on in that mind of yours?"

Pulling on her jeans, she answers, a forced smile on her lips. "Nothing. Just getting moving. It's the afternoon. Ya' know? Figured we shouldn't just lay around in bed."

I lean back on her bed. Throw pillows are stacked four or five deep against her headboard. There's a wet spot on the comforter, and I slide a pillow over it. "So, we're good?"

She answers as she slides her top back on so her answer comes out muffled and rushed. "Yeah. Definitely. Incredible. I've definitely missed sex."

"Yeah?"

She nods, fully dressed. Well, that's good news. I decide to follow her lead and get dressed too. She leaves the room before I've located my boxers.

When I enter the den, she's in the kitchen, pouring herself something to drink. "Do you want anything?"

"Water. Thanks."

I take the water from her and sip. "I guess this means next time we have to work on spending some time together in bed afterward?"

She raises her eyebrows inquisitively.

"To get you comfortable so you can have sex and not have to bolt from the room immediately."

She pulls out a dish towel from the drawer, sprays the counter, and wipes away at something I can't see. "Does it matter in a friends with benefits situation?"

She has a good point, but something tells me something else is going on. Or maybe friends with benefits means no snuggling. Who am I to judge? I can't remember the last time I snuggled with someone after sex. It was probably with Anna. Why am I pressing for snuggling? What am I doing?

She flops down on her futon. The futon we did naughty things on yesterday.

She gives me an unsure look. "So, you want to keep doing this?"

Without hesitation, I answer, "Absolutely."

She squirms. "I think we might be improving with age." Her cheeks glow with a haze of pink. Damn. She's so sexy.

I sit down beside her. "Yeah? Well, I guess we can work on

improving each time. I like goals." I wiggle my eyebrows sugges-tively. She giggles. I want to pull her against me and hold her, but suppress the urge. Something tells me that's not what she wants right now. It's probably not the best tactic for keeping it to the friendship level.

"All right. What do you want to do now?" I ask.

"Watch the Carolina game? After the game, take Chewie for a walk down by the river."

"Sounds perfect." I don't want a girlfriend, but if I did, Anna would be it. Hot as hell, great in bed, and she wants to watch the Carolina football game then go outside. The perfect Sunday after-noon. Oh, wait, her ankle. "You don't have any business going on a walk. After the game, I'll take her."

She rolls her eyes. "You may be right, but just so you know, I don't want you to start feeling like you can tell me what to do. That pisses me off. And you don't want to piss me off." She points her finger at me, and she sounds like she's joking and mimicking Arnold Schwarzenegger. But something in her eyes tells me in this case, I'd be smart to listen.

"Yes, ma'am," I respond, suppressing my grin in an attempt to appear sincere. Don't step on her independence. Message received. I'm not looking to control her. I don't want a girlfriend. We're good friends blowing off steam together. This might be the biggest win-win scenario I have ever encountered in my life.

sixteen

ANNA

All six elevators are on the top floors of the building. I flick my wrist, and my Apple watch lights up. 11:30 p.m. Exhaustion sets in under the fluorescent lights. I usually aim to get home by ten. This week's been intense. I've had to pay the dog walker for an evening outing every day this week.

I roll my head back and forth, the muscles in my neck tight. I've run in the morning with Jackson every day this week. Running is becoming an addiction. Seeing Jackson every morning is an extra perk. It's not awkward between us. It's been simply two friends meeting up for a run. He's been working long hours this week too, and like me, our morning run has been his only time outdoors.

Impatient, I push the elevator button again, and my skin tingles. I whip around. Jackson approaches. Wrinkled shirt, tired eyes, briefcase slung bicycle style across his chest, curving around the slope of his pectoral muscle. He grins. "You can push the button as many times as you like, but it doesn't speed the elevator up."

Funny man. I grin back at him.

"You just now getting back from the office?" he asks.

"Yeah. Helping out on a new business pitch." The elevator dings, the door opens, and we both enter.

Jackson presses our floor. As the doors close, his dark hazel eyes roam my body. Goosebumps rise along my arms. He looks at me like he wants to devour me. I swallow. His power suit fits him well and screams *successful*. A tie hangs loosely from his neck, and the top button of his shirt is unbuttoned. A five o'clock shadow darkens his face. Damn. So hot. Attraction to a friends with benefits partner is normal. Right? I mean, why else have benefits? This is why we're doing this. High levels of attraction. No issues.

The elevator rises. He takes two steps forward and grasps my neck, pulling me to him. He kisses me with a passion and longing so intense it knocks the breath out of me. A surge of heat flushes through my core, and my panties dampen. I reach up, pulling him tighter to me, trying to rub my needy channel against him, seeking release. His hand moves up my shirt, onto my breast, and his thumb flicks across my nipple.

The elevator dings, and we stumble apart.

Wordlessly, he follows me into my apartment. *It's a work night, and it's late*, the disciplined part of me scolds, telling me I shouldn't let this happen. Before I blink, my alarm will be going off, telling me it's time for my run. But the carefree part of me that wants to live life tells me to go with it and enjoy it. My traitorous body begs for release.

Jackson drops his briefcase, grabs my hand, and pulls me toward the bedroom. He closes the door on Chewie as she tries to follow.

We rip clothes off each other as if it's been weeks since we've been together and not mere days. In minutes, we're both naked, clothes scattered across the floor, our hands roaming each other's body. My hand wraps around his hard erection, stroking. His finger dips into me, finding me wet and ready.

He carries me to the wall and lifts me, wrapping my legs around his waist. He positions himself at my entrance, and with one powerful push, slides full hilt into me. Against the wall, he's deeper. He fills me. I moan, the pressure and fullness a welcome sensation. Slowly, he slides in and out then increases his pace, hammering me against the wall. Holy shit. So hot. His body presses against my clit with each thrust. I convulse, my muscles tightening from the strain and the ecstasy. I scream, "Jacks! Right there. Right…" My muscles contract, throb and quake. He pinches my nipple, and I scream louder from the initial pain and the intensity he brought to my orgasm by doing so. His mouth comes down over mine, his tongue plunging, demanding, as his thrusts become quicker and more urgent. His back arches, and he thrusts one last time as he finds his release. His head falls to my shoulder as his cock pulses deep within me.

My legs slowly fall to the floor, trembling. He picks me up, sends throw pillows flying, pulls back the covers, lays me in bed, and kisses me. The tender touch is a stark contrast to the animal pounding from moments before.

He goes to the other side of the bed and pulls back the covers, sliding in.

What's he doing? Is he planning on staying here? That's not part of the plan.

He rests his back against my headboard and pulls me up against his chest. His fingers play with my hair, sending tingling sensations down my back. "You are incredible." He angles my head up, forcing my eyes to meet his. "You doing okay?"

I'm fine, but sleeping over isn't okay. He's not worried about emotions developing. He's a guy. But if I have any hope of keeping this at a friends game level, then I can't hold him after having sex. I need the space. The reminder it's a physical release, nothing more. At the same time, kicking him out of my bed doesn't seem right. I'm not the kind of woman who fucks someone and kicks them out of the bed.

He sighs and rubs a hand over his face. "I didn't use a condom. I didn't think about anything other than getting inside of you." He places a soft kiss on my forehead. "I never do that. Do you still have your IUD?"

Oh, shit. I forgot the condom. *I know better.* "Yeah." I had an IUD inserted freshman year in college, and I've never had it removed. "Um, I'm clean." I had gone and gotten tested after my blackout night with Nick. With no memory of the night, I had no idea if he'd used a condom and had no desire to discuss the night to that level of detail with him.

"I'm clean too. It's been a while since I've been with anyone. Shit, I'm so sorry Anna. I lost control, got carried away."

"It's okay." I caress the strong lines of his toned chest then circle my thumb around his nipple. I've watched him toy with mine a few times now. The sensation always turns me on, intensifies my arousal. I press a kiss to his chest. "We both kind of lost our minds." Feeling a little timid, I bury my face against his throat, breathing him in. A hint of his cedar soap comes through, as well as the much stronger scent of our sex. "Maybe we just needed to blow off some steam. Tough work week and all."

His hand runs through my hair. He kisses me on my mouth, then my forehead, the tip of my nose, then brushes his lips across mine. "Yeah, maybe. So, IUD still?"

I settle against him, resting my head on his chest. "It's a ten-year non-hormonal one. So, it's still in. The failure rates on the pill aren't good. I don't trust myself to remember the pill at the same time every day." I pinch his nipple, teasing. "I remember you asking me why I didn't use the pill like the other college girls."

"It might make me an ignorant fool, but I've never researched birth control stats. But then again, I've always used condoms and felt covered." He pauses. "Pun intended."

I lean down and nip his nipple, teasing him. He tickles me a bit until I settle back into his chest. "Well, you can be happy your friends with benefits partner has done her research. But, um, as nice as this feels right now, I don't think you staying over is a good idea." I don't want to hurt his feelings, but I've got to be firm on this. This crazy scheme we have going can only work if we aren't spending the night together, and lying here naked in his arms feels too good, too comfortable.

"Really? You want me to head home? You don't like having someone sleeping in your bed?" He sounds curious, even surprised. Something tells me he's used to his hookups wanting to stay the night. It's definitely more of a normal girl reaction. When the girl is seeking a relationship.

"It's not that. It just feels like a slippery slope. Right now, we're friends with benefits. Great benefits. Don't get me wrong. But if we start staying over at each other's places, running in the morning, hanging out on weekends, where will we draw the line?" Past experience creates a nagging teacher. I know all too well how easily one can find herself with a boyfriend, without a single conversation. He doesn't want a relationship, but still. If we expect friends with benefits to work, we've got to limit cuddling and keep emotions in check.

Jackson squints and frowns. "I guess we've taken the next step, and we're sitting here talking after sex. You haven't jumped out of the bed. But I think sometimes we will stay over, and we can agree it doesn't mean anything. If one weekend I get to do everything with you I want, I'm not going to have the energy to walk back to my place. And I do like to snuggle sometimes afterward."

As he says this, I realize he hasn't stopped touching me. He's drawn me close to him, our naked bodies lying against each other. Yes, he has a roaming hand and a snuggle side. But I have to figure out how to convince him, because I'm right. It's too easy to slip. For me to slip.

"Look, I care about you, Anna, but I don't have time to dedicate to a relationship. You don't have to worry about falling into a relationship with me. It's not gonna happen."

I flinch at his statement. Yes, he's addressing my unspoken fear, but his direct statement hits hard. I don't want a relationship either. Why does his honesty hurt?

I lower my head onto his chest and listen to his heartbeat. The sound calms my pain and soothes my vulnerability.

"What was so bad about the relationship you were in?"

"Well, it lasted four years. I was miserable. I don't like who I am when I'm in a relationship. I become submissive. A lot like my mom. I never went out, lost my high school friends, and never found any real college friends. I did exactly what he wanted me to do. My mom was the same way with my dad. I hated it. I don't even know how I ended up dating Evan. It was like we went out on two dates, and he started introducing me as his girlfriend without us ever talking about it. I wasn't happy about it, but I went along with it, not wanting to hurt him and taking the easiest path. Our parents were super close. My parents loved him. Our parents loved us together. Our families did stuff together all the time. I had a hard time finding the courage to stand up to my parents and end things with him."

I pause, hating I sound weak. Anyone else would have just ended the relationship. Anyone else wouldn't have stayed in a relationship as the best years of her life passed by. But I hadn't been able to do the right thing. To end things. A public marriage proposal forced me to stand up for myself. To decide, in that case, I needed to be selfish.

I take deep breaths, remembering my past mistakes. My head stills on his chest, and his fingers entwine with mine.

"I'm twenty-six. I want to listen to bands on the weekends. I want to enjoy New York when I have extra time. I want a career. I'm not ready to get married and move to the 'burbs. I don't want the 'burbs. I don't even know if I want kids." At this point, the tone of my voice hits a high pitch, not unlike a whiny kid.

"Okay. Okay. I hear you. You're committed to not dating. Although, for the record, there is such a thing as a healthy relationship. A relationship where two independent individuals make it work. And dating doesn't mean an immediate move to the 'burbs."

"I know. In theory. But I don't trust myself. If I'm dating someone and he tells me he wants a relationship, I'm the kind of person who will say yes, whether I want it or not." It sucks. I'm such a pleaser, always trying not to ruffle feathers or hurt feelings. Anna, the girl everyone likes. Somehow, it's ingrained in me. Growing up, teachers thought it was wonderful how kind I was to other kids. Always the peacemaker. Kids could steal my cookies, and I'd never get upset. I'd say that was fine and smile and forget about it. But really, it wasn't okay for kids to be pilfering through my lunch.

I stretch, leaning my body into him as I reach to fondle his hair. I love the feel of his hair in my fingers. "What about you? Bad relationship in the past?"

His hand glides down my arm, giving me goosebumps. He traces my stomach, my bellybutton, and then caresses my breast. I clench my center, throbbing. My body reacts to his touch, every single time. His hand works magic as he talks. "No. I don't have the time. Making partner requires crazy hours. To some degree, it's all about how many hours you clock. I want to make name partner by the time I'm forty. Once I'm partner, I'll have more time. But I don't have the time for a relationship with the hours I work. I've tried. It gets ugly. Not worth it."

He sounds sincere. My fingers graze the hard stubble along his jaw. "Do you think we can pull this off? Sex and friends? Not wanting too much from each other?"

His phone vibrates, and he reaches over to read the incoming text before responding. "I think we can. It sounds like our arrangement is perfect for both of us. And I won't stay tonight. But one day, I might. It doesn't have to mean more than we want it to."

Right.

He leans down and kisses me then rolls on top of me, rubbing his body against mine. His erection presses against my belly, and I wrap my legs around him.

"If we aren't going to be using protection, then you can't fuck anyone else." I'm not familiar with the rules concerning friends with benefits and exclusivity, but we can't be going bare unless we have a commitment to be exclusive.

He shifts, lining his cock up with my drenched entrance, sighing. "I don't want to fuck anyone else, Anna. Only you."

I tilt my hips, encouraging him to enter, as he teases my wet folds with his tip. I watch, mesmerized.

He groans. "That goes for you too."

"Okay."

His hand slides between us and rubs circles over my clit. Heaven.

"Oh, Jackson." Using my sultriest come-hither voice, I murmur, "So, round two?"

In answer, he takes me.

seventeen

ANNA

"The girls are out tonight!" Delilah belts in synch with the music, pulling Stacy and me laughing toward the dance floor. It's Friday. After what felt like one of the longest weeks ever, Delilah declared it a night to go out dancing. A cab delivered us to the House of Yes. We survived the manic, nonstop week, and it's gonna be a good night.

The music pulses. Blue lights flash. Bodies hum. The packed dance floor throbs with a frenetic energy. The music pulses through my body, no cares or concerns to hold me back. We're alive and young and free.

A college friend once told me I'd been born to dance in front of a band. Back then, I'd spent countless nights standing right in front of him and his band, jumping around, singing lyrics along with them, and dancing with the crowd. I'll never forget his words because it's my favorite thing anyone has ever said about me.

In New York, I'm as likely to be dancing in a club with a DJ as in front of a band. For bands, I prefer the small venues. The bands that haven't hit the bigtime yet. Shows about the music, not the spectacle. I love watching the band's faces during the sets and the thrill of catching a bandmate's eye and sharing a mutual appreciation for the liberating musical moment.

A skinhead in black leather pants, stacked leather bracelets with silver spikes, a tight white t-shirt, and a nose ring dances up to me. He pulls my back to his front, his hands on my hips, moving us to the beat together. After the song ends, we move on to a new dance partner. It doesn't matter who I dance with. To me, dancing isn't about meeting people, it's about losing myself. Forgetting all my worries and letting go. Mr. Black Leather isn't my type, and I'm pretty sure I'm not his either. Like me, he was there to dance. Likeminded hipsters pack the dance floor. Drag queens, men, women, grinding, groping, spinning. Lost in the music. Lost in the scene.

A song with a heavy techno beat and too much bass comes on, and head to the bar. After getting a glass of water filled with ice, I search the crowd for Delilah or Stacy.

I don't see them, so I pull my phone out and check. No text from either of them, which means they haven't been hunting for me. It's three o'clock in the morning. I do have a couple of texts from Jackson.

Jackson:
Hey, what are you up to tonight?

Jackson:
Are you still out?

Is he worried? Did I tell him I was going out tonight? Wait. It doesn't matter if I told him or not. We're not dating, and I don't owe him a thing. He needs to understand our little arrangement doesn't give him dictatorial rights to my activities. I have no interest in having someone in my life telling me what to do.

Women in tight dresses and sky-high heels writhe on the dance floor. The lights blur, the edges of this massive cavern dark. My first dance comes to mind. The dancers' apparel differs, but the lights, the loud music, the cavernous room with dark edges bear a similarity.

Prom night. My senior year. Evan tugs on my hand. "Let's get out of here. You've got a promise to fulfill." He conveys plenty with his eyes and I understand exactly what he wants to go do. I watch the scene in front of me, longing to dance with my friends.

"We just got here. This will be our only prom. You didn't want to go last year. Please? Just a few dances."

He tugs me to him and grinds his erection against me. "You promised. Tonight's the night. I've been waiting for two years, Anna baby. Why do you want to hang with these losers? Let's go."

I push the memory away. Tonight, I'm dancing. I shove the phone into my clutch and shimmy back onto the dance floor.

Hours later, Delilah circles her arm around my waist. Stacy shakes her booty on my other side, and another friend, Elle, dances in front of us. I hadn't even realized Elle was here. The music shifts, signaling the end of the night. This DJ likes to throw in singalong type songs right before closing. *Hey, Bartender* comes on, and we dance in our circle, belting out the lyrics. Once the oldies hit, we know the lights will be coming on soon. The floor has cleared out, leaving us with much more room. Only extremely inebriated or strung-out dancers remain.

The four of us giggle our way out of the club and jerk back immediately when the door opens to the street. Our hands shield our eyes, like vampires fearing the rising sun's rays. What time is it? I glance at my watch. "Holy shit, girls! It's after six a.m.! When was the last time we closed out a club?"

Delilah giggles and falls straight down to her knees. Oh, shit. She didn't stick with water. Stacy and I each pick a side and loop her arms around our shoulders. Elle giggles, sways a bit, and stumbles.

Stacy and I look at each other, Delilah between us. Which of us is going to take Elle? And can one person manage Delilah?

Elle stumbles forward, and we follow. She reaches the end of the sidewalk and raises her hand. A yellow cab pulls up, and she jumps in. As the cab pulls away, I see her lie down on the back seat. "What you want to bet that cabbie is regretting picking her up right about now?"

Stacy laughs. "Think we could get another cab to come along and pick this one up?" she asks, angling her head at Delilah. At this point, Delilah's hanging on us, face down, staring at the concrete on the sidewalk, incoherent.

"Let's go to the ABC Diner and get some food in her." I point down the street. It's about two blocks away, but the black sign stands out against the brick building.

When we enter, it's clear that six o'clock on a Saturday morning is a slow period. We have our choice of any booth in the place.

The waitress approaches us, takes one look at Delilah, and demands, "If she's gonna puke, bathroom's that way. Please don't let her puke out here."

Delilah peers up at her, eyes red and glassy. "Not gonna puke. Just tired. Need coffee. And hash browns. Cheese. Hash browns with cheese. French fries!"

"No French fries right now. Coffee and hash browns with cheese. What will you ladies have?"

Stacy and I order coffees and egg and cheese biscuits. By the time the coffee arrives, we're recapping the night. Delilah sits with her head on the table, eyes closed.

"Who was the guy in black leather? He was grinding on you for*ever*!"

"No idea. Not my type at all, though. Nose rings, I mean. Fun to dance with, look at, and all. Just not what I'm into these days."

The waitress stops by to deliver food and refill our coffee mugs. Then she leaves the coffee pitcher on the table. Smart.

"What is your type these days?" Stacy asks.

"Hmmm. Off the top of my head? An REI kind of guy? Or any of the models in the Sundance Catalog. What about you?" What I won't admit to these girls is that my type is weekend Jackson. Jackson before and after work. I'm into a hybrid version of Jackson that doesn't exist.

Stacy sips her coffee, reflecting. "Well, I have to say, I wouldn't think I'd find my type in a club. My type is going to be at a Deadhead cover band show. I like them with long hair, cool t-shirts, ripped jeans, Birks."

"Yeah, we are so not going to find your man at a club. You find the show, and I'll go with you."

She nods. "Maybe. There is this bartender I've been eyeing."

"What bar?"

"Sullivan's. It's near my place."

The rest of our breakfast, Stacy shares the full scoop on Ryder from the pub while intermittently forcing Delilah to raise her head and eat.

We all share a cab Uptown. Stacy said she'd bring Delilah back to her apartment, so they drop me off first. I wave goodbye, close the door, and see Jackson in his morning running gear. He flicks his wrist, reading the time.

"Seven twenty a.m.? You're getting home at seven twenty a.m.?" he asks, glaring, anger and irritation soaking his words.

"Yeah." In the back of my mind, I can almost see Delilah waving her finger, taunting me with a "someone's in trouble." *Glare away, Jackson. I can do what I want.*

"Don't you need to walk your dog?"

"Yep. Heading up now."

I tilt my chin up, defiant, and charge past him. He's right. My dog needs to be let out. Bad dog mom, right here. There's some truth to his words, but his angry face pisses me off. He's not my dad. Not my keeper. Not my boyfriend. I don't need to sit around and get grilled by a prosecuting attorney.

Five minutes later, Chewie pulls me outside, tugging full force on her leash. In my place I changed into sweats and tennis shoes before coming out with her. My feet throb from a night out in sky-high heels. Chu pulls me hard toward the bushes along the side of our apartment building. As soon as we reach the patch of dirt, she squats.

"Where'd you go out last night?"

"Holy fuck!" I jump. "Where did you come from? You scared me."

"I scared you?" Anger ripples through his words.

"Yeah. I didn't see anyone out here. Where did you come from?"

"I scared you?" he repeats, still glaring. "You never answered my text last night."

Oh. That. Remorse is swift. I probably should have at least sent an all good or a TTYL. "I'm sorry. I didn't see your text until three in the morning and figured you'd already gone to sleep. We were out dancing. I told you I sometimes go out dancing on Fridays."

"Until seven?"

"Well, last night was on the late side for us. Delilah had a bit too much to drink, so we went to the diner to get her some food."

"What about you?" I really do not appreciate his tone.

"What about me?"

"Did you have too much to drink?"

"Nah. I mostly drank water. We danced for hours. It's been an insane week. Left from the office." I fiddle with the leash in my hand. "Anyway, I'm going to walk Chewie around the block and crash."

Jackson jogs away toward the park.

"Wait, are you mad at me?" I call.

Friends with benefits don't get mad. Anger courses through me. He thinks he has a right to get mad? So mad he would walk away? The equivalent of a hang-up mad?

Jackson flips around, walking backward to the intersection so he faces me. "Nope. Why would I be mad? See ya later," he shouts, right as the light changes and he runs across the intersection.

eighteen

JACKSON

"Hey, man, let's head to White Horse instead. I'm not up for this tonight." The line wraps around the corner at the Corner Bistro. I love a Corner Bistro burger as much as anyone, but their refusal to accept reservations, forcing patrons to circle the place for empty tables, irks me. Today, my patience level nears zero. It is not a Corner Bistro night.

Chase looks like he's about to argue but changes his mind. Smart man. Today is not the day to piss me off. "Okay, but you're buying," he snaps.

We don't speak again until we're seated with beers in hand at the White Horse. Chase has been playing with his phone the whole time. I pull mine out too and flip through email.

After we've both swallowed long drags of our beer, Chase breaks the silence. "So, what has your panties in a wad?"

"Fuck you."

Chase holds his hands up in the air. "Hey, man. I'm sorry. That was supposed to be a chill way of asking what's wrong."

I don't say anything.

"Something's clearly wrong. I haven't seen you in weeks, so I know it's not something I did."

What is wrong with me? Why have I been in such a piss-poor mood all day? Yes, it pissed me off to see Anna hopping out of a cab at seven fucking o'clock in the morning. In a tight black sexy-as-fuck dress and fuck-me heels. But it's not like she'd been with a guy. I saw two girls in the cab with her. She could have fucking responded to my text. I'd had crazy scenarios going through my head all night. Worried something had happened to her. Worried she'd gotten drunk and was hooking up with someone. Remembering those days at Carolina where she'd be drinking with guys and practically climbing them while dancing.

"If you don't plan on speaking at all, then I'm gonna head out after we eat. I'd rather stare at a TV tonight."

"Fuck, man. You're right. I'm not sure why I'm so out of it. Guess it's just been a long day working on this merger I've been busy with."

Chase squints at me, sipping his beer. "Nope. Don't buy it."

He's right. A stressful case wouldn't put me in a bad mood. A stressful case might have me working through the night, but I wouldn't be angry. Not unless I lost a case. And I don't lose cases. I don't lose negotiations.

I focus on my breathing, catch the eye of our waitress, and signal for another round. "You're right. That's not it. I don't feel like talking about it. But I'll carry on a conversation. Deal?"

"Whatever, dude. If you wanted someone to harp on you about feelings, you'd have a girl sitting in my chair. How you getting settled?"

"It's good. There are things I like. Central Park. All the restaurants. Not having to drive everywhere. Not dealing with traffic. Being able to drink at dinner and walk outside and grab a cab."

"Yeah, the city has good stuff. How's the apartment?"

I snort. "Yeah, that's where the city sucks. I mean, my apartment is fine. It's a sublet, though. There's a Realtor who's been sending me listings. I'm thinking I want to buy in the Lower West Side."

"Not an Upper East Side guy?"

"It's fine. When I move, I'll miss Central Park. But it'd make more sense to be closer to work."

"Not digging the packed subway?"

I smirk. "I don't take the subway."

He looks at me like I've lost my mind. "What do you do? Bus?"

"I'm a junior partner. The firm has a driver for me."

"You take a fucking car?"

"I make calls and read on the way to work."

"You lucky bastard!"

"What can I say? The firm takes care of its own."

"Yeah, well. My firm does not take care of its accountants. I guess the free crappy coffee is their version of taking care of us."

The beer and conversation seem to be loosening me up. My tense muscles relax a bit. "So, yeah, I'm thinking Lower West Side might not be so bad. They have good running trails along the Hudson. Some good choices between condos and some brownstones. Once my place in Atlanta sells, I'll focus on buying here to roll those proceeds over."

"Yeah, I like it down there. Not a bad choice."

"What about you? You and Angela gonna move in together soon?"

Chase grimaces. "Not a good topic."

I catch the waitress's eye and signal for another round. "She putting pressure on?"

"Dude, you have no idea."

"With rent like it is, it's not such a bad idea."

"Maybe with some girls. But trust me, the moment we move in together, the pressure would increase tenfold to put a ring on it."

"Is she not the one?" I'm not the kind of guy to dive deep with friends, but that's the crux of the issue.

"Nah, she's not."

"How long have you been together?"

"Over a year."

"And why, exactly, are you still together if she's not the one?"

He taps his knuckle on the table. "I don't know. She wants to do something every single night. I make excuses. She gets angry. It's a vicious cycle."

Interesting. I jump at the chance these days to see Anna after work. Hell, if I hadn't been so angry at her today, I'd be doing something with her tonight. And she's just a friend. "Man, you've got to end it. None of that sounds good."

"I've been hoping she'd end it." He sounds exasperated.

I don't know what to advise him, but I know someone who will. "You want a woman's perspective on this?" I flip my phone over on the table and hand it to him. "Call Anna and have her meet us here. She'll tell you."

He rocks back in his chair. "Anna?"

"Yeah, you said you guys are friends, right?"

"Well, yeah. Have you seen her much?"

I nod. "Yeah. We go running together each morning before work. We've been hanging out sometimes after work too. She's right down the hall. You know."

"What's she up to tonight?"

"Well, she was out last night until seven in the morning. Usually, when she pulls a hard Friday night, she stays in Saturday. But I bet you could talk her into coming out for a beer."

"To the Lower West Side? You clearly don't know Anna. If she's staying in, she's curled up with Chu, and she's already topped at least one bottle of wine by now."

I tap my fingers against the table. How exactly does he know that about her?

Ignoring my phone, he picks his up and taps away. I scan the pub, hunting for our waitress and our drinks.

"Anna says to come on up. Let's pay and go."

———

Anna's door opens as we step off the elevator. She must have been listening for the ding. Doesn't want Chewie to start barking when we approach. It's after ten o'clock, a little late for a loud dog.

Chewie pushes past her, and I hold out my hand with a sit command. She sits, and I bend to scratch behind her ears. I don't have her treats, but she doesn't seem to mind. Anna's honey brown eyes lock with mine. This is what I needed. To see her. The tightness in my chest I hadn't realized was there eases.

Chase gives her a brief hug and heads into the apartment, leaving the two of us in the hall. "Hey, thanks for letting us come up."

"Is he okay?" she asks.

"I think he needs a female perspective."

"What about you? Are you okay?"

She's asking if I'm still pissed. Without thinking, I brush a kiss against her soft lips. "Yeah. I am now."

She shoots me a shy smile and pushes the door wide open. I let her hand go when I see Chase standing in her kitchen. It's not that I want to hide anything between us, but I sure as hell don't want to try to explain friends with benefits to Chase.

An empty bottle of wine sits on her kitchen counter. She's out of vino, so I step out to get her a bottle of mine. Chase and I brought a twelve-pack from a deli with us. I'd told him a six-pack was more than enough, but he wanted to be sure we didn't run out.

I use my key to let myself back in. Anna's giving Chase a hug, her back to me. His arms circle her like a friend. It's a friendly hug. My free hand still rolls into a fist, and I grit my teeth, forcing the muscles in my cheeks to flex. Damn. What the hell is wrong with me?

But if I'm honest with myself, I've never liked the idea of Chase having his hands on her. Four years ago, the thought sent me into a tailspin. I sure as hell don't like it now. She's mine.

The thought springs unbidden. And it's wrong. She's not mine. We're friends. I don't want a relationship. I don't have time for one. Obligations and guilt are not on my docket. Yet, emotions roil inside. Anger. Jealousy. This shit's gonna fuck me up if I'm not careful. This little thing between us is casual. I need to chill.

They break apart—finally--and she pats his arm like he's a dog.

"You guys talk it out?" I ask, as much to remind them of my presence as anything.

Chase flops down on her big chair. "Yeah. Seems she's on the same page as you. If I don't like spending time with her, then it's time to end things."

Anna sits down on one end of the futon, leaving plenty of room for me to sit too. "Not exactly what I said." She crosses her legs, a half smile on her face. "I said if you don't like spending time with her, then you need to figure out why. And if you can't fix whatever the issue is, then it's probably time to end things. You're almost thirty years old. None of this is rocket science."

I head into the kitchen to pour Anna a glass of wine. Then I decide I'll switch over to wine as well and pour myself a glass.

Chase runs his hand through his hair. "I'm just tired of all the fighting. I like her. Hell, I love her. But we used to be friends, you know? We used to like hanging out. Now it's an endless stream of fights, and most of those fights are about her wanting more. But I want less, not more. Like, if we get married, are we going to magically start getting along?"

We may have come for a female perspective, but I jump in anyway. "No, dude. I've never been married, but I did learn a little from marriage law. It can be rock solid awesome and still end up in divorce. But if it's rocky before the marriage, you can bet your ass it'll end in divorce. Marriage is not the answer to a relationship with issues. Ever."

Chase and Anna both look surprised at my outburst.

"Hey, just telling it like it is."

Chase bends forward, putting his elbows on his knees and his head in his hands.

Anna quietly adds, "I agree with Jackson."

Chase lifts his head. "You don't think she'll break up with me? Because I'd so much prefer that. I don't want to hurt her."

Anna gives him a sad smile. "Eventually, yeah, she'll end things. But if you wait around until then, you may hate each other by the time she does. And isn't it kind of leading her on, if she thinks you guys have a chance at forever, and you don't?" Anna speaks with the wisdom of experience.

He sets his beer down on the coffee table and stands. His phone has been vibrating the whole night. He holds it out for us to see. "She has texted me, like, fifty times tonight." He sighs. "It's time." He throws his empty beer in the garbage.

"Wait, you are going to do it now?" Anna asks, flicking her wrist to see the time.

"Might as well get it over with. She's texting me nonstop to come over. What am I gonna do? Go over and pretend everything's okay? I mean, you're right. Putting off the inevitable isn't fair to her."

Anna follows Chase to the door and gives him a hug. "I'm here for you if you need anything." She tosses her head my direction. "So is that guy."

Chase nods at us both, a sad expression on his face, and raps the door with his hand. "See you guys later."

Anna closes the door and returns to the futon. I pull her close to my side, and she starts *Saturday Night Live.*

We don't speak. She curls her legs up under her, and I hold her close. This is what I've needed the whole day. To sit here, holding her, breathing her in. If timing were different, could Anna and I have a chance at forever? Because when I think about what I want in my life partner, Anna is it. Just not right now. We wouldn't be dating long at all before Anna would be the girl texting me, like, fifty times, asking when I'm leaving the office or what I'm doing.

She falls asleep against me. *Saturday Night Live* ends, and another show comes on. I sit there, holding her until I fear she might wake up and wonder why I'm still sitting there. The last thing I want is to make her uncomfortable, so I turn the TV off and pick her up. I carry her into her bedroom and pull the covers over her, leaning down to kiss her forehead once. With her eyes closed, she looks angelic. I brush my lips over hers to wish her goodnight.

Her eyes flutter open. She reaches up and fingers my hair, pulling me down for another soft kiss. Our tongues play in a seductive dance that sends blood coursing southward. I flip the comforter away and climb on the bed, fully clothed, positioning myself between her legs. I lift her shirt, moving it out of the way, then push the cups of her bra below her breasts. Her breasts spill over, her nipples erect. I drop my head, taking first one then the other into my mouth. Biting, then softly sucking, eliciting a purring noise.

My hand wanders farther down, and I mentally curse jeans and how hard they are to maneuver. I sit up and unbutton her jeans, grabbing both her panties and jeans, and wrestle them off. Wanting her completely naked, I reach behind her to unsnap her bra and she removes her shirt. Her dark, wavy hair falls down around her shoulders, almost to her breasts. Her bare pussy glistens. She plays with her folds while her chocolate eyes stay on me. She moves in slow circles then inserts her index finger. She moans, seductive eyes still on me. Damn. Could she be any sexier? Any more beautiful?

My jeans hurt because my cock has no space. I had planned to go down on her, but I can't wait. I grab the hem of my shirt and send it flying across the room. Unbuttoning my jeans, I push them down and kick them off. She pulls her wet finger out and sucks on it.

"Fuck!" I climb onto the bed and drive into her. One thrust, and I'm balls deep, my stroke slamming her head against the headboard. "Put your hands on the headboard and push back."

She does as I say. I ram into her like an animal. Owning her. Making her mine. I loop my arm around her leg and lift it higher, adjusting the angle to hit her deep. The headboard repeatedly thumps against the wall with each thrust.

Her orgasm comes hard and fast, her muscles tightening all around me in waves, forcing my climax. An explosion. My body shudders, and my erection pulses as her muscles milk my wasted cock.

I collapse onto Anna, breathing in her hair, placing my lips against her neck, feeling our rapid heartbeats gradually slow and intermingle. Our sweaty bodies press together.

A loud bang sounds. Followed by another bang. I raise my head, staring at the wall, the source of the noise. Anna giggles, and I reluctantly pull out of her, groaning as I roll onto my side.

"We may have been a little too loud for Lester." She presses kisses along my throat and her fingers lightly roam my side.

"Damn. I don't know what came over me. I was going to put you in bed and let you sleep."

"Well, personally, I'm glad I woke up."

"Yeah?"

"Yeah. It's not like I'm going to turn an orgasm down." She smiles her honest, big smile. My insides muddle in the strangest way, and my chest burns.

"It was too fast. I should've taken more time. Taken it slowly."

She's so beautiful. I take her in, sprawled on the bed. Her dark, mussed up hair, those golden-brown eyes, full lips and flushed cheeks. Natural. And god, that fit body. Flat stomach, lean legs. She bites her lower lip in the little way she does. She is sexy perfection. Still. I set the pillows so I can lean back against them and pull her up to rest on my chest.

Twisting soft tangled strands through my fingers, I sigh. We went into this with no expectations. Zero parameters. That did not work for me. "Look. It's fine when you go out with your friends. It's good. You need your girlfriends. I get it. But please do me the favor of texting me back if you read my text. My mind goes crazy sometimes. Yeah, we aren't official. You aren't *my* girlfriend. But can you respond? Please? So I don't worry about you."

Anna rolls to her side, her bare breasts dragging across my chest as she shifts so we are eye to eye. She presses a soft sweet kiss to my lips. "Yeah, I can respond. I'm sorry for making you worry. I didn't think about how you would feel. Next time, I promise I'll respond and let you know I'm okay."

nineteen

ANNA

The soothing sound of waves crashing on a beach rouses me from sleep. It's a relaxing, soothing sound that lulls me into a faraway land...until realization strikes. That's my alarm. It's time to wake up. Jackson's leg wraps over mine, and one arm curves along my waist.

Last night, we had sex three times. First against the wall. Then on the futon. Then on my bed. I fell asleep sometime after the last round of bone-liquifying orgasms. And he's still here.

He's never stayed over before. His hair is a mess and I brush my fingers through his unruly strands. In his sleep, he's peaceful and relaxed. I curl into his side, breathing him in. There's a hint of his cedar scented soap, but there's also a strong, manly scent mixed with the smell of sex.

The last couple of weeks have been kind of perfect. He never complains when I go out with friends, and of course, I always let him know I'm safe when I'm out. Maybe seeing Chase in his misery forced us to treat each other with more consideration. Or maybe our agreement eliminates expectations, and without holding one another up to some sort of performance bar, we end up treating each other with kindness and care. Or maybe we do that because our friendship has strengthened.

Every time we part, I look forward to seeing him again. While it's good, it's also unnerving. A little voice in my head nags, telling me that I'm slipping into a relationship. But I do my best to ignore it. This is what we both want. Our friends thing works for us. We're here for each other without all the crap and responsibility of a relationship. Work remains our number one priority. It's only a big deal if we make it a big deal, and we've agreed this is the opposite of a big deal. We're having fun. And it's convenient and easy.

I place a kiss right below his ear. To make our morning run, we need to get moving. Clearly my nature sounds alarm doesn't work for him, as he's still conked out. Chewie jumps on the end of the bed, eyes alert, tail wagging, ready to go.

The shaking mattress does it. Jackson's eyes flutter open. Instantly awake, he snaps his fingers at Chu, and she jumps off the bed and trots into the den. I run my fingers along his jaw, scratching his morning stubble. With a lazy morning smile, he lowers the sheet and takes my nipple in his mouth as his hand wanders lower. My lower body contracts, my nipples erect, anticipating what's to come. But there's no time to play.

I pull away with a sad sigh, but he growls, pulling me back and situating himself between my legs with his enormous erection rubbing my entrance.

"But we don't have time."

If he hears my faint whine, he ignores me. He strokes the tip of his cock up and down my folds. I watch, mesmerized as his hard cock dips then pulls out. I circle his precum with my thumb, then suck the salty juice.

"Fuck, Anna." He plunges in.

Oh, holy hell. What a way to wake up.

———

My phone vibrates as I rush down the hall to my office, late.

Jackson:
Pick you up at 8, k?

Me:
Might have to work late.

Jackson:
We're supposed to be in the West Village by 8:30.

Oh, snap. I bite my thumbnail as panic sets in. I need to shower and blow out my hair since I rushed to the office with my hair in a messy bun. How did I forget tonight?

Me:
I'll be ready.

Jackson:
Did you forget?

Me:
Someone kept me up all night. Brain a little slow.

Jackson:
Was it worth it?

I roll my eyes.

Today's not a good day to be punch-drunk. I tried to explain that to Jackson when he came over last night, but reason vacated after his lips took possession. I seem to lose control around him, which is not really a good thing.

Today, my team presents our plan to the agency partners. If they don't like what we created, it will mean a weekend of fixing what they didn't like. The pitch is Monday morning in Atlanta.

It's seven-thirty. Not as early as I aimed to be in the office, but I'm still the first person opening our agency doors. Most people don't arrive until nine.

My team meets in my office, and we prepare with one last run-through of our presentation.

During the presentation, the panel, consisting of the two owners and agency founders, two group account directors, and two group creative directors, all maintain stoic expressions. My team does a solid job presenting the creative. After we complete our presentations, we take our seats at the conference table. Nick speaks first.

"Thanks, Anna. Would you and your team mind if we discuss the creative privately?"

"Of course." I force a smile, but my optimism wanes. A private meeting is not a good sign. Feedback, including negative feedback, is usually given in front of the team.

As I follow my team out, I study the executives. John, the creative part of the two-person founding team, opens his mouth but then closes it after Benton, his account half, stares him down. I close the door behind me, leaving the panel to their private discussion.

Delilah follows me to my office. "Has that ever happened before?"

"Not to my knowledge. Maybe they're trying something new." My team deserves at least a "great effort, guys" even if the end result needs work.

Should I have pushed back in the meeting? Did I let my team down? I'd shown the creative to my other colleagues, and all initial feedback had been positive. At twenty-six, I'm young to be in this role. A more experienced creative director might have refused to leave. Should I have refused to leave? Should I have asked questions before agreeing to leave?

If they had liked the creative, they would have said so. If requested changes were minor, we would have received those requests in the room. My stomach churns. Delilah sits in my office, and we run through theories. Delilah eventually returns to her desk, and I open Pinterest. I should work, but I can't.

About an hour later, John walks into my office, followed by Nick and Christian. Christian, our new business VP, acts more or less like an account person on all new business accounts. He developed the strategy and has worked closely with us over the last few weeks on this pitch.

John speaks first. "Anna, the work you did was impressive. But Nick has convinced us we need an alternative strategy with at least two campaigns behind it. He wants to spend the weekend working with your team on the new strategy and creative concepts. He's convinced us that if we let him do this, we'll end up with a stronger pitch."

Christian stands beside John, livid, his face beet red thanks to an Irish temper.

"It's almost noon on Friday," I say, attempting to reason with John. "The presentation and boards we presented took over two weeks to complete. Any work we complete this weekend on a new strategy won't be as polished as what we've already completed."

John nods in agreement. He's a creative. Of course, he agrees with me. He doesn't get in the trenches anymore, but every single creative in this agency ultimately reports to him. We're his people; he's been in my shoes before.

Nick's expression is a combination of leer and derision, and instantly I know I am not going to like what he says. "If you don't think you can do it, we'll get another team to tackle it and do it right. The creative was weak and off strategy. We need more options to show our breadth and abilities."

"We have a solid presentation. If you had concerns about the direction we were headed, you could have stepped in last week when we went through concepts." Christian's response is professional and on-point, but he glowers at Nick, but Nick being Nick, doesn't back down.

John interrupts their glare-fest. "Anna, I'm gonna be honest. This is all bullshit. I'd personally like to strangle Nick."

That comment wipes the smug expression off Nick's face. Something tells me he expected to be seen as the hero, the leader pushing to be the best.

John continues. "But Nick convinced Benton. This is an important pitch. It gives us a chance to get our foot in the door at Coca-Cola." He pauses. "I'll stay and work the weekend with your team. We'll work together. We already have the alternate strategy the executive team just agreed on. If we can work tonight on concepts and agree on everything tomorrow morning, then Saturday afternoon, we can present revised work. Sunday, we can complete the presentation boards and the digital presentation."

It crosses my mind to suggest a different team. Fresh blood that hasn't worked insane hours the past two weeks. Fresh eyes. But my pride won't let me get the words out. Plus, suggesting another group risks me coming across like a defensive brat. It's an insane schedule. But it's also a chance to work hand-in-hand with John. So maybe that's the silver lining I can sell my team. And give them Monday off.

Nick addresses John. "John, you don't have to work this weekend. I'll stay and oversee the project. I want to see us win this account, which is why I pushed for the absolute best we can do in today's meeting. Trust me."

John's skin flushes and his nostrils flare. I understand. His team, his people, stand in the crossfire of this mess. "No, this isn't your project. It's Christian's. I'll work with Anna and her team. They need the extra creative help. Anna, can you look to see if we can pull in some extra ADs and staff the graphics studio for the weekend?" He then turns to Christian. "You and Anna did good work on this. It's solid. Christian, you remain in control from the account side." John checks his watch. "Anna, can you clear your calendar for the rest of the day?"

In an upbeat voice, I respond, "Absolutely."

My frustration surges sky-high, and I want to close my office door and scream. But John built this agency. A part of me thrills to be working on a project with our founder. And I don't quit. I dig in and keep going.

John never utters a word out loud to Christian, but Christian answers his questioning expression with a strong, "Me too. I'm here on this."

A heavy sigh escapes John. "Okay. Let's meet in my office in thirty minutes. I need to call my wife and tell her about this change in plans for the weekend. Anna, please talk to your team and prepare the graphics studio. Then we'll review the alternate strategy, and we'll have a brief to share with the team soon. We'll order dinner in. It's gonna be a long night and weekend."

Nick's cheeks flush crimson. Anger? Embarrassment? I'm not

sure which, and I don't care. He had every chance to change the direction before now if he didn't like it.

After Nick leaves, Christian frowns while staring at the papers on my desk. My gut says he wants to unload. We've worked together quite a bit on this pitch. But Christian is a professional. Right now, time is of the essence. Maybe one day after work, when this is all over, he'll unload over a beer. Nick's a snake. I don't doubt he orchestrated this whole thing as some sort of political play, attempting to take over the new business group or some nonsense.

"Anna, let's go tell your team together. They lost their weekend. You shouldn't have to tell them alone."

Christian's a good account guy. He understands that even people who aren't married with kids have lives outside the office.

"Thanks. We'll get through this. It's frustrating, but we'll dig in and get through it."

He exhales loudly. "Nick." He says his name like it's an expletive. "In that private meeting, he was trying to play some sort of crazy game to take over this pitch. But the way he did it, stepping in so late, he'd prepped those guys before the presentation. He had to have." He stares up at the ceiling and huffs. "Let's go. Let's do this. We don't have much time before we need to be in John's office."

We meet with the team and update everyone. They aren't shocked.

Then I stop by for an unpleasant talk with the studio manager. Jerry had a few choice words to express his displeasure at being asked at the eleventh hour to have the studio staffed over the weekend.

Next, I meander through the cubicles to recruit a few extra art directors and copywriters for weekend duty. It's not a super tough sell, because it's an opportunity to do work for another brand to put in a person's portfolio. But it also means losing the weekend.

By the time I've recruited four more people and ensured staffing for the studio, forty-five minutes have passed and I'm late walking into John's office.

The three of us spend the afternoon coming up with a creative brief based on the alternative strategy. Usually, Christian would have written the creative brief on his own, but given how little time we had, John wanted us all working on it together. Then the three of us brainstorm concepts together.

I've never had the chance to work with John before. He's brilliant. We bounce ideas off each other like teammates. Any anger or frustration about losing my weekend filters away. This is why I work at a smaller agency—to learn from experienced, gifted creatives. I love my job. These people. This agency. I'd never get this experience at a big agency. Not at my age.

Delilah knocks on John's office door and announces food is set up in the conference room.

Christian briefs the team over dinner, then I assign each art director with a copywriter and send them off to concept. We agree to review initial concepts at 9:00 p.m.

As everyone's filing out of the conference room, I glance at my phone and mutter a low, "Fuck!"

Christian frowns. "Everything okay?"

"I forgot I'm supposed to go out with someone tonight." Christian is still sitting with me in the conference room, and John's about to return. I look up from my phone. "I need to go call someone."

Christian chuckles. "If I'd known you were dating someone, I would have reminded you to call when John and I went and made our calls."

I roll my eyes at his comment, choosing not to respond. Shit. It's almost seven o'clock, and I'm supposed to meet Jackson in an hour. We're not dating, but it's rude to bail last minute. Dating? These last few weeks, he's become my person. I see him daily and I want to see him every day. The slipping I hadn't wanted to do? I've pretty much fallen. Relationship or not, I feel more for Jackson than I've ever felt for anyone. And he's not going to be happy with me. Nor should he be.

Jackson picks up on the first ring, and I brace myself. I don't want to make this call. He sounds out of breath, like he's been rushing around. "Hey, there. I'm in my apartment getting ready. Where are you?"

"Jackson, I'm so sorry. I'm still at work. We have a new business pitch on Monday, and everything got derailed. I've got to work tonight and through the weekend."

Silence.

"I really am so sorry. It's not my fault. We gained some new information on the account, and we have to change the pitch."

Silence.

He asked me to attend his work event weeks ago. Almost two months ago. I told him I'd go with him, and I want to be there for him, but I have no choice.

"When did you realize you couldn't make it tonight?" His voice quivers across the line with ill-concealed anger.

I hesitate before answering because I am so in the wrong. "Earlier today. We had a presentation to executives. It's been a shit storm since. I've been working nonstop. It's been insane."

"You forgot about tonight. Or are you doing this because I stayed over? Are you making this up to avoid me? Is this you freaking out?"

Whoa. What? "I'm not going to dignify your question with a response. It's a huge pitch, and by the way, you made me late to the presentation this morning. But of course, why would I expect you to take my job seriously?" *Guilt, hit the bench. Anger, you're up to bat.*

"Are you serious right now?"

"Are you?" I counter, outrage spurring me on. Only a man would expect the world to fucking revolve around him.

"Yeah, I'm serious. I don't know what to think. You knew I needed you tonight. It's been on your calendar for ages."

"Jesus, Jackson. You can go to a work function by yourself. Just lie and tell the old ladies you have a girlfriend. Then they won't set you up. It's not that big of a deal."

He snaps, "Got it. No problem." The line goes dead.

Christian taps on the frame of my office door. "Everything okay?"

"Yeah." *No.*

He grins. "You look shell-shocked. Like someone just tore you a new one. I'm pretty sure I've worn the same look a few times when my wife lit into me. You ready to head back to the conference room?"

It's a little after 2:00 a.m. when we all call it a night. I jump into a cab, waving goodnight to other colleagues also grabbing cabs. We're in a good place on the concepts, and we agree to meet back at the office at 10:00 a.m.

I pull out my phone and read the one text from Jackson.

> **Jackson:**
> Found someone else to go. Hope work
> goes well.

My chest aches as if he plowed a knife through it. Why? We aren't dating. He said he needed a date to this. Of course, he found someone to go. He probably has a little black book full of interested and available women. He and I agreed to sexual exclusivity, so at least he isn't going to sleep with his date tonight. There's that. Unless he decides to move on and tell me tomorrow. Friends with benefits. There's no reason to be jealous. We were having fun and if he finds someone real then that will be good for him.

It's 2:30 in the morning when the elevator to my floor opens. I push open my apartment door, and one giant mound of fur wiggles and waggles in her happy welcome home dance. I don't bother washing my face or taking off clothes. I call Chewie up to the bed to sleep with me, and within moments, I'm out.

twenty

ANNA

Waves crash. Then a siren sounds. I slam my hand down to shut off my backup alarm. The two-alarm system sucks as far as day starters go. But after yesterday's marathon, sounds of the ocean might lull me deeper into dreamland instead of waking me.

I listen to the soothing sounds of waves crashing for a few minutes. Awake but resistant. I grab my phone. No new texts.

Steaming coffee in hand, I stand scribbling a note on the outside of my door for the dog walker. She's already texted confirmation she's coming today. But I'm writing a thank you note since she added me into her rotation last minute.

Jackson's apartment door opens, and I stop writing.

A young woman in her twenties steps into the hall, wearing one of Jackson's frayed UVA baseball hats. It's one of the ones that hangs on the inside of his closet door. I've debated secretly borrowing it but decided he might notice it missing. It's worn and looks like a favorite.

She glances down the hall as she meanders to the elevator, texting someone on her phone while walking.

Tears spring to my eyes. My chest aches. It's like someone punched me so hard I can't breathe for a moment.

The elevator door opens, and the woman holds the door, glancing my way. "You getting on?"

I shake my head and turn back to my notepad hanging outside my door, pretending to be finishing up my note. I can't get on the elevator with her.

He found a date, and she didn't have any problem staying over. Clearly. They also plan on seeing each other again, given she's wearing his hat. His baseball hat from undergrad. One night, and she's wearing his twelve-year-old baseball hat that hangs like valued art in his bedroom.

My commute to work is a blur. The office lights are off when I enter. I flip switches, and the hallway lights up. All the offices remain dark.

"Hey, there you are. Brought you a bagel," Delilah shouts from her cubicle as I pass.

I keep marching to my office but yell back, "Thanks. Give it to someone else. I've already had one." That's a lie, but I have zero appetite. Tears fall down my cheeks, an irrational reaction. Jackson can do what he wants. That's our agreement because that works for both of us. I don't need someone in my life who doesn't support me, someone who doesn't see my work as important.

Bagel and coffee in hand, Delilah opens my office door without knocking. She gasps. "What happened? Why are you crying?"

I sniffle and hunt for a tissue to stem the tide of snot flowing from my nose. "I'm an idiot. That's all."

"You're an idiot?" She pauses, angling her head. "Does this have to do with the pitch?"

I mumble out a "no" then blow into the tissue. I need to pull myself together. John and Christian will be here soon.

"Does this have to do with a certain well-dressed executive who's met us out after work a few times?"

I nod as I reach for a new tissue.

She closes my office door and sits on the edge of my sofa. "What happened?"

"I can't talk about it right now. I need to pull myself together."

"Have you been seeing each other? For real?"

I snort into my tissue. "No, and that's why I'm an idiot. We were doing the friends with benefits thing. I told myself I could handle it. That neither of us wanted a relationship. But we agreed to not have sex with anyone else."

Delilah nods and mutters a slow "Riiight." She leans over and in a stealth move places the wrapped bagel on my desk.

"This morning, another woman came out of his apartment." A new burst of tears flows. Jeez. What is this? I've never been one to cry over guys. "And she was wearing his clothes."

"That scumbag! You deserve better than that," Delilah exclaims. She watches me as she sips her coffee. "Did you have any idea he was cheating on you?"

I scoot onto my desk and cross my legs, sitting directly on top of piles of papers. Not exactly professional, but professional Anna hasn't arrived at work yet. "I don't think he's been cheating. He was pissed because I canceled on him last night. I guess he just had a really good time last night with my replacement." And you can't cheat when you're not dating, but I don't have the energy to say it out loud. At least as long as he tells me about her the next time I see him, he hasn't done anything wrong. I breathe in, and my lungs expand. Deep breathing helps control the emotions. Right then, my phone pings.

Jackson:
You at the office?

I flip my phone over so I can't see the text. "I'm gonna go splash some water on my face. I'll see you in the conference room. And, D?" I pause until she stops staring at her phone. "Thanks for the bagel."

She jumps up to hug me, and I put my arms out, blocking her. "No hugs. I've got to pull it together." Hugs will make me cry harder. Past experience taught me. Two funerals under my belt. I can't avoid everything that brings on tears, but I learned from my past. I know how to rein in emotion and move forward.

twenty-one

JACKSON

"Nope, not a word." I stare out the window, frustration seeping through my pores and a sense of helplessness strangling me. My sister, Joanna, sits across from me at brunch on Sunday. By chance, she'd been in New York on Friday when Anna bailed. She was supposed to stay with a friend, but since I had a guest room with a bed and her friend had a sofa, she'd ended up staying overnight with me. She's heading back to DC this afternoon.

My sister eyes me over her Diet Coke. "She hasn't responded to any of your texts?"

"Nope." I know better than to keep texting and calling. I did that back in the day when we had our big fight. Some people will eventually text back or return a phone call. Not Anna. She'll go days and days. "Dammit." I stare out the window. "I can't believe I fell for this shit twice."

Joanna studies me. "There could be an explanation."

I roll my eyes and snap, "Yeah? An explanation? She texted me an hour before we were supposed to be there to say she had to work late. I never received any kind of text the next day. Nothing. It's all bullshit, anyway. We weren't in a relationship."

"It seems to me like you were."

I run my hand through my hair. "No, no relationship. We talked about it. We had an agreement. I told her I don't have the time or desire for a relationship and she said she was in the same boat. But here's the thing. The first time I stay over, she's MIA the next day. Blows me off. Don't you think that's a little coincidental?"

Joanna's eyes bug out a bit, and she gapes at me as if I'm the crazy one. "You told the woman you've been sleeping with for over a month you don't have the time or desire for a relationship?"

I sigh. "She doesn't want a relationship either. Clearly." I emphasize the word *clearly* and grit my teeth.

"Why doesn't she want a relationship?"

I don't want to talk about this, but I'm also about to explode. Angry at Anna. Angry at myself. It was one thing to get burned by someone once. But twice? By the same person? "She had a bad relationship. She's never shared all the details, but it was bad. She has this idea that it's too easy to slip into a relationship and too hard to get out of one when things aren't going well. She wants to focus on her career." I pause and add, "And I get it. But," I slam my palms down on the table, "here's the thing. Four years ago, we got in a massive fight because I wanted her to move to Atlanta." I leave out the shit with Chase. "Here, she's been adamant about me not staying over. The moment I do, she's MIA. It's the same shit as at Carolina. She's got relationship issues."

Joanna spreads jelly on her toast. "That could be. Did you do something to make her turn away from you? Is it possible she's mad at you for something?"

I run my hand through my hair for the umpteenth time today. This is such *déjà vu*. How many times did I dissect our fight, wondering if I pushed her to Chase, if I was out of line?

"I stayed the night. Thursday was the first time I stayed the entire night at her place. I thought she was fine. She must have freaked out the next day. That's when she blew me off."

Joanna gives me a curious look. "Are you sure you don't want a relationship with her?"

My annoyance with my sister grows because she isn't paying attention to what I'm saying. "No, I've told you I don't have time one. That's why Anna and I were supposed to be great together. Two friends hanging out. We live right down the hall from each other. It's convenient. Fun. We agreed. There's no reason for her to react this way. None."

Joanna puts her hand up. "Hey, got it. And you are my brother. There is no need to overshare." I half smile, and she questions me. "But I don't understand you. You're, like, thirty years old. Don't you want something serious one day? Get married? Have a family?"

"Jo, I work insane hours. To make partner, you've got to put in the hours."

"Jackson," she says, exasperation painting her words. "Life is short. You're going to get named partner eventually. But if you spend years without living your life, is it worth it? We watched Dad put in all the hours too. Remember what he said when Mom was sick?"

Mom's stage four breast cancer diagnosis left us reeling, shocked it could happen to our rock. It had been touch and go for a while, but she survived.

I hadn't been around for a lot of Mom's sickness because I'd been working. But it had gotten bad. Our healthy, vibrant mother transformed into a frail, sick skeleton almost overnight. She'd survived, though. To look at her now, you'd never know how feeble she had once been or how close we came to losing her.

"You may not remember it. Maybe he didn't tell you, but he told me if he had to do it all again, he would've been there for her more. He got teary-eyed and said he wished he'd been around for us kids more too."

"He was building his business. A successful business. He was providing for his family."

"Yeah, but you know what? Realizing he might lose Mom forced him to think about life. And he realized that at the end of the day, the business didn't mean nearly as much to him as Mom… or us. He sold his company right around then. He missed so much of our lives. Birthday parties, games, and for what?"

Dad hadn't said any of this to me. But then again, I haven't been around much. We don't speak much on the phone either. He and I don't have a phone kind of relationship.

Joanna continues. "They say that on a person's deathbed, no one ever says he wishes he'd spent more time at the office."

"On some level, I know you're right." Mom's always telling me I work too hard. Reminding me there's more to life than work. But at a law firm, so much comes down to billable hours, and I'm so close to making partner, I can taste it.

"Tell me about this Anna."

I stare over my coffee mug at my sister. What can I say? And does it matter now?

"What does she look like?"

"Hmmm…about five foot six. Long, dark, curly hair. Not tight curls, loose curls like waves. Straight if she blow dries it. Golden-brown eyes. She's funky and creative. I'm not sure she can decide if she wants to be a painter or a photographer or a graphic designer. She's always working on something, creating something." I pause, careful in my words so my sister sees her as I see her. "Big, beautiful smile. She's the kind of person who makes everyone around her feel good. Everyone, and I mean even random dog walkers around here love her. She lives in my building, so I see it all the time. Random people greet her on the sidewalk."

Joanna's eyes widen with surprise.

"What?"

"Well, first of all, you definitely like her. You sound like a guy who has it bad. Like love bad. Which means you're a fool if you keep this no relationship, friends with benefits shit going. And two, I may know why she hasn't texted you back."

I sit back in the booth, waiting to hear my sister's theory. I wave my hand for her to go on. I'll fight her on the whole love bit later. Or maybe I won't. I want to hear why she thinks Anna hasn't texted me back. Why she's fucking ghosting me.

"By chance, does she live on your floor?"

"Yeah, other end of the hall."

"When I came out of your apartment Saturday morning, it must have been Anna that was standing at the end of the hall. Did you tell her I was staying with you this weekend?"

twenty-two

ANNA

"Call me."

The yellow Post-it note covers the notes I've posted for my dog walker. He set in the middle of the board as if he owns it. Fuck him.

I unlock my door and push it open. Chewie wiggles and waggles and shakes. I drop to the floor and bury my face into her side. My girl.

I've had a lot of messages from Jackson on my cell, but I haven't had the time or desire to listen to them. I'm in avoidance mode. He needs to tell me about his overnight lady friend, but I'm not up for hearing it. Not yet. I'll be damned if I'm going to cry when he tells me. And if he chooses to keep it a secret, then I'm not in a place to deal with that either.

John, Christian, and I flew out early this morning for the presentation in Atlanta. The meeting went well. My heart felt like someone took a sledgehammer to it, but at the same time, impressing the hell out of the agency founders felt pretty damn good. John told me and my team to take extra time off since we worked nonstop over the weekend.

I sit down on the floor and scratch Chewie all over, giving her all the love such a good doggie deserves. Light tapping sounds on my door. Chewie jumps up and lunges at the door while barking with a resounding furor. Crap. It has to be Jackson. Anyone else would have to call up.

On impulse, I snatch the handle of my bag and run into my bedroom. I hear the door open and Jackson's deep voice. "Hey, there, girl. Is your Mommy not home yet? You want me to take you for a walk?"

He's taking her for a walk?

I remain hidden in my bedroom. Frozen in place. I hear the sound of the door closing and feel the absence of Chewie. I remain squatting by the side of the bed. I'm not ready to face him.

I pull my phone out and text my brother.

Me:
Are you around?

It's Monday evening. Stranger things have happened.

Bobby:
Yeah. About to order pizza. You want to come over?

Me:
Y. Be there soon.

. . .

I find a small tote bag from the top of my closet and throw in some clothes. I'd rather crash at Bobby's than be on high alert for the door unlocking and Jackson coming in.

I sit on the floor of my room, hidden by my bed, kike a kid hiding from her parents.

"Anna, where are you?"

I lift up on the floor and peer over the bed. "Bobby? Over here."

"What're you doing?"

"Hiding."

"What'd you do now?"

"Nothing."

He punches my leg.

"Ow. Stop it."

"What'd you do?"

"Nothing. I went to the library."

"And now you're hiding?"

"Mom's mad. I didn't tell her where I was going."

"Why not?"

"Because she'd find something else for me to do. Mom and Dad only want me to get married. It's you they want to go to college. Haven't you noticed?"

"They want you to go to college...and they want you to marry Evan. Can't you do both?"

"Bobby! I want to go to college. I don't want to marry Evan. Don't I get a choice?"

"Of course, you do. They just think you want to marry him. Just tell them."

. . .

Tell them. Yeah, that worked out well.

A long tongue licks my face. Chewie. Jackson must have let her back in while I was off in Memory Lane. I sit up on my knees and peer over the bed. The apartment's empty.

I stand, grab my bag and Chewie's leash, and head out to my brother's apartment.

I buzz up, and the door unlocks. Bobby's head comes into view as I climb the stairs to get to the third floor.

"Hey, Anna." He pulls me into a bear hug the moment I reach his landing. He lifts the tote off my shoulder and asks, "You staying the night? Everything okay?"

"It's fine."

After we enter his apartment, he hands me a beer and a pizza slice. "Who're you hiding from?"

I roll my eyes. "I'm not hiding from anyone. I worked all weekend and don't have to work tomorrow, so figured I'd crash here tonight. Is that okay?"

He narrows his eyes, and a wrinkle forms between his eyebrows. "You can stay here anytime. But something's up. You're not fooling me."

Given I can't remember the last time I crashed at Bobby's place, he's not crazy to suspect something's wrong. My phone vibrates.

"You not going to answer that?"

"No."

"Anna. What. Is. Going. On?"

"Nothing."

He punches my leg.

"Ow! Asshole."

"Anna!"

I tilt my head back and stare at his whitish popcorn ceiling. "Fine. I was kind of seeing someone. My neighbor. He brought someone else home, and I saw her coming out of his apartment in the morning. I'm not ready to talk to him about it."

"The guy you've been running with?"

"Yes."

"Why do you think she was more than a friend?"

"Why do you always see the good in everyone? How many women friends do you have who sleep over?"

"Well, it would appear my sister and her dog are sleeping over tonight. And it might surprise you, but I have had out-of-town friends come to visit. Friends with tits. Who are just friends."

I point my index finger at Bobby and aim it like I'm wielding a big stick. "I told you what's wrong. I don't want to think about it anymore. I'll think about it tomorrow. Now, pick a movie."

twenty-three

ANNA

"Chewbacca, my love, look at you. Out for an afternoon walk on a Wednesday!"

Al and Chewie greet each other in their normal way, ending with treat crumbs scattering Al's button-down shirt.

"You love your walks, don't you, girl? Such a good girl. Good, good girl. You're the only girl who can get Mr. Hendricks to smile. Isn't that right?" Al's baby talk has Chewie doing the butt shake, wagging her tail like it's a happy stick.

I roll my eyes. I know Al's baiting me, but I'll bite. "Jackson smiles when he takes her out for a walk?"

"They both do. Chewie loves your man."

"Not my man, Al." I snap my fingers to get Chewie's attention and to signal it's time to head upstairs. She falls in line like the well-trained dog she's becoming. She does defy Jackson in some ways. Dirty paw marks grace the front of Al's shirt, offering proof.

Al calls after me, "You sure about that, Anna girl?"

I press the elevator call button repeatedly. Al hovers nearby until the swish of the lobby door resonates. Then I hear his cheerful greeting echo through the lobby. "Good afternoon!"

Two yellow Post-it notes now adorn my bulletin board. The first one that stated "Call me" has a new friend that reads "Please call me. It's not what you think."

I wait until evening for Jackson to get home from work. I'm done hiding. I tap my knuckle lightly on his door. Heavy footfalls grow louder. The door opens, and bloodshot eyes stare back at me. His hair points in different directions, as if his hands have been running through it nonstop all day.

We stare at each other for a moment. Words escape me, which is ridiculous since I prepared a speech. He reaches out and pulls me against his chest and wraps his arms around me.

I plant both hands on his chest and push back hard, instantly creating distance.

"I saw the note on my door."

"Did you listen to my messages?"

"No."

"Why not?"

"I've been busy." And I haven't wanted to hear them.

"Do you know that was my sister you saw Saturday morning?"

"Your sister?" Holy shit. Bobby's theory. I've been a freaking wreck over his *sister*.

His hand engulfs mine, and he tugs me out of the way so he can close the door. Still holding my hand, he leads me to his sofa. The city lights twinkle through the window behind him.

"Yeah, my sister. After you stood me up last minute, I asked Joanna—*my sister*—to come with me. She was in town visiting friends. Her friend only had a sofa, and I have a spare bed, so she decided to stay at my place."

"Oh." All those tears and all that anger over nothing. Do those dark circles under his eyes mean he's been upset too? Or has he been working long hours? A part of me wants to finger the rough stubble lining his jaw and breathe him in, but I lean back instead.

"Yeah. Oh." He plays with my fingers. "Is she why you didn't return my calls or texts? Were you angry?"

I lower my head. I'd been so ready to let him have it. To tell him I don't want anything to do with him. Only now, what does this mean? I don't have any reason to be angry at him. No, he should be angry at me. I've been acting like a jilted girlfriend.

Today, with his gray t-shirt on, his eyes are shaded blue, almost a gray-blue. "Joanna thought you were the one in the hall when she came out of my apartment Saturday morning. But we didn't figure it out until Sunday. Have you been angry this whole time?"

"Yeah." I take a calming breath, trying to sort out my circling thoughts and emotions. "But I had no right to be. We're friends. Just friends." I stare at his socked feet, feeling ridiculous and a little shell-shocked. His sister. I've been a teary-eyed, emotional, fucking mess over nothing.

He sits straighter but continues to hold my hand. "Yeah, but we had an agreement to be exclusive. You'd have every right to be angry if I had someone stay over. I'd probably break down your door if I thought you did." His slightly upturned lips hold my attention. Is he amused?

I rub both hands over my face, absorbing this new information. "I came over here planning to let you have it. I was going to tell you I don't want to see you again. And now there's no need. But I was too emotional. The emotion didn't make sense. Maybe there is a need."

He frowns. "What do you mean?"

"I'm getting too involved. My emotions are too intense. I need to take a step back from this. From us. I thought I could do this. Friends with extra. But I can't."

He brushes through my hair with his fingers, almost absentmindedly. My whole body tingles as I gaze into his hazel eyes that shine like dark orbs in the dimly lit room. He leans forward and presses his lips to mine. Slow. Cautious. I open my mouth for him as he deepens the kiss and wraps his arms around me. Our kiss is tender to start. A kiss so intense that I never want it to end. God, I've missed him.

His hand caresses my neck then glides down to my chest. His thumb circles my nipple through my blouse. My nipples harden in response, and my core tightens, needy.

His fingers fumble with the tiny buttons on my shirt, and then, in frustration, he yanks, sending buttons flying everywhere. His mouth drops to my breast, and I hum as heat courses through me and I squeeze my thighs together.

My body shivers in need. I want him. But I place a hand against his chest and push him back. "We can't do this. Jackson, I want to, but we can't. I'm in too deep." I need to end things now, or the pain when it does end will be unbearable. Tears fall from my eyes. What I won't tell him, because I know he doesn't want to hear it, is I've already fallen. To say it out loud, to tell him I love him, would make it real. Too real. And our friendship would be irrevocably shattered.

His hand coasts along my thigh. "One last time?" His hands toy with the hem of my mini-skirt. He shifts the skirt upward, and his hands finds my center. He rubs and circles. His gray-blue eyes find mine and he whispers, "Please."

What would one more time hurt? Saying goodbye is going to hurt like hell anyway. I did try not to slip. I thought I could do this, told myself I could be strong, but the damage is done.

Just one more time together. One more time like this. One more time before we stop this and push ourselves back into the only friends zone, the safe zone.

I push him onto his back and straddle him. I press my center against his bulging erection and shift my hips, finding friction. He growls. I gaze into those mercurial eyes while tugging on his shirt. "One last time."

twenty-four

JACKSON

"Hey, man, thanks for meeting me for dinner tonight." I sink into the opposite side of the booth Chase claimed at Finn's, our favorite neighborhood Irish bar.

"The legal eagle wants to grab dinner? How can I say no?" Chase asks. Judging by his half empty pint glass, he's been here for at least ten minutes.

Thankfully, a waitress comes up and takes my order. It is out of the ordinary for me to ask him to meet for dinner on a weeknight. I don't want to talk about anything serious or stressful, but I need to get out of the apartment building.

"How are you doing these days? Have you recovered from your breakup?" I ask, aiming to keep it light.

Chase raises his eyebrows, surprised at my question. Okay. Not as light as I want. Crap. My head's so screwed up I'm violating Bro Code. "Yeah, Angela's not talking to me. She's pissed. Understandably, I guess. Her mom's not talking to my mom. My mom's pretty pissed at me. But, yeah, all good."

"Oh, shit. I didn't realize the moms were involved."

He nods and drinks his beer. "Yep. Take it from me. Introducing the parents before you're engaged is never a good idea."

I laugh out loud. This is why I invited Chase out. Sometimes it's nice to hang out with an old friend and hear about someone else's problems.

"What are your plans for Thanksgiving?" he asks.

"Headed home. You?"

"My parents always host a dinner. Anna's brother is working, but if he gets the chance, he may stop by. If you're around, we'd love to have you. As long as my mom doesn't exile me, that is."

"Thanks, but I'll be in Virginia. Where's Anna spending Thanksgiving?"

"Prague. Remember? But last year, she and her brother joined my family for turkey. The invitation stands for both Bobby and Anna." I nod as I absorb this new information. Her parents both passed away, so it all makes sense. She mentioned a while ago she was planning to visit her old roommate. I forgot she booked the trip over Thanksgiving.

Chase studies me as he drinks his beer. "Okay, dude. What's going on there? Angela told me she suspected something was up with you guys."

I shrug, aiming for nonchalance. "Nothing, man."

"Bullshit."

"We've spent a lot of time together. That's it."

"Yeah, you guys still running buddies?"

"Yeah, we were." Anna told me she wouldn't be doing that now. Not for a while. She needs time. It makes sense but still sucks. Best she figured it out now, though, before we couldn't even be friends.

"Were?" He drinks his beer. "What did you do?"

I exhale with a loud blow. Who am I kidding? Talking about it is inevitable. "Well, we blurred lines and became more like friends with benefits." I brace for his laughter, but he sits there, waiting for me to continue. "Anna wants to take a break. Says she's getting too emotional."

"Dammit, man. I told you not to hurt her."

I snap back, defensive. "I didn't hurt her. She's the one who wants to take a step back, not me. Besides, even if I wanted a relationship, she doesn't want one."

He angles his head. "Do you want more?"

I pause, weighing Chase's question. I'm being ridiculous. There's no reason to weigh anything. "Nah, man. I've told you. I don't have the time. My hours are insane. You think Angela complained. Women hate dating me."

He leans back, making room for the waitress to deposit our fish and chips dinners. After she rushes away to another table, he glances up while cutting his fish and pouring vinegar over it. "You keep saying you don't want a relationship, but is that what you really want? These are some of the best years of your life. You want to spend all of them between an office and an empty apartment? You love contract law that much? M&A really that thrilling?" His tone is both incredulous and sarcastic.

I don't say anything as I sit and stare at my food. He sounds like my sister. The last time I wanted a relationship was four years ago, and it was with Anna. But neither of us was willing to change our plans and give up the jobs we'd already lined up for something that started during the end of our last semester.

"How long were you two benefiting each other?"

I roll my eyes. His snide question annoys me to no end. He can be such an ass. "A couple of months?"

"And did your work suffer during that time?"

I rub my chin, reflecting on recent successes at work. I'm kicking ass. "No."

He chugs his beer and looks at me like I'm a moron. There's an awkward silence, and he raises his eyebrows.

"But we weren't dating."

"No? You ran together every day, right?"

"Yeah, before work." And I'd make her coffee every morning too. Not gonna mention that.

"And how often did you guys get together after work? And on weekends?"

"Mmmm. A lot, I guess. If we got home in time, we'd order in together." No reason to share if we got in late at night I still usually ended up at her place, at least until she'd kick me out.

"And weekends?"

"Usually one night she'd go out with her friends, one night we'd stay in. Typical weekend." I drink my beer, eyeing him with suspicion. I can see where he's going with his line of questioning. Despite all appearances, I'm not a moron. My chest hurts so damn bad. The fish and chips are greasy and unappetizing. I push the plate away.

"You dumbnut. No matter what label you gave it, you were dating. How the hell do you think that's any different than dating?" He pauses to shove a few fries in his mouth. "Were you dating other people?"

"No. We agreed we'd be…" I trail off before saying *exclusive*, because if I say that out loud, I'll sound like the world's biggest dumbass.

"You'd be?"

He's not going to let it go. I huff. "We weren't seeing other people."

He drinks his beer and slams it down on the table. "You fucktard. You were dating her! Did you ever tell her you'd be open to a relationship?"

"You aren't hearing me. She doesn't want to date. Yes, we've been close for a while, but the first time I stayed over the whole night, she freaked out. She canceled on me the next day for a work function I needed her at." Of course, it's possible work had forced her to cancel. I'd never pressed her on that. Never discussed it because the next discussion we had, she was telling me she was too emotional. Kind of pointless to talk more about that fucking day.

"You mean she canceled this past weekend? This past weekend when she had to work nonstop? Anna told me all about work. Insane, if you ask me. At the office until, like, two o'clock in the morning on a Friday night…well, Saturday morning." Annoyance radiates off him as he grips his pint. "She told you she needed time away because she's getting too emotional. Sounds to me like Anna fell for you, and she's asking for distance because you don't want a relationship."

"Well, I don't want a relationship."

"Fucktard. You are a fucktard!" He points his index finger at me. "Throw away your life. I just hope whenever you reach that magical day when you decide you can have a life, you find someone half as cool and awesome as Anna. In the meantime, if this is the way you are going to fucking play it, you stay the hell away from her."

"Man, I'm telling you. We weren't in a relationship. It's been working because we haven't applied the label and so haven't dealt with any expectations."

He glares at me while downing his beer, so I continue my defense.

"Really. She doesn't nag me. There's no pressure. She never asks where it's going. Never makes me feel guilty when I work until ten o'clock at night. You just got out of a relationship. You fucking know what I'm talking about."

Chase tips his head back and stares up at the ceiling. "Maybe. Or maybe I was in a relationship with the wrong person. Maybe that's why I didn't want to see so much of Angela. Maybe that's why she had to nag. Maybe when it's the right person, you get each other. You make time."

As I listen to Chase, it occurs to me he might have a point. I'd never been with anyone I wanted to be with. No one I'd been crazy about. Eager to see. Blamed it on work, my goals. But would I be different with someone I was into? Did Anna not seem disappointed in me because I made an effort to be near her, to see her? Because any spare time I had, I spent with her. The nights we were apart were almost always because she was out with the girls.

My beer finished, I place it down on the edge of the table so our waitress will see the need for a refill. Meeting Chase's eyes, I tug on my chin as I consider his points. "Maybe. Is that your take? The Chase philosophy?"

He grins. "I don't know, man. I mean, but, yeah. Yeah. That's what I believe. Not so much from my experience. Clearly. But from watching other guys. That's what I hope, anyway. No one would ever get married if it was always so fucking difficult."

Could he be right? Did Anna and I have a relationship? Was our issue with a label? Or did she have other issues? Maybe something from her past I'd never asked about?

I wave the waitress over for another round. On me.

twenty-five

ANNA

Sleep has not been my friend. I bounce back and forth between regretting saying goodbye and regretting ever spending time with Jackson. I should have known having sex on the regular would make me emotional. Tears. Lack of focus. Confusion. On the bright side, I didn't cave. I decided to end it, and I did. I didn't let it last for four years and let my family fall in love with Jackson. The only heart broken is mine.

With the big pitch behind us and Thanksgiving in front of us, we don't have any pressing deadlines. It's a good thing because my productivity has fallen to an all-time low. My chest aches. Damn heart. When my dad died, my mom said she'd read a research paper claiming the shape of a surviving spouse's heart sometimes changes in the year or two after their life partner passes. Is this pain my heart shapeshifting? I hope not. My mom died from a heart attack about six months after sharing that little nugget of knowledge with me.

A soft rap sounds outside my office door. "Hey, there. Want some company?" Delilah stands in my office doorway, two steaming Starbucks cups in her hand.

"Oh, you are a goddess."

"Now, only in exchange for company." She grins as she hands over my grande.

I point to my sofa. "Sit." It's late. I could leave the office now, but I can stay and hang. I have nowhere to rush to. I've almost finished packing for my upcoming trip to visit Olivia.

Delilah sits on my sofa and studies me. "You look tired. Everything okay?"

"Yeah, sure." I plop down on the sofa beside her then kick my feet up on the coffee table.

"You sure? That doesn't sound convincing. What's going on? Have you seen Jackson since you ended things?"

I'd told her I'd ended our arrangement. But I'll still see him again. "We're still friends. It's not an end. It's a transition. I'm just taking some space right now."

"Uh huh. Space for what? To fall out of love with him?" She beams at me as if she told me it's a sunny day, and for a moment I consider picking up one of my art books and throwing it at her.

"Delilah, I don't know what you're trying to do, but stop."

She reaches out and grabs my hand, and her eyes are all doe-like and serious. "You need to give it a chance."

"That's not what he wants!" I lower my head. My voice was far louder than I intended. In a more controlled volume, I continue. "It's not what I want either. There is no giving it a chance."

Nick taps on the doorframe. I get the sense he's been listening for a while. Smirking, he strolls in and leans back on the front of my desk to face us. "So, you and your boyfriend part ways?"

Fuck. Cover blown. I should've closed the office door. "Not really. Just working through some things."

He keeps grinning. "Not what it sounds like to me. Anyway,

that's not why I stopped by." He hands over the paper he's holding. "I wanted to give you a creative brief so you can review it with your team. Was thinking we'd schedule the brief for tomorrow?" He directs his attention to Delilah. "Can I break up your girl powwow long enough to go over this with Anna?"

Delilah stands and stretches. "Sure. I've got to get out of here, anyway. Yoga class." She points a finger at me as she walks out. "Tomorrow. Lunch, okay?"

I nod. "Sure thing." Car service picks me up from the office tomorrow at 3:00 p.m. to drive me to the airport. Departure time cannot get here soon enough.

After she leaves, I scan Nick's brief and don't notice any issues. It's our standard brief based on the existing campaign for some new subway billboard ads.

I place the brief on the sofa beside me. "I don't see any issues. Looks good." I hop up, intending to send a quick email to the team. But as I pass Nick, his large hand grips my wrist to stop me.

"What?"

"I'm here for you if you need someone."

I snap my wrist back and move quickly, placing my desk between us. "I'm fine, Nick." I give him a small smile, wanting to hide how uncomfortable his touch makes me. "You know, it doesn't make sense to start this project until after Thanksgiving break. Almost everyone on the team is out next week."

"Where are you gonna be for Thanksgiving?" He plants his fists on my desk and leans forward, across my desk and into my space.

"I'm leaving for Prague tomorrow. I'll be gone all next week too."

He squints his beady eyes. "Let's regroup when you're back from Prague. It'll give you time to get over your little boy toy."

"What?" I grit my teeth and point to the door. "Nick. Just..." I want to tell him to get the fuck out of my office, but he's a senior executive, and instead I inhale. And exhale. "I'll see you when I get back."

twenty-six

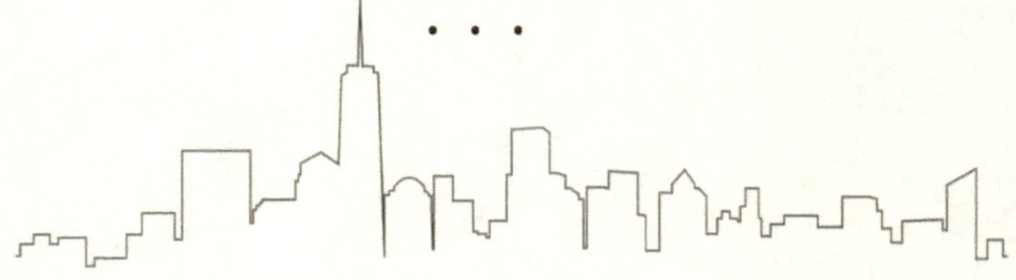

ANNA

As soon as I land in Prague, I text Olivia to let her know. My low battery alert shows five percent remaining thanks to a malfunctioning charging plug.

Lovely. I write down Olivia's address on paper in case my phone dies before I wade through customs and the taxi line. My brain's too foggy from the red-eye flight to trust myself to remember much of anything.

Olivia lives in Old Town, a big touristy part of Prague. She said it had been love at first sight. On the first day of looking for furnished rentals with an agent, she found this place. The third place she checked out. She regrets her quick decision. She says the crowds of tourists get old, and she wishes she had found something in New Town, somewhere near the park.

Me:
Phone about to die. Be at your place in
thirty minutes to an hour depending on
customs and traffic.

Olivia:
Can't wait to see you!

Excitement and wanderlust dance across the fringes of my consciousness. Traveling on my own always feeds my soul and my independence. But the bulk of my being post red-eye craves a pillow and solitude. The line through customs moves quickly, and after collecting my suitcase from baggage claim, I wander out to the taxi line. Multi-lingual signs, with English prominently displayed, guide me through the airport, and relief fills me when I tentatively speak in English to the man in charge of the taxi line, and he responds in my native language without missing a beat.

Staring out the window of my taxi, I rub my hand over my face. Random tears stream down my overtired cheeks as the driver navigates through a rundown area. Graffiti mars the sides of the high fences barricading in back yards. There are few pedestrians out and about.

As the cab moves farther away from the airport, the bleak urban scenery of graffiti walls and billboards changes. As we drive farther into Prague, the homes give off a statelier appearance. These homes are also surrounded by walls, but these walls are elegant and well-maintained. Pedestrians are out in greater numbers, walking dogs. Packs of kids roam free. Then we drive over a river, and everything takes on a storybook feel. The medieval style buildings are centuries old. The cab bounces along uneven cobblestone.

The cab stops at the corner of Kozi Street. The James Dean

Diner sits across the street, a red and white 1950s style diner with American icons in black and white. On the other side of the street, there's a place called Bake Shop. Farther down, there's a quaint cafe called Nostress with the sign "Best Coffee Since 2001" in the window. Yes, that'll be my first stop. Tomorrow morning.

All the restaurants and the windows of the apartments above boast window boxes. Greenery spills out. Many feature arranged Christmas tree limbs, some with large glittery balls. As gorgeous as the holiday window boxes are, a part of me wishes I'd come in the summertime. The summer window boxes must overflow with fragrant, colorful flowers, enhancing the European storybook vibe.

I find Olivia's address on the street and ring the bell, standing back to wait. Olivia opens the gigantic door, takes one look at me, and pulls me into her arms. Like always, a hug at such a weak moment rips me apart, and I can't stop the tears from falling. My shoulders tremble as I melt into my best friend's warm embrace.

She holds me without saying a word, rendered speechless by my tears. I shouldn't be crying. It has to be a side effect of exhaustion and the madness of the last couple of weeks. Her apartments is on the second floor, and once I've pulled myself together, she helps me with getting my luggage up the stairs.

Set in an art nouveau building with soaring high ceilings, her apartment reminds me of the pre-war buildings in New York. The pinewood floors are laid down in a chevron pattern, and the walls, ceiling, and trim are painted a monochromatic white. The furniture, which came with the rental, is a well-thought-out combination of modern and art deco.

I survey the room as I collect my emotions. Enormous windows highlight the kitchen and living area, bringing in light and the sights of Kozi Street. The kitchen is all white with a thick, mammoth white marble island. On one end, four chairs surround the island to create a table. The opposite end of the island features a stove.

Two deep blue velvet sofas and an oval white marble coffee table adorn the living room. Abstract art pops color throughout, but I'm too tired to spend time taking in the art. The place evokes clean and calm. It's simply gorgeous, *Architectural Digest*-worthy.

Olivia leads me down the hall, opening a door into a bedroom with a queen-size bed. The room is so narrow, only about three feet exists between the side of the bed and the wall. One large window overlooks the bed. Stepping closer to the window, the view is of a spacious natural area filled with trees and park benches. It appears several buildings open up into this quaint private courtyard.

Olivia yanks on a string, and a shade falls to cover the window and block outside light. "I know you're exhausted. Lay down. Take a nap. Whenever you wake up, I'll be outside. I'm working from home today. After you sleep, we'll talk." She smooths wayward hairs and gently tucks them behind my ear. "Yes?"

Tears well up in my overtired eyes again. I collapse on the bed, rolling onto my side into a fetal position. She gathers the pale blue comforter from the end of the bed and bundles me in it. I close my eyes.

twenty-seven

JACKSON

The elevator doors open. On reflex, my eyes wander to Anna's place.

A tall man in scrubs stands outside her door. His head is down, and he's fumbling with keys on a keyring.

"Can I help you?"

He jerks his head up, startled. "Nah, I got it." He inserts a key into the lock and turns.

"Do you know Anna?"

He pushes the door open then kicks his foot up against it to keep it open. Exhaustion paints his appearance. Slightly bloodshot eyes with dark circles. A five o'clock shadow mars his jaw. I recognize the signs of exhaustion as I've seen them reflected back at me in the mirror too many times. His pants are splattered with a dark brown substance. Maybe blood? He must have come here straight from the hospital.

"I'm Anna's brother. Are you her neighbor?"

The tension I hadn't even realized I was carrying eases. Her brother is here. That's right. He's a resident. I hold out my hand in greeting. "I'm her neighbor, Jackson. I live down the hall."

With a firm handshake, he says, "Bobby."

With his back to me as he enters the apartment, he says, "Sorry, man. I just came off a double shift. Just stopping by to grab some of Chewie's treats."

I follow him into her apartment. "Is Anna already in Prague?"

He opens up cabinet doors, searching for something, and mumbles, "Yeah. Arrived last night. Or yesterday. Or this morning." He's mumbling more to himself than to me.

I huff and slide past him to the tall cabinet in the corner and reach for the snack bin. Chewie's not in the apartment. A yellow Post-it note with scribbled handwriting reads "Dr. Herriot" with a phone number. Her vet. I place the Post-it on the treats and hand them over.

"Thanks, man." He twists the bin in his hand, and the treats tumbling around make a low drumming sound. "You know where things are. I take it you've spent time here. Are you by chance the guy she's been seeing?"

"Yes." At least, I'd better be. No, we hadn't phrased it like that, but we had agreed to be exclusive. If her brother heard about a guy, I sure as hell better be that guy.

"Well, it's good to meet you. I probably smell, so stand away from me. I'm a resident, and right now I'm on ER rotation. My last shift involved bodily fluids." He rests his back on the counter to face me. "Should've showered before leaving, but I just wanted to get home."

"I'm gone over Thanksgiving to visit my family, but if you need help with Chewie before I leave, or when I get back, let me know."

"Thanks. I have roommates to help out, so it should be okay." He runs his hand through his hair and blinks as if trying to force his eyes open.

"She's doing good? Landed safely?"

He squints and pulls out his phone. "I think so. But I don't have a text from her." He types a message into his phone. "Look, man, I've got to head home. I'm about to fall on my face, and I still have to walk that dog. You seem like a good guy. My sister's been through a lot. Take care of her, okay?"

He holds the door open, waiting for me to leave so he can lock up.

As he waits for the elevator, I reiterate my offer. "If you need help, I am more than willing to take Chewie. The dog walker already knows to come to this building. Chewie and I run together. It's not a big deal."

"Thanks, man. I have two roommates, so between us, we should be okay." He hesitates. "But here, you know what? Let's swap numbers in case I need to take you up on your offer. With Thanksgiving coming up, there's definitely a window there where all three of us will be working. It's pretty much a hard and fast rule residents work holidays."

As I input my number in his cell, I ask, "When is she coming back again?"

"The Sunday after Thanksgiving." The elevator door opens, and he holds it. "For the record, I think you've been good for her. It's been a long time since she's been this happy with someone. It's been a long time since she's been with anyone."

I can't stop myself from asking, "She told you we're together?"

He squints. I can't tell if he's about to close his eyes to fall asleep or if that's a confused expression. "Not in so many words. In her own way, she told me. Be good to her."

The elevator door closes. I stand, staring at my blurry reflection in the door. His words, "Be good to her," play through my head.

I pull out my phone and send a text.

Me:
Did you land safely? How's Prague? I met
Bobby. I told him I'm here to take care of
Chu if he needs me to. I'm here for you too.
Always.

twenty-eight

ANNA

I wake to a dark room. Disoriented, it takes me a few minutes for my eyes to adjust to the foreign surroundings and for me to remember where I am. After stretching and clearing sleep out of my eyes, I step out of the room to search for Olivia. I find her sitting with crossed legs, a laptop on her lap, and papers stacked beside her.

"Hey, sleepyhead," she says.

"What time is it?"

"Close to six. Early evening. I wasn't sure if you'd sleep straight through to the morning. Thought about waking you but decided sleep might be the best thing for you."

Olivia's black hair is longer now. She's cut long bangs across her brow, reminiscent of Amelie or a trendy French girl. She's always been so put-together and perfect. Our close friendship never really made sense. She's the epitome of sophistication, whereas I favor a bohemian style. We're opposites in a lot of ways but that's never mattered.

"Let me brush my teeth and fix myself up so I don't embarrass you, and I'll take you out to dinner. My treat as a thank you for hosting me."

———

"So, you want to tell me what's going on?" Olivia asks after we've ordered and she's filled me in on how she's spending her time in her newly adopted city. She came here after her ex cheated on her, but from everything she's said, she's moved on. Both physically and emotionally.

We're in the John Lennon Pub, located close to the Charles Bridge, and our window seat offers a view of the cobblestone path along the river. It's not super close to Olivia's rental, but she picked the restaurant for its location. Built in 1357, the Charles Bridge is one of the oldest in Prague. Artisans sell paintings, ceramics, and jewelry all along it, and tourists flock to it for views of the Vltava River and the bridge itself. Musicians camp out in different places along the bridge, spaced far enough apart their songs do not blend into cacophony. Exhaustion prevented me from snapping photos on our walk over, but I'll be back before I leave.

Pedestrians pass by on the sidewalk and I stare at each passing stranger without reservation as they aren't looking at the window.

"Anna?"

I rub my eyes and stifle a yawn. "I don't really know where to start."

"Well, first, tell me why the tears. Let's start there."

"Jackson."

She gasps. "Did he cheat on you?" A mixture of disbelief and anger rings through her tone.

I bow my head and focus on the graffiti etched into the wood. "I thought he did. But he didn't. The whole thing made me realize I can't do it."

"Do what?"

"The whole friends with benefits thing. I'm just too emotional about him."

"Do you love him?"

I stare out the window for a long time before answering. "I think so." And that was not the deal.

Olivia squeezes my hand and sips her beer. Then she excuses herself to go to the bathroom.

Night has fallen, and the streetlamps cast a mystical glow on the crowded tourist street outside. Lights crisscross over an outside patio across the street. The lights dance over a group crowded under heat lamps. The view reminds me of a tented holiday from my past in a festive pavilion with a canopy of lights.

Evan holds my hand and leads me to the front of the tent. He taps his wine glass filled with sparkling grape juice. Neither of us is twenty-one yet. Around a hundred people stand before us. Some are our friends, but most are our parents' friends. Our parents have been throwing the Annual Hart-Daughtridge Holiday Festivus for as long as I can remember.

I try to pull my hand away and stand with the crowd. Evan grips me tighter and gives me a reprimanding glare. I bow my head. Satisfied I'll remain by his side, he addresses the crowd.

"Dear friends, tonight marks twenty years our parents have been throwing this holiday party. Every year, the celebration grows. It's a Hart-Daughtridge tradition. A tradition I hope Anna and I continue long into the future."

The crowd fills with smiles. Someone shouts, "Hear, hear." I stand beside Evan, eyes cast down. I want to get off this stage and away from the microphone. Our parents come and stand near us. My mom has tears in her eyes. My lips pinch together, and my throat grows thick.

Evan falls to one knee, and I hear a few gasps from the crowd. Evan's mom places her palms over her heart. I struggle to breathe. "Anna Elizabeth, we've loved each other for as long as I can remember. You are my first love, and I want you to be my last. Marry me."

I stare out on a sea of expectant faces. My chest aches. He knows I don't want this. We talked about this. The lights overhead, strings of Edison bulbs glowing warm, blur as I push my way through the crowd and run.

"Hey, daydreamer. Dinner's here." Olivia's voice brings me back to the here and now. A cheeseburger on grilled potato bread sits before me. "You okay?"

I rub my hands over my face in an attempt to rid myself of the memory. The day of the unwanted public proposal. The worst part had been the shouting match with my parents. They'd been angry and hurt. How could I be so selfish? What's wrong with me? Evan will take care of me. Why don't I want Evan? He's a good southern gentleman. I'll never find anyone to love me the way Evan loves me!

I rest my forehead on my hand. There are too many voices. Too many emotions. I need more sleep.

Olivia's gentle voice breaks through my inner turmoil. "If you love him, why aren't you with him?"

I slam my head back against the wooden booth so hard it hurts. "Ow." I smooth the back of my head and laugh at Olivia's bewildered expression. "Shit, that hurt."

She sort of laughs with me but doesn't speak, waiting for my answer.

"He doesn't want a relationship. It's a moot point." She squeezes my hand in a way that says she understands. Then we dig into our burgers and drink up.

twenty-nine

JACKSON

The football game plays on both the large TV in our den and the smaller TV in the kitchen. My parents knocked down the walls between the two rooms ages ago to create one large open space living area. The giant TV in the den can be seen from the kitchen, making the second TV complete overkill. But at least today it's on a game instead of streaming news.

I stand indecisively in the middle of the space, between my dad sprawled on one of the sofas and my mom and sister hard at work in the kitchen. The sofa summons me. No one would bat an eye if I joined Dad. But instead, I make my way to my mom, kiss her on the cheek, and ask what I can do to help.

She runs her hand through my hair as if I'm a school age kid and pats my shoulder. "Do you mind chopping the onions for the dressing? They make me tear up."

With steady precision, I dice the onions. I move on to peel and dice the carrots while my Mom and sister flit around each other. It feels like any other Thanksgiving in our home. Would Anna like it here? She'd fit in. She'd be at home in the kitchen with my mom and sister. Then, when all the work's completed, she'd gladly flop on the sofa to hang with my dad. That's Anna. She can fit into any world—with women or men. She's comfortable in her own skin.

Damnit. She should be here. With me.

As if on cue, my younger sister glances up from her task of creating the cranberry relish and asks, "What's Anna up to today?"

I pause. I had expected she'd ask, but I hadn't expected it would hit like a punch to the gut when she did. "She's in Prague."

"Wow! That's awesome. Who's she there with?" she asks, her focus on the chef's knife she's using to chop walnuts.

"Her old roommate lives there. She's coming back Sunday." I rattle off answers to her questions. I don't know much, though. Other than one brief text, I haven't heard anything from Anna.

After making an excuse about checking voicemail, I head into my room and shut the door. It's my childhood bedroom and it still looks like it. My bug collection sits in small glass jars on shelves. Star Wars Legos line up on proud display over my desk. Mom kept everything exactly as I'd left it. It's a bit disturbing, as the room's starting to take on a museum feel. She needs to convert it into a guest room or use the space in some way she'd enjoy.

I sit in my desk chair and pick up an old Dungeons and Dragons book. Flipping through the pages, I remember the last day I held this book. I sat here, in this same chair, tears streaming down my face, the graphic images a blur. Betsy had told me she didn't want to be my girlfriend anymore because I was too fat. I didn't cry at school. It wasn't until I'd closed my bedroom door and picked up this book that the tears had started to fall. Fifth grade. Joanna could tell something was wrong. She barged in, hugged me, then asked if I wanted to play Legos. As a kindergartener, she preferred dolls, but she knew Legos were my thing. That's when I knew I had a pretty great kid sister. It was also the start of my running career and my addiction to healthy eating.

So many memories in this room. I'd sat here, on this bed with the same comforter, right after graduation. Torn between reaching out to Anna and deleting her contact info from my phone. I rub my hand over my face. Instead of doing anything about Anna, I'd packed and moved to Atlanta. I closed the door and never looked back.

I pick up my cell. No new texts. No new calls. I throw it down on the bed. Stare at it. Then pick it up and press her name. My heartrate kicks up a notch and my chest expands when she answers.

"Hey, you."

My throat thickens. "Hey. Happy Thanksgiving."

"Happy Thanksgiving to you too."

"Are you okay?" It's the most important question I can ask.

"Yeah. I am."

She sounds good. Really good. "What have you been up to?" *Did you need to go so fucking far away?*

"I've been spending time with Olivia. Exploring Prague. They don't celebrate Thanksgiving here, but Olivia took the day off, and we went out to eat at a nice restaurant. We shared two bottles of wine at dinner." She sort of giggles, and I think I hear a door close.

"What time is it there?"

"Nine o'clock. We just got home." She sighs loud enough it carries through the phone line. "It's been a good day, but we've walked a ton and had a lot to drink. Time to call it a night."

"Are you in the room by yourself now?"

"Yeah." Static and her soft exhales are the only sounds through the line. I close my eyes.

"I miss you."

"I miss you too."

I squeeze my eyes shut and hold on to her response. A silence fills the line, prompting me to give a little more. "I wish you were here. You'd like my family."

"I'm sure I would. They're probably a lot like you."

Maybe they are, maybe they aren't, but I don't want to talk about my family, so I say, "Tell me about Prague. What's it like?"

———

"Hey, have you been following Anna's Instagram posts? I searched for her when you told me she's in Prague. She's an awesome photographer." I glance over from my suitcase. Joanna stands in my doorway, a coffee mug in hand.

I'm in the middle of packing my clothes and straightening my bedroom. Thanksgiving takes a lot out of Mom, and I don't want her to have to clean up after me.

"Yeah. She's making Prague look amazing." I don't think I've ever checked Instagram with such frequency. Her posts capture Prague's architecture, landscape, and people with a photographer's eye. Unfortunately, she doesn't post selfies.

"Tell me about it. Czechoslovakia moved up a dozen spots on my travel wish list. Have you been talking to her?"

My dad joins Joanna at the doorway and places his arm around her shoulders.

"Not much." I have a lot to say to her, but I want to say it in person.

I close my suitcase, ready to roll it out and get on the road. I had planned to stay until Sunday, but Bobby and I have been texting. I get the sense he'd like for me to get Chewie out of his apartment. She's not getting regular exercise, and as her energy level rises, so do her destructive tendencies. A football, the corner of the sofa, a running shoe, and the garbage are among the casualty list.

"You guys here to see me off?" I ask, a little self-conscious with them both watching me pack. My dad's eyes shine. He's not an emotional man, so it's probably allergies.

My dad lifts Joanna's hair and twists it around like he used to do when she was little. She leans against him and smiles. He tugs her hair and asks, "Hey, do you mind if I talk to Jackson for a bit?"

Joanna gives Dad a warm smile and hug before responding, "Sure thing." She addresses me with a stern, "Don't you dare leave without saying goodbye."

"You got it, sis."

My dad watches her go then takes a seat in my desk chair. I sit down on my bed, preparing for a father-son talk. Seeing him in my chair, it hits me this is a bit of a role reversal. When I was growing up, I'd sit in the chair. He'd either stop by the doorway and say something quick, or if something big had to be addressed, he'd sit on my bed. When I knocked over Mom's lamp playing forbidden indoor soccer, for example, he sat on my bed for a small eternity.

"I hear you're dating a girl."

Is this what he's here to talk to me about? Girls? I'm almost thirty. *Come on, now, Dad.* I smirk, amused. "Yeah. Well, kind of. I want to date her. The whole thing is still a little TBD." I see now we are more than friends with benefits. I'm not about to tell Dad the woman I've fallen for wants sex with no relationship.

My dad nods and fingers his college ring. It's a nervous habit of his, but I suspect he started doing it to make other people nervous. At least, when I was a kid, he'd always twist the substantial ring when he was trying to come up with a cruel punishment.

I straighten my back and stretch out my legs. Awkwardness fills the room. Dad and I don't talk much. Our conversations often center around sports or business. There's something about him broaching the girls subject with me now that amuses me. I could tell him it's a little late for the birds and bees talk, crack a joke, but that's not us.

He swallows and shifts in his seat. "Well, I'm glad to hear that.

Your mom's been after me to talk to you. She thinks you've been holding off on living life, focusing solely on your work ambitions. She's worried you might be trying to be like me." He lifts his shoulders, resigned. "Apparently that's a bad thing."

"Is that what Mom said?" The vision of her berating him for my choices has me laughing out loud.

Dad nods and shifts in his chair. "More or less." He gives me a sheepish grin. "But she's not wrong. If I could go back and redo things, I would. You kids and—well, your mom—you are my world. I'm not sure you guys know that. And you should. Every kid should know that. I was always working when you were growing up, and now, in the blink of an eye, you guys are grown and gone out of the house. We get to see you a handful of times a year. I thought I'd have more time. When you were kids, it didn't feel temporary." He studies his right palm, traces one of the lines with his other thumb. His voice quakes with emotion. "I didn't know how fleeting it would be. Your childhood. So, yeah, I'd redo your childhood. In a heartbeat. And I certainly hope you don't repeat my mistakes."

When he tilts his head up, tears fill his eyes, and he sniffles. This is not the dad I had growing up. I want to gather him into a hug but stay on the bed instead. We've never been touchy-feely men, and I'm not sure I can handle watching my dad cry. "Dad, I love you. You know that, right?" He nods, and his lips curl into each other, holding back emotion. "You were building a company. I understand. Joanna kind of mentioned some of this stuff to me. I get it. And, yeah, I've been following in your footsteps. In my own way. Putting off the whole marriage and family thing until further in my career. But I'm rethinking my plan."

The bedroom walls blur, and I breathe in deeply for a minute until my vision clears. Dad's sitting there, patiently waiting.

"Dad, I know we don't do a lot of stuff together, but it's not too late to change that. You guys live in Virginia. It's not that far away.

Why don't you come up one weekend, and we'll catch a game? Or we can plan a ski weekend together?"

Shock covers my Dad's face, as if I proposed we take a space shuttle to the moon. He sniffles. "I'd love that." He stands, signifying the conversation has ended. There may be a limit to how long he can handle an emotional discussion. "If you and this Anna girl work things out, maybe your mom and I can come for a weekend to meet her. I'm sure your mom would love some time getting to know her. So would I."

"Let's take it day by day. When she's ready, I'd like that too." I'd like that an awful lot, actually. The question of the hour is how to sell Anna on it. A new plan. A new arrangement for us.

Four years ago, we closed the door on us. I don't want to close the door this time. I don't want to let her go.

thirty

. . .

ANNA

"Hey, you! Happy belated Thanksgiving."

"Hey, sis. How's the wandering solo traveler?" Bobby's voice brings a smile to my face. I couldn't catch him on Thanksgiving. Today's my last day in Prague. I return home tomorrow. The whole trip has blown by in the blink of an eye.

"It's good. Olivia's taken a few days off, so I haven't been solo the whole time, but I love it here. If you ever get the chance to get away, I recommend it. How're things there? Did you get any turkey?"

"If you count the hospital cafeteria turkey, then, yes."

"Ugh. Chase didn't bring you by a plate of food?"

"No. Don't be ridiculous. Chase didn't hand deliver a plate of food. I did go out with him for beer Friday night. And I saw Jackson this morning."

I tilt my head forward to hear him better, even though I'm

holding a phone and shifting my head won't improve acoustics. "What? Why?"

"Because that dog of yours is not trained, Anna. She has destroyed my apartment."

"No! I'm so sorry. What did she do?"

"Don't worry about it. Just thank your boyfriend because I was about ten seconds away from taking that chew monster to the pound."

I gasp. "You would do no such thing."

"You did name her well." he snaps back, humor ringing through his tone.

"Har. Har. Why Jackson? How did that happen?" I don't address the boyfriend comment. I'm too confused.

"We met at your apartment. He offered. Kept in touch this past week. You've got a good guy there. Don't blow it."

I roll my eyes. "He's not my boyfriend. There's nothing to blow."

"'Anna, why do you do that?"

"Do what?"

"Block a good guy. I get that Evan did a number on you, but you've got to move on."

"I've moved on."

"Bullshit."

"You know what? You're talking out of your ass right now. Jackson doesn't want to date me. I fell for him. I told him too. And you know what? He didn't say a word when I said goodbye. If he's helping with Chu, then he's just trying to prove we're still friends. I can promise you, he's not into me, not in that way. It might be Mom was right. Maybe Evan is the only guy who will ever be into me. Have you ever thought about that? Maybe I screwed up more than just our family when I said no to Evan." Tears well up as my words flow out in rapid-fire and stream of consciousness. Defenses up and crumbling in an incongruous battle.

"Whoa. Whoa, little sis. Take a deep breath. Calm down. I've only got a few minutes before I need to do rounds, so I'm gonna respond to all your bullshit in bullet points. Then I'm texting you those points for you to reread. Got it?"

I set the phone down and blow my nose. When I pick it back up, Bobby's voice echoes through the line, "Anna? Got it?"

"Fire away." I sniffle.

"First, Jackson loves you. He may not have said it out loud yet, but no man cuts his vacation to take care of a girl's disobedient mutt unless he loves her. Two, you made the right choice when you broke up with Evan. The guy's an insecure asshat, and I've heard he's going through a divorce right now. That could've been you. Listen closely. Mom and Dad would still be dead. Their deaths had nothing to do with you choosing not to marry him. Saying no to a marriage you don't want will always be a valid choice. The smartest choice. If you had married Evan for Mom and Dad, it would've been an enormous mistake."

"Believe me, I know. But the thing is, saying no destroyed my relationship with Mom and Dad. They never forgave me. They never understood." I jam a tissue against my nose to blot the steady stream of snot and tears.

"Anna, there was nothing to forgive. Your life. Your choices." He pauses then continues. "Have you ever thought about what would've happened if you had married Evan? Because here's the scenario that plays through my mind. You'd marry him. Drop out of college. Have a kid. At some point, you'd get a divorce. You still would've had issues with Mom and Dad. Either from their over-involvement in your marriage or blaming you for your failed marriage."

Deep down, I know he's right. Our parents were best friends. From the time I could crawl, they'd been pushing Evan and me together. And I always wanted to please my parents. Make them happy. But, in the end, I chose me. My life. My choice. His words bang around in my head and chest tightens.

"Anna, you still there?"

"Yeah, sorry. Ah, when did you hear Evan's getting divorced?"

"A while ago. He got caught cheating." Rumors had flown in high school and college that he was hooking up with random girls. I never gave them credence. But it could explain why he was so controlling and possessive of me. He never wanted me to go out with friends. Perhaps he was worried I'd behave like him if given the chance.

"And, last point, little sis. You are a beautiful person. One day, a good guy is going to see all you are and love you with everything he has. If it's not Jackson, then it'll be another guy."

———

For my last night in Prague, Olivia made reservations for us at Restaurant Mlynic on the Vltava river. The lights from ships glitter along the waterway. The streetlamps cast a golden glow and amplify the storybook aesthetic. Inside the restaurant, the contemporary lighting and design contrast with the view outside. The blending of historical with contemporary yields an alluring atmosphere.

The restaurant boasts three terraces overlooking the river. Tables line the windows. Boats carry tourists up and down the river below the stunning European architecture.

Olivia flips through a leather book filled with hundreds of wines, while I stare out the window at the boat lights floating along the river. "Hello, daydreamer. What's going on in that mind of yours?" Olivia asks after our waiter takes our order.

My patient friend sits. Expectant. The waiter pours a red French wine I don't recognize. Olivia swirls the dark liquid in the glass, smells it, sips, and nods her approval. The waiter fills our glasses.

Olivia lifts her glass to toast. "Here's to us both finding our way."

Our glasses clink, and we savor the wine.

"Jackson's picking me up from the airport. He texted me today. He's also taking care of Chewie right now."

"I thought Bobby had your dog."

"Word on the street is she's been a bad girl."

Olivia laughs. "And Mr. I-Don't-Want-a-Relationship swooped in to save the day?"

I bite my lip. "Something like that."

"And he's picking you up from the airport?" A knowing grin spreads across Olivia's face, and I can't suppress my smile. I get what she's insinuating.

I exhale loudly, releasing uncertainty and general unease with the idea of hoping. "He says he wants to talk." I don't add that Bobby believes he's in love with me. That's a bit of an over-the-top theory. One I can't bear to say out loud as it's too risky.

Olivia raises her eyebrows. With a dose of dramatic flair, she asks, "So, when he tells you he wants to date, and he should've never let you walk out the door, what are you going to say?"

I sip my wine and when I set it back on the table, notice the light reflect on the dark maroon liquid. "I'm scared. I don't like me in a relationship."

Olivia points her index finger at my face. "Here's the thing. At different points in our lives, we are different people. You were a kid in your last relationship."

I open my mouth to disagree, but she stabs her finger in the air to hush me.

"No! Let me finish. From age seventeen to twenty is a kid. A big kid, yes, but significantly different than the woman you are now. You moved to a city on your own. You are the youngest creative director at your agency. You are successful in your own right. You are not the same kid dependent on her parents and trying to please them. You're a different person now."

I swirl my wine thoughtfully. She's right. Knowing she's right doesn't make trusting myself any easier.

"You aren't going to know what kind of person you will be in the next relationship. I'd bet who you are with Jackson this year will be a totally different person with someone else next year."

"Someone else?" I can't fathom dating another man. Not right now, especially with Jackson living on my hall.

A mischievous smile flits across her face. "Yeah, like, what if you and Chase start dating?"

"Chase and I are just friends." She kind of laughs, and so do I. She's friends with him too, and she understands. I might have been lying to myself about Jackson. But Chase falls squarely in the friend zone.

"My point is, a relationship requires two people. Sometimes the other person helps us to be a better person. Sometimes the other person can have a toxic, poisonous effect. Such as bringing out our insecurities and weaknesses. It's what the other person brings out in us. It's not who we necessarily are with every person we date. Can you see that? Our goal is to find the person who brings out the person we want to be. And we bring out their best self. It's not who you are in a relationship. It's who you are with that someone else in a relationship. Make sense?"

"It does. I guess. I'm not sure I agree that Jackson's changed his mind, but if he has, I'll give it a try. See where it goes."

Olivia clinks her wine glass to mine. "That's my girl. You only live once. So, live." She raises her glass. "A toast. To finding our way. To finding happiness."

She raises her hand to attract our waiter's attention. "We'll take another bottle, *dekuji*."

We both sip our wine. My thoughts go to Olivia. Running from a bad relationship. "The toast. Finding our own way. Does this mean you're on your way to happiness?"

"I am. I've put relationships on the back burner, and all my focus has been on me. Not just work but finding things I like. Books I like. Exercises and museums I like. And you know what I'm discovering?"

She's glowing, and there's a cheerfulness and confidence to her that's stirring. "What are you discovering?"

She dramatically lifts her wine glass out to the side in a *ta da!* fashion and says, "I like me."

I snort. "I like you too, babe."

I'm a little lightheaded from all the wine, so I pick up the food menu, and the wine menu catches my eye. "Holy shit! You ordered us a one-hundred-and twenty-five-dollar bottle of wine. Are you out of your mind? Two of them!"

Olivia grins. "I figured tonight is a night to celebrate. To celebrate our friendship. The end of a fantastic week together. And good things coming our way." She lifts her glass for another toast. "Here's to finding our own success and enjoying it. Whatever success might look like."

I clink my glass with hers. "I guess you're doing well here, huh?" We sure as hell didn't order bottles over a hundred dollars back in the States before she left.

She smiles and winks. "Let's just say I'm coming into my own."

thirty-one

JACKSON

I pace outside the baggage claim. My mouth has gone completely dry, but I'm not about to leave to get a bottle of water. My heart pounds with such vigor and strength I'm conscious of each beat.

She texted twenty minutes ago to say the line in customs is short, and I can meet her on the curb outside. As if.

At some point over Thanksgiving, the truth hit me. I'm in love. Maybe I loved Anna four years ago. But this is a deeper love, something new to me. I am willing to make adjustments for her. I want to make her a priority. But what do I do if she doesn't feel the same way? If she's not willing to take the same risks?

She told me she's too emotional and therefore couldn't keep seeing me. What if I tell her how I feel, and it doesn't change anything?

I did consider playing it safe. Picking her up from the airport as her friend. Taking it day by day, searching for signs she might be willing to take a chance on me. On us. But waiting to see is a weak approach.

I'm not weak. I go after what I want. I've got to lay it all out there. The crazy thing is I shouldn't be this nervous picking her up from the airport. It's not like I'm asking her to marry me. I'm only asking her to date me, which is something we've already been doing if we get analytical. But I am asking her to take a chance. Because things didn't work out before, and they might not work out again.

I check my phone for the thousandth time.

A crowd of people pours through the international baggage area. I search the crowd. Families. Kids with stuffed animals in tow. One man hugs a woman who's been standing outside waiting near me. Several business travelers hustle through and out of the building.

My skin tingles. She's near. I've always sensed when she's near. I scan the crowd, and there she is, one hand pulling her suitcase, the other holding her phone, texting as she walks. My phone vibrates. I slip it in my pocket, swallow, and reach out to her.

Surprised brown eyes stare into mine. Electricity burns through where I'm touching her arm then her hip. I pull her to me and embrace her. There's a moment of hesitation. Her arms circle my waist and pull me close. Her hands press against my back, and I close my eyes. I have missed her in a way I didn't know I could, and holding her calms the ache and relieves the physical pain I've carried in my chest.

The hustle and bustle of the airport fades into the background. I hold her close to me, breathing her in, before asking, "Can we sit and talk?"

She agrees with a slight nod, and I guide her to a nearby vacant bench. She's wearing black leggings, running shoes, and a worn gray sweatshirt. Natural. Beautiful. Perfect. Real.

We sit together on the bench, thighs touching. She tightens her grip on my hand, as if she's giving me courage to say whatever it is I need to say. *Here goes.* "I've done a lot of thinking since we last said goodbye, and here's the thing. You aren't the only one who's become emotional. I love you, Anna. I never said it four years ago, but I think I loved you then. I don't want to end this. I want to try. I can't promise it will be perfect. I can't promise you I'll be the best boyfriend. But I can promise you I'll try. You will be a priority in my life and I promise to do my best to make you happy."

Those golden-brown eyes gaze into mine. She tilts her head, and my lungs contract. Time stops. Everything around us fades to black. Her lips touch mine. Soft.

A single tear falls down her cheek. "I love you too, Jackson. So much."

———

I unlock my apartment door and push it open. A brown, shaggy beast bounds through the door, leaping and twisting her body in the air. I watch the mother and child reunion with a smile plastered on my face. I've been smiling nonstop like a goon the whole way home from the airport. Anna has more to say, but she's processing. I'll wait. She told me she loves me, and that's all I need to hear. I drove one-handed the whole way home, her hand in mine.

I grab two bottles of water and head to the sofa. There are many things I want to do right now, but I wait for Chewie to calm down.

Anna's running her hands all over her dog, as if she's checking for any signs of harm. She laughs. "I'm not sure she can see. This hair falls all over her eyes. She needs to go to the dog groomer, stat."

"When she runs, she seems to be able to see. But I'll admit, it has crossed my mind that all that hair might be impeding her vision."

"Yeah, she needs the groomer." Greeting completed, Anna slides up onto the sofa next to me. She runs her hand along my chest, and I inhale. Her lavender scent floods my senses.

She fingers along my jaw, my hair, and as she stares into my eyes, she pulls my head down to hers. My pulse races. Then her lips meet mine.

It's a soft brush of lips at first. Tentative and uncertain. She opens, and our tongues dance, hopeful. I don't want to rush things. I want to take my time getting reacquainted. She fingers my hair and I explore her curves. But when she climbs onto my lap and straddles me, it becomes much harder to go slow. Her core rocks against me. My hands explore her muscular ass and guide her hips. The tightness in my jeans and the sensation of her rubbing my cock through our clothes create a heady pain-ecstasy combination.

She pulls back, both hands touching my face. "I've missed you."

I close my eyes and move to kiss her again as my hands grip her hips to move her.

She breaks the kiss. Her hips softly undulate along my erection, teasing. "Do you think maybe we should talk first?"

I exhale. "Probably. But now that I have you on my lap, maybe we can talk later?" There are more urgent matters at hand.

"Well, I'll make this quick, then." She presses her hands against my chest and seems to be preparing to speak. She might be unaware, but her pelvis continues to rock back and forth.

With a groan, I grip her hips to still them. "If you want to talk, you've got to stop grinding on me."

She climbs off and moves to sit on the opposite side of the sofa.

"Ah, I didn't say to do that."

She holds up an index finger. "Here's the thing. I do want to be your girlfriend."

She pauses. I nod for her to continue. She's captured my attention. Our sofa reunion and exchange of I love yous had me thinking we're a done deal. Uncertainty hits hard. "Is there a but?"

"No. I do love you. I do want to date you. But there's something you need to know about me. I'm a pleaser."

I can't handle not touching her so reach for her hand. "Anna, that's one of the things I love about you." I attempt to suppress my smile so I don't come off like a jackass.

"No. Seriously. It can be problematic. You see. Before."

"With Evan?"

"Yes. With Evan. He was controlling. And possessive. But I never once told him I wasn't happy. Never once told him I wanted something different. So, in a way, I'm as responsible as he is for things not working out. I played along with my parents, his parents, him. I shocked the hell out of them when I told them the truth. And that's kind of me. So, with you, if I'm going to do this..."

I squeeze her hand. "And you are going to do this."

She smiles and warmth blooms below my sternum. "I need you to understand I might struggle to be honest with you."

"To communicate, you mean? To talk to me? Yeah, I kind of know this about you."

She gives me a playful shove. "I'm serious."

I return her stare. "So am I."

She climbs back onto my lap. "Does this mean you're my boyfriend?"

"Yes, it does." I press my lips to her neck. "You are my girl-friend. And we are giving this a go. And we'll both make mistakes. I'll piss you off. And you'll tell me about it. And you'll piss me off."

She wrinkles her nose in that cute way she has. "And you'll tell me about it. Like you always do. It's called communicating."

"And debating," I counter.

She raises her eyebrows. "And you love to debate."

"I love to persuade."

"But you won't push too hard, right? You'll let me stand up for myself?"

I nip at her chin. "Always."

I lose patience and lift her sweatshirt then send it sailing across the room. Her cheeks glow. She leans in and nuzzles my neck. "I really like my boyfriend."

"Is that so? Because I really love my girlfriend."

Her bra hits the floor. My mouth falls to her nipple, sucking and biting. Her hips grind me, rubbing almost painfully against my hard cock. If I'm not careful, she's gonna make me come fully clothed. With a groan, I pick her up and lay her down on my sofa, lying by her side so I can remove her leggings. She grabs my t-shirt and tosses it. Then her hands work the buttons on my jeans. In seconds, we're naked, clothes scattered across the room. Her hand grips my cock and strokes. I slip a finger into her drenched pussy. I let her ride my fingers and grunt, "You are so wet. Is that for me?"

"Only for you."

Her words, hearing her say it, intensify the need to be inside her. But I work her with my fingers, watching her closely as my fingers drive into her channel and I knead her clit. Her long brown hair spreads across the sofa, and her eyelids half close as she rides my fingers. Her thighs clamp together and she curls forward off the sofa.

"Feel good?"

She mewls. Her hand on my cock had stilled, but she begins stroking me again. Her thumb circles my juices on the end of my cock, and with a coy smile, she sucks her thumb clean. And that's it.

I reposition us so I'm between her legs. She's so wet, and ready, and so am I. With one hard thrust, I slam into her. We both moan, overcome. "God, I have missed you." I press into her, balls deep, and I still, savoring her tight pussy and long legs wrapped around me.

"Open your eyes, Anna. Look at me." Those golden-brown eyes open, and I start to move. To thrust.

"You. Feel. So. Good. I'm never going to let you go."

Her eyes lock with mine as we move together. Her nails scrape my back as her hips urge me on, meeting me with each thrust. I angle forward, giving her pressure where I know she needs it. Her back arches, and her muscles clench my cock. She's close. I reach between us, press right along her clit, and she shatters around me. I let go and the world goes black as I pulse out my release. Deep inside her. A vortex of emotion swirls.

She's mine. Mine. I will not fuck this up.

I hold her close. Our breathing slows. And then a long, wet tongue slides along the side of my face and Anna's. Chewie pushes her furry, smelly face between us. We both laugh.

thirty-two

ANNA

The Edison light bulbs dangling from the ceiling and industrial modern design capture my interest. I whip out my iPhone to snap some photos. The Goldwater, Brooke, and Associates offices aren't at all what I expected.

A polished woman wearing a skin-tight black skirt, white silk camisole, and a power red jacket saunters past. I don't mean to gawk, but she's wearing sky-high black heels in the office. Her dark hair hangs in a sophisticated, low, sleek pony. She's television-worthy gorgeous.

I reach the reception desk and ask for Jackson. I'm meeting him for lunch because he wanted his colleagues to meet his girlfriend. Only now that I'm here, I'm second-guessing my outfit. I'm wearing dark jeans, tall black Frye boots with wedge heels, a form-fitting sweater, and a camel swing coat. A thick camel scarf wraps around my neck. I loosen it. Either the heat runs rampant in this building, or my nerves are skyrocketing.

The receptionist's black sheath dress could double for an elegant evening out. On her chair rests her black suit jacket. Her shoes are not in my line of sight, but I'd bet a hundred dollars she's wearing gorgeous heels. When I ask to speak to Jackson, her gaze roams up and down my outfit, as if she's questioning if I'm a vagabond off the street and if she should throw me out.

Within moments, Jackson enters the hall and whisks me away from the reception desk. He slips his fingers through mine and leads me down the hall. As I glance back, I catch the receptionist's glare. I can't really blame her though. Jackson's gorgeous. No doubt she hoped he was single.

Two men in custom bespoke suits approach. "Bill and Tom, I'd like to introduce you to my girlfriend, Anna." This is the first time he's introduced me as his girlfriend and it's something I could definitely get used to. I tap down the giddy grin that's itching to break out and shake hands with both men.

Bill, the older of the two gentlemen, has a twinkle in his eye and there's something about him that reminds me of my dad. "It's a pleasure to meet you, Anna. Jackson needs a young lady like you by his side." I have no idea how to respond to that, so I simply smile.

When we reach Jackson's office, he pushes the door open and directs me to a conference table in the corner of the room. Before I can sit, a woman in gray slacks and a winter white silk blouse taps on the doorframe. "Jack, do you want to grab lunch?"

Jackson places a possessive hand on my lower back and disregards her question. "Eleanor, I'd like you to meet my girlfriend, Anna."

Eleanor peers around the corner at me and cocks her head as if she's unsure what kind of bug has flown into the office. She extends a professional hand in greeting. "It's nice to meet you." Her ice-cold hand takes mine with a firm, powerful grip. "Jack," she quips as she waltzes out of the office, her hair swinging along her back.

"They call you Jack here?" Jackson closes his door, draws his shades closed, and pulls me into his arms.

"They do not. I prefer Jackson. Only people trying to get under my skin call me Jack."

"Hmmm. I call you Jack."

He nuzzles along my neck and whispers, "When my cock's inside you, filling you up, you can call me anything you like."

Then he steps away and picks up a paper bag. He sets out two chef's salads, a selection of dressings, and two lime waters. "I hope this works for you. I don't have much time. I had my assistant pick up lunch for us."

"It's great. Perfect."

We gaze at each other a bit as we dig into the salads.

"You never told me you work with such good-looking women."

He raises his eyebrows and smirks. "Vipers. I'm surrounded by vipers."

"Maybe. Still gorgeous." I don't particularly like that he's surrounded by beautiful women. Polished perfectionists.

His lips spread into a cocky grin. "Are you jealous?"

I bite my lip. "Maybe."

"Babe, you have no reason to be. You are so much more beautiful. Outside and inside. Those women out there? I won't turn my back on them for fear I'm going to have a stiletto sinking into me."

"Eleanor? Is she one you don't turn your back on?"

His gaze turns thoughtful. "She's not a friend."

My phone buzzes, and I pull it out. It's the middle of the workday, so of course I'll check it.

> **Nick:**
> Drinks after work?

He's told me twice in the hall this week he wants to talk. My stomach churns. I type a quick text back.

> **Me:**
> Still getting caught up from being gone.
> Can't.

Now, or ever. Jackson leans and reads my text.

"He's still asking you out?"

"He's not asking me out that way."

Jackson rests his chin on his joined hands, elbows planted on the table. "I don't like how he treats you."

Me neither. The guy gives me the heebie-jeebies, but he's harmless. "It's fine. It's the way he is. And at least I don't have to worry about him nailing a stiletto into my back."

Jackson chuckles. "Yeah, you might have me there."

I narrow my eyes. "Be honest. When you wanted me to go on a date with you to an office function, it had nothing to do with old ladies setting you up. You didn't want your colleagues throwing themselves at you."

He shrugs and gives me this you-caught-me look. "Office politics."

I smirk. "Yeah, it must be tough being so gorgeous that you know with a little alcohol these hot women are going to hit on you."

"Actually, it is tough. I don't do office romance. Way too many dangers. And turning down a woman's advances can be tricky. I think of it as an emotional minefield. Only, in the office, when the bomb goes off, you don't lose a limb, you create an enemy."

"Sounds like the voice of experience."

Jackson glances at his watch. "It is. Remind me at home later, and I'll tell you what happened in Atlanta."

Jackson guides me to the elevator bank, a protective hand resting on my lower back. He kisses me goodbye, and I step into the elevator. As the doors slide close, I hear a feminine voice echo through the hall. "Jack, do you have a minute?"

thirty-three

ANNA

"Hey, there! How was lunch at Jackson's office?" Delilah stands outside my door, two steaming Starbucks cups in hand.

"Oh, you are a goddess."

"Only in exchange for company." She grins as she delivers my grande.

I point to my sofa. "Sit." It's after six o'clock. It's the best time of the day to sit and gab. "So, Jackson's office. Where do I begin? The office itself is way cool. Industrial modern design." I whip out my phone to share my photos of the building.

"Nice," she responds, flicking through the photos.

"Uber professional. Everyone's in a super nice suit. The women wear heels. The difference between his office and ours is like night and day. And those women…they are so put together. Like they could be the cast of Suits."

"Uh huh. Anyone inspire jealousy?" The tilt of her head and twerk in her lips show she's teasing.

"Not really." Jackson and I are in a good place. "He described them as vipers. I get the sense it's a cutthroat kind of place to work. I don't think I'd be happy working there. I definitely wouldn't fit in. And I can't help but wonder if Jackson's happy there."

Delilah grabs the latest *Adweek* and flips through it. "Heels everyday wouldn't work for me. That's for sure." A Mr. Clean ad gets her attention, and she flings the magazine at me. "Did you see the latest Mr. Clean commercial? I love where they are taking the campaign. It's a play off my favorite romance novels."

A tap sounds out on my door. Nick stands in the doorway, watching us on the sofa. "What you ladies up to?"

"Coffee break. If I'd known you were still around, I would've gotten you some."

"Thank you, Delilah. Watch and learn from Delilah, Anna. She'll show you how to treat a colleague."

"Thanks, D," I say as I toss a throw pillow in Delilah's direction. She snorts and dives to catch the pillow, sending her messy bun in a tailspin.

With his usual confident swagger, Nick waves a piece of paper. "I didn't stop by to give out etiquette pointers. Do you have a minute to review this brief? It's for an online campaign for National Geographic."

I reach for the brief and Nick taps his foot against Delilah's leg. "Can I break up your girl powwow long enough to go over this with Anna?"

Delilah stands and stretches her arms out to the ceiling. "Sure. I've got to get out of here, anyway. Gotta hit the gym." She points at me as she heads out. "Tomorrow. Lunch, okay? You and me."

I give her the thumbs up sign and mutter, "Sure thing. Have a good night."

Reading through the brief, I don't notice any issues. It's our standard brief based on the existing campaign for banner ads.

Still sitting on the sofa, I glance up at Nick. "I don't see any issues with it. I'll schedule the creative brief for tomorrow." I hop up to send a quick email to the team about the brief. When I pass Nick, he grabs my wrist and whips me around to face him.

"What?"

"I'm here for you, if you need someone."

I back up, moving outside of his reach to regain my space cushion. "What do you mean?"

He takes a step closer, head down so I see more of his eyebrows than his eyes. "You broke up with your boyfriend? I want you to know, I'm here for you."

"Oh, that. Jackson and I worked everything out." I give him a small smile, attempting to mask my discomfort. I take two steps backward, edging toward my computer.

He takes two steps forward. Then he straightens, turns, and heads to the door.

I breathe a sigh of relief.

He pushes the door closed.

My heartrate increases.

"Nick, what are you doing? Open the door." This guy. His demeanor can be so unnerving.

He stalks over to me, eyes dark, head down. Determined. It's not lost on me he didn't open the door like I asked him to. While it's not unusual for him to ignore me, this doesn't feel right.

An inside voice tells me to run. But my professional voice says to stand my ground. I don't want him to have the satisfaction of knowing he makes me uncomfortable. He'll think I'm too young for my role.

He moves around the corner of my desk and towers over me. "Go to dinner with me tonight. I've been thinking about you. Don't you remember how good it was?"

"Nick. Really, enough." This whole thing is getting absurd. "You should go."

In one quick move, he grabs both wrists and pulls them above my head, pressing his body hard against mine.

"Nick, stop!"

"No, think about it. Don't you remember how good we were together? I've been waiting a long time, Anna. This whole waiting game you've got going is getting old. You've been a little fucking cock tease."

I blink. I'm pressed against the wall, both wrists held high above my head.

I try to knee him, but I can't move my legs, my hands captive. I pull on my arms, but I can't move them. I'm trapped. What is he doing?

Nick's sinister glare is new. Trapping me against a wall, is new. His grip on my wrists tightens and hurts. But we are in the office. *Think.* It's not late. Other people will still be in the office. It can't be much past six o'clock. Talk to him. Calm him down. If that fails, scream.

"Nick, stop. Let me go."

"No. Listen. It's time we explore this thing between us. I've been standing by, waiting. That guy, he's not right for you. Don't be afraid of a good thing. What we have. Don't be afraid." He growls into my ear, "Do you get off on teasing me?" His weight presses me into the wall. The helplessness of my situation hits me hard. My heart thunders as desperation threatens to overwhelm me.

"Nick, there is nothing between us. Let. Me. Go. Or I will scream," I say, aiming to sound commanding and firm.

"Yeah?" He twists his head and gives me an eerie half grin.

The point of his nose touches the base of my neck, and revulsion surges. His wet tongue licks up along my neck. Nausea, fear, and helplessness intermingle. I jerk, and his hands grip my wrists harder. Pain radiates through my hands and arms. I squirm, and he presses his full weight against me. A hardness that might be his erection presses into my belly, and I freeze. I do not want to turn him on.

He sneers. "Scream. Who are they going to believe? Your version of the story or mine? I'm best friends with the owners. I play with their kids. Know their wives. You think they'll pick you over me?" He pauses and nips at my earlobe. "You want me. Give in to us."

I flatten my head against the wall. Tears spring to my eyes. I knew Nick was creepy, but I never thought he would hurt me. Never saw him as demented. Crazy. He places both of my wrists under the hold of one his large hands. His free hand drops along my side then squeezes my breast.

Holy shit. What is he going to do? Rape me in my office at work with people right outside? What defense moves do I know? I wriggle more, trying to get away. But he's too big, and I don't have any room. I need more space to get a leg free and kick him hard with my boots or to at least knee up, but I can't. He physically overpowers me. Helpless. I'm helpless.

His grip intensifies as I struggle. Pain shoots through my wrists. "Ow. You're hurting me!" I need him to back off enough so I can fight.

An angry deep voice shoots through the room, "Let her go. *Now!*"

Nick startles. He drops my wrist and steps backward, as if stung. Jackson stands in the doorway. Silent tears stream down my cheeks, and my knees wobble.

I stumble past Nick to reach Jackson.

Nick taunts, "Well, if it isn't the little boyfriend."

Jackson lunges past me, fist in the air, free-falling straight into Nick.

I scream.

Jackson's fists keep flying, pushing Nick down over my desk.

Nick's fists swing, but within seconds he's huddled, hands over his face in a defensive stance.

I back out in the hall and scream, "Help!" Someone has to be in the office.

John comes running down the hall. "Anna?"

I point toward my office door. The sound of glass shattering rings from inside as my lamp crashes to the floor. John rushes past me into my office with his assistant Jamie following close behind.

John pulls Jackson back, and Jamie spreads his arms out to block Nick. Blood runs down Nick's face near his left eye and under his hairline on his forehead.

John yells, "What the fuck is going on?"

Nick points at Jackson and screams, "He attacked me!"

Jackson growls at him, anger pouring off in waves. John grips Jackson's shoulder, forcing him back. "Who are you?"

Jackson points to me as he gasps for air, and I step forward. "He's my boyfriend."

John whips his head around, taking in the scene. The broken lamp on the floor, the mess on my desk, a bloody Nick. "What the hell is going on in here?"

Jackson steps back to rest against the wall. John keeps one arm pinned to him, as if he's a loose wild animal.

"I opened the door to her office and found Nick holding her against the wall, wrists pinned above her head."

John glares at Nick then lets Jackson go. He pulls his phone out of his back jeans pocket and dials. "Hey, Margaret. Have you made it to the station yet?" Pause. "Can you come back here? We have an urgent situation." Pause. "Thanks."

John shifts his attention to Nick. "Head to my office and wait in there."

Nick scowls but he does as directed. After taking a couple of steps into the hall, he turns around and grumbles, "This is bullshit.

She's been coming on to me for months. You can't believe anything that crazy bitch says."

John raises his arm to point down the hall and commands, "Nick. Now. To my office. Margaret will be here shortly, and she'll talk to you. Jamie, can you go with him and get something to put on his cuts?"

Eyes big as saucers, Jamie nods and follows Nick down the hall.

After they are out of sight, John places a gentle hand on my shoulder and in a quiet, calm voice, asks, "What happened, Anna?"

My hands tremble, and tears fall without control. "I'm sorry I'm crying. This is crazy."

John leads me to the sofa and picks up a tissue box and hands it to me. "Margaret will be here soon. She'll handle this from an HR perspective. I just want to know…what happened?"

Jackson leans back against my desk, his cheeks still flushed red. He clearly wants to hear too. Blood shines on the edge of his knuckles as his hands grip my desk.

I try to calm my breathing and my sniffles. My fingers quiver. "It happened so fast. Nick came in with a creative brief. I told him it was fine, and I was walking past him to schedule the brief with my team, and he grabbed me and pushed me up against the wall." I think back. Trying to remember the order of things. It's a sort of dark blur. "He kissed me. Licked my throat." I grimace remembering how disgusting his saliva felt. "I tried to get away. I told him I'd scream. He told me no one would believe my side." I stare at the carpet then up at Jackson. "Then Jackson told him to let me go."

Nothing happened. Not really. He didn't hurt me. Hit me. Rape me. But I can't stop the tears.

"Is this the first time he's come on to you?" John asks.

Jackson speaks up, his voice firm and angry. "No."

No part of me wants to tell John everything that has happened between Nick and me. Jackson doesn't even know a fraction of it.

And I don't want to tell him either. I focus on the leg of the coffee table and the thick gray carpet.

Jackson takes my silence as opportunity to speak. He points at John and demands, "Nick needs to go. Fire him. Fire him, or Anna quits. Fire him, or you will have one hell of a sexual harassment case against your company."

I snap my head up. What gives him the right to make demands at my workplace? Lawyer Jackson needs to leave.

John pushes out his chest and moves to stand in front of Jackson. "This is my company. I'll find out what's going on, and it will be handled," John responds in a calm tone laced with anger. The two men face each other, shoulders back, hands to their sides, like two cowboys in a ridiculous western.

A flurry of emotions rips through me. Embarrassment. Relief. Residual fear. No part of me wants to be weak, and this whole situation made me weak. I try to stifle the tears, but they keep falling.

The tension in the room between Jackson and John rises. A wave of exhaustion settles over me. "Jackson, what are you even doing here? You need to leave."

"Anna, I won't allow you to keep working here. Not if he's here. No way." He's angry. Possessive. Dominating. He's treating me like a possession. Something he owns.

Anger surges to become my dominant emotion, crushing all the others swirling within. "You won't allow me? Are you out of your mind? On what planet do you own me?"

He scowls. "It's not about owning you. I care about you. You don't know what that sick fuck might've done. He trapped you against a wall. There was nothing you could've done."

I stand and shriek, "I had it handled! Get out! You don't own me. Get. Out!"

Jackson's eyes widen, and he jerks back away from me, as if punched.

John places his hand on Jackson's shoulder. "Come on. If you don't mind, I'll have Margaret talk to you first. But after talking to HR, you need to respect Anna's wishes and leave." John squeezes Jackson's shoulder with a fatherly kindness I don't understand. A moment ago, the two men were on the precipice of flinging fists.

Once both men are gone, I curl up on my sofa and sob, hugging a pillow to my chest.

———

Margaret, our head of HR, taps on my door. She wears her white hair up in a grandmotherly high bun, but her smooth skin and sharp eyes are those of a younger woman. She's kind but can be quite stern. I don't know her well, but I liked her from the moment I met her when I was first hired.

With a gentle, kind touch, she pulls the hair away from my face and offers me another tissue. "It sounds like you have a lot to tell me."

I exhale in a loud, calming puff. Might as well get this over with. "There's not a lot to tell. Do you want me to start from the beginning?"

She nods. An open notebook rests on her lap, a pen in hand.

I start from the moment Nick came into my office and tell her everything. I mention he asked Delilah to leave. I blow my nose after I finish and think of one more thing. "That brief was so standard and straightforward, he could have emailed it to me."

Margaret nods. She's been silent up until now. "Now, tell me everything, going back to the first time he acted inappropriately."

I close my eyes. This is what I hadn't wanted to get into. "It's really just little stuff. Nothing big or worth reporting to HR. He asked me out, and I always said no. He'd touch me, but not in such a way I was scared, just annoyed. He just doesn't seem to respect personal space."

Margaret nods repeatedly, scribbling away in her notebook. Her bright blue eyes pierce me. "I need you to tell me everything. You need to be aware I have already met with your friend Jackson, and I've also met with Nick. I have Nick's full version of events. I need to have everything from your perspective."

Shit. He told her. He used that one drunken night to make it look like I wanted him. Like I asked for him. My chin trembles and heat radiates from my cheeks. "I never wanted anyone at work to know about this, but I guess…" Great. I have to tell her. I feel like I'm telling my mom about the night I lost control and did bad things.

Margaret sets her pen down on the notebook and waits.

"A long time ago, like over eight or nine months ago, maybe longer, I went to one of Nick's apartment parties. I don't…" I pause, twisting my hands in my lap. "I came from the office and hadn't eaten. I drank. A lot. Blacked out. Woke up in Nick's bed." I'm not Catholic, but this is how I suspect a confessional feels. "I don't remember it at all, but I slept with Nick."

She does not look surprised. In her kind voice, she asks, "What happened in the morning?"

"I left without waking him."

She scribbles in her notebook then asks, "How did you feel?"

I stare at the wall as I try to remember what I've tried so hard to forget. "I felt horrible. Extremely hungover. I don't think I've been that hungover ever in my life." I pause and gaze out my office window. "And that's saying a lot. I was so sick."

Her lips turn up in a semblance of a smile while she writes. "How many drinks do you remember having that night?"

My gaze returns to Margaret. I've thought a lot about the party, trying to piece together how it went so wrong. "I only remember my second beer. He had a keg, and I was on my second beer in a red Solo cup." Almost speaking to myself, I tell her, "It's a bit of a mystery. You would think I'd remember taking shots or something." Frustration and annoyance with myself mingle when I ponder my stupidity around colleagues. I made it through college without doing something so foolish. Then when I do screw up, I risk my career. "I must have switched to liquor."

"Did the two of you talk about it afterward?"

I swallow. "Yeah. He came up to me at work. Told me he'd enjoyed, well, he'd had fun the night before. I told him it couldn't happen again. It was after that that things started getting more, I don't know...I avoided him. He didn't seem to want to accept I wasn't interested in him. Delilah has witnessed some things. She did encourage me to go to HR a few times."

Margaret tilts her head, questioning. "Why didn't you?"

Tears well up once again and I stare out the window in a vain attempt to not cry. "It didn't feel like it was that bad. I felt like I had it under control. And I don't want to have this on my record. For people to think of me as the woman who filed sexual harassment."

No matter what people want to think, it's naive to believe a sexual harassment case doesn't put a blemish on a person. It's not that companies wouldn't hire someone with that shadow. But any hiring manager in her right mind, when comparing similarly qualified candidates, is going to go with the one without any legal risk. The candidate who plays well in the sandbox. And in an incestuous industry like advertising...well, rumors fly.

Margaret's face contorts in a way I suspect means she disagrees with me. Maybe everyone disagrees with me. But I have good reasons. Who would have ever thought he'd go psycho? A jerk? Yes, he was a jerk. But not a rapist.

I mutter defensively, "I really did have it under control. Until today. I don't know why Jackson was here." Damn him for being right. I didn't have it under control. Not today. Not really. I'd been fucking helpless. The tears I tried to hold back stream down my cheeks unchecked once again.

Margaret spreads her hands out over her notes. "Well, it sounds like you are lucky he was here."

"I really thought I had it under control." I need to defend myself, so I ramble on. "At first, I thought he was just being his normal pushy self. Then, before I knew it, he had me trapped." That helpless sensation. I never want to experience it again. "I threatened to scream, and he told me to scream, that everyone would take his side." And hadn't that been the root of my fear from the beginning of this mess? That I'd be made out to be the bad person? They'd believe him over me? I rub my hand over my face and smear the tears. More to myself than to Margaret, I say, "If Jackson hadn't come in right then, would I have screamed?"

The question hits me like a wrecking ball. Would I have screamed? Or would I have been so scared of losing my job, of others not believing me, would I have let him rape me? Or would I have been too stunned to scream? Or would he have covered my mouth and taken the choice away? My body shivers as the questions boomerang through my head.

"Listen, we won't ever know what might have happened. But if you had come to HR earlier, then what happened in your office probably would never have happened. If someone is out of line, I'm here to help you."

"I know. I do know that. I just didn't feel it necessary, and I felt…" I pause, searching for the right words.

Margaret surveys me. "You felt responsible for what was happening because of what happened at his apartment?"

I sniffle. "Yes." My voice quivers, and yet more tears fall.

"Anna, look at me." She squeezes my arm. "You did nothing wrong. Having a history with you does not give him the right to force himself on you. He had no right to treat you in any way other than in a professional manner. If it's okay with you, I'm going to talk to Delilah tomorrow."

She sounds like she's asking a question, so I offer an answer, although it's difficult to imagine I have a say. "Yeah, that's fine." I pause. Hold my breath. Then ask, "Am I in trouble?" My boyfriend attacked an executive, and that executive has a different version of events than I do. This is the big stain on my career I didn't want, in an agency where I love working.

"No, you are not in trouble. But I was going to ask you if you might want to take some time off. A day or two? When these things happen, it can be emotional. I'd like to encourage you to at least take the rest of this week off."

Given I can't seem to stop crying, I can't argue against taking time off.

She wraps her arms around me in a gentle, warm hug. Tears unleash. Again. Exactly why I usually refuse hugs when emotional.

She uses her thumb to wipe tears away then passes me the box of tissue.

"Thank you, Margaret."

With a sad smile, she offers, "You can call me Maggie."

thirty-four

ANNA

Margaret leads me down the hall to reception. Jackson sits in a chair, head resting in his hands, elbows on his knees. When he hears us, he lifts his head.

"Hey, what are you still doing here?" I had no idea he'd been waiting this whole time.

"Waiting for you. I have a car service sitting outside waiting to take us home." Of course, he does. The gesture strikes me as thoughtful and sweet. And those are some of the reasons I love him. He is a really good guy and I love he wants to be here for me. But I've got to talk to him. Going caveman in my business and with my career is not okay.

Margaret says goodnight and heads back into the agency. He wraps his strong arms around me as we wait for the elevator and I sink into his chest.

Neither of us speaks as we get into the back of a black sedan. The city streets pass by, and I gaze out the window, watching the myriad of pedestrians rushing along the sidewalks. Did they have a good day at work? Are they rushing home to a loved one?

Jackson's deep, calm voice breaks into the random thoughts swirling around. "John had security escort Nick out. He had a box of personal belongings. I overheard John mention he hoped Nick would take them up on their offer for therapy. It sounds like they are offering to get him help in the form of therapy. Can you believe that?"

I close my eyes. A sense of relief percolates. It's over. I may never have to see Nick again. I rest my head against Jackson's chest and cuddle into his side. "Do you think that means they believe me?"

"I threatened legal action. I'm the last person they would share information with. But I suspect you aren't the first employee who has had issues with Nick."

"Really?" I vaguely recall Delilah mentioning someone in accounting, but had she gone to HR? I don't think so. Could it have been someone else?

Jackson kisses my forehead. "I expect they are going to handle the situation correctly. If they don't, I'll handle it." His tone smacks of authority and determination.

"You," I say. I don't want to fight. I need him near me, and I don't want to create distance between us. Not tonight. But we have to talk this out. "You can't do that."

He shifts so he can see me better. Cautious.

I soften my tone but remain serious. "I make my career decisions. You do not."

He lifts my hand to his lips and kisses it. Closes his eyes. When he opens them, sincerity and love pour out. "I don't want to force decisions on you. Christ, Anna. Can you understand at all what it did to me to walk into your office and see him holding you against the wall? I stood there, shocked, trying to comprehend what I was walking in on. I heard him threaten you. Tell you no one would believe your side. The anger. Anna, seeing someone hurt you. I could have killed him. Thank god John broke us up. I…I've never done that, Anna." His shoulders slump as he stares out the car window. "Attacked someone."

I lift his hands and examine his knuckles and place soft kisses along the broken skin. "I'm so sorry," I whisper.

He lifts my chin. "No. You have nothing to be sorry for. You didn't do anything wrong."

I lean my head back against the car seat. I could have handled things differently. Maybe.

I open my eyes. A question has lingered in my mind. "What were you doing at my office?"

A sheepish expression I've never seen before flits across his face. "I wanted to surprise you for dinner. I thought you might have heard Eleanor in the hallway. She asked me to dinner. I didn't want you to worry."

"I trust you." I tighten my hold on him.

"Good."

"Do you have your own little issue going on in the office?"

He exhales a half laugh. "Not a Nick situation. Our office orders dinner in all the time when working late on a case. Eleanor and I are finishing up a contract. When I couldn't do lunch, she asked about dinner. I told her no for tonight. Told her I had plans with my girlfriend."

A weight hangs over me. I gently hold on to Jackson's hand, aware of the broken skin, but needing to touch him as I unload. "Jackson, what happened with Nick? It might…some of it might have been my fault."

"What do you mean?"

"Nick and I. Almost a year ago, we hooked up at an office party at his condo. I was really drunk. I don't remember it." I brace myself, preparing for Jackson to pull away, but he doesn't. Shame and humiliation prevent me from looking up at him.

His hold on me tightens. "That doesn't make this your fault. One drunken hook-up does not give him any rights to you. Anna, believe me. You did not deserve this." He places a soft kiss on my forehead. "Anna, I love you so much."

"Still?"

"Yes, still. For always. A drunken mistake doesn't change who you are. I love you. And I will stand by you. Always."

The car pulls up to our apartment building on 82nd Street. The streetlights cast a warm glow on the winter night. Bundled up for the cold, we hustle to get into the warm lobby. The glass doors slide open as we approach, and we enter, hand in hand.

epilogue - anna

10 Months Later

Anna

"The last box! We. Are. Done!" Jackson shouts.

With a dramatic salute, Chase raises an arm sky-high, and the two men high-five over a stack of boxes.

Yes, we could have afforded movers, but given all we're moving is boxes, we opted for the friends and U-Haul route. There's no furniture to move, only boxes. One U-Haul rental, one afternoon with friends, plus the promise of beer and pizza, and our whole life moved from the Upper East Side to the Lower West Side.

Jackson and I have officially been living together for the last six months. Ever practical, he kept pointing out it's ridiculous to pay two New York rents. His apartment felt larger and was a true two-bedroom, but it came furnished. It couldn't hold my furniture, so he moved into my apartment.

Then our relationship faced its biggest trial to date. Not living together. House hunting together.

Jackson insisted on buying an apartment. He sold his place in Atlanta, so he needed to buy something to avoid capital gains tax penalties. Our house hunting disagreements did lead me to question if we were meant to be. He loved the new modern glass building by the river, the XI. The new construction building boasts huge windows with amazing views, an indoor pool, and a full gym. The building is a dream, but all the white marble feels cold to me. Not to mention it's crazy expensive.

I insisted I would pay half of whatever we bought. I told him it was important to me and I inherited money from my parents and can afford to invest. I debated the wisdom of buying a place with my boyfriend. A joint mortgage would complicate a breakup.

But somewhere during our home search is when I knew without a doubt I was in it with Jackson for the absolute long haul. Because, one, every time we visited a place I didn't like, I stood up to him. I asked him to lower his target price so I could go in 50/50. We approached it like partners, real partners. When I had an issue, I told him. We worked through it all.

He helped me be my best self. We worked through each disagreement. Jackson loves to cover all points of an argument, so he had no issues with rounds and rounds of discussions. I needed to prove to myself I could be with someone and be strong and maintain my identity. Possibly to Jackson's chagrin, I have no issue at all standing up to him now.

"Hello, peoples!" Olivia calls from the hall. She and Delilah wander in through the open door, weighed down with pizza boxes and beer.

"Come on in. Let's head up to the terrace," I say, directing everyone to the stairs. Yep, our new penthouse apartment has stairs. I never thought I'd live in such an incredible space.

Our compromise, an older doorman building on 28th Street, lies near the Hudson River. Our apartment boasts huge windows with views of the river and city. The nine-hundred-square-foot private rooftop terrace sold us both. The terrace alone is bigger than our entire apartment on 82nd Street. The moment we saw it, we knew we'd found our home.

Of course, wallpaper hung on every single wall. I had no idea people still used wallpaper. So while we closed two weeks ago, we're only moving in now. I insisted we remove all wallpaper and paint before moving in. While the renovation magic happened, we decked out the terrace. New outdoor furniture, heat lamps, and Jackson's dream grill. I may have gone a little insane on plants and hanging lights.

Everyone follows me up the iron stairs.

"Wow!" Olivia exclaims when she steps onto the roof. This is the first time our friends are seeing our place. I knew they'd be pretty impressed.

Olivia arrived back from Prague two days ago. She's currently staying with Delilah but will be moving into my old apartment tomorrow. Well, our old apartment. All of her old furniture awaits her, including the lumpy, stained futon. Her MBA program at Columbia University starts next week.

Delilah is now a fellow creative director. I celebrated her promotion more than mine, because I'd much prefer my close friend not be reporting to me.

I never saw Nick again. It did turn out I wasn't the only employee at Evolve he'd harassed. Margaret shared she suspected Nick had used a date rape drug on me. No evidence existed, and I chose not to pursue charges. But Evolve didn't need any further proof to fire him for sexual harassment and inappropriate conduct since I had a witness in the office.

At Margaret's insistence, I did meet with a therapist for several sessions. I found the experience to be positive. Hearing a third party tell me I wasn't in the wrong meant more to me than I would have ever imagined. Talking through my emotions helped to mitigate my pain and fear.

Chase, Delilah, Olivia, Bobby, Jackson, and I gather around our outdoor picnic table. Back in the day when we were at Chapel Hill, we never hired movers. It was always a friends-helping-friends thing. This moment, drinking beer and eating pizza straight from the box, it's bittersweet. This might be the last time we gather friends together to move. Next time, we'll have real adult furniture. Like real, heavier-than-Ikea furniture that requires a moving truck and professional can-wrap-it-in-quilts movers.

Bobby holds up a glass. "A toast! Here's to Anna and Jackson. Here's to you finding such an insane apartment with a kick-ass terrace."

Everyone clinks glasses. Chase holds his up and adds, "And just so you two are clear, we will be over here. A lot."

The sound of laughter rings across the terrace. Jackson wraps his arm around me and softly kisses my forehead. Chewie moves from spot to spot on the terrace, sniffing. Our furry beast may love the terrace more than any of us.

"So, when are you two going to make this whole thing official?" Chase asks.

Jackson gazes at me and grins. He answers Chase, but those hazel eyes stay with me. "We are official. This is it." His hand finds mine under the table and squeezes as I lean into him.

Yeah, he's absolutely right. This is it. *It* being the relationship for me. The relationship where I am the best me. Maybe we could have had this four—well, now, five—years ago if I'd been less afraid of the whole relationship thing, of turning into who I was in a relationship with my high school boyfriend, of repeating mistakes. Maybe. But timing played a big part too. I don't think I would have been strong enough or confident enough to be a good partner back then. I believe I would have slipped into old habits. Become dependent. Lost myself. I needed to walk away from Jackson before I could be with Jackson. I had to find myself on my own before I could find myself with someone else.

The sun sets, and the city lights grow brighter as day transitions to night. I sit back in Jackson's arms, listening to our friends. The low hum of heat lamps surrounds us. Bobby kicks back, legs stretched out, beer in hand. Olivia entertains everyone with stories of her adventures in Prague. Delilah tells us about a recent speed dating event. Chase joins in the conversation from time to time. He's working on lining up late-night plans with his flavor of the week.

Jackson kisses my ear and whispers, "We are official, right?"

I smile up at him. He doesn't need to ask that. We're cosigners on a mortgage. I whisper back, "Yeah, we're official. I'm all yours. And you're mine."

His lips graze my cheek as he grumbles, "It's about time."

epilogue - jackson

1 year later

Jackson

On my first date with Anna, I knew I'd marry her. Or, at least, I was fairly certain. A few months later, I was fairly certain I'd never been more wrong in my life.

Four years later, when those elevator doors opened, I had to blink several times. I couldn't believe it was her. I'd seen her as a bad judgment call from my law school days. Someone I had no desire to cross paths with again.

I couldn't believe I'd ended up in her apartment building. On her floor. Somewhere around the time I discovered she didn't sleep with my roommate, it started to feel like kismet. Not that I believe in that kind of thing. But still, what are the odds?

I took it slow. Did I really want friends with benefits? Hell, no. Does anyone really believe friends with benefits works? It seemed like an excellent strategy, a way for me to get Anna without the timing obligation of a girlfriend. Who am I kidding? It was a way for me to get Anna without scaring her off. Without facing up to my feelings. Intense feelings that terrified me.

The day I left work early to surprise her and take her out to dinner…well, I knew then. I knew I wanted more than a girlfriend. I wanted her for life.

We've been living together for almost two years now, one year in this Chelsea apartment we bought together. I would have been more than happy to buy us a place, but that's not how my girl rolls. And I'm okay with that. While, yes, I would like to take care of her, I'll take her any way I can get her. I want her as my partner in life.

I bought a ring before we ever moved into the Chelsea apartment. It was kind of a backup Hail Mary plan if I pushed too hard and pissed her off during the stressful apartment hunting process.

Every day, I love coming home to her. Waking up with her. Going on our morning runs together. Watching her while she works at her computer or when she's painting. Hearing about her day. Telling her about mine. If I leave for the office before she does, I still leave her a Post-it note by the coffee machine. Because, tradition.

She's the love of my life. I've known this since our first date. I've questioned it at times, sure, but I haven't questioned it since we've been living together. Even during heated disputes during sofa selection, I've never questioned it.

The ring sat in the back of my drawer for over a year. Not because I questioned us. Life just got busy.

I've been waiting for signs. Signs Anna is ready for the next step. Proof the timing's right. I don't walk on eggshells around her. That's not me. And I know she's all in. She's committed to us. There's no confusion on that point. Blurred lines are a thing of our past. But I haven't wanted to rush her.

She was recently promoted to group creative director. The promotion did come with more responsibility, managing more teams, and overseeing more accounts. From my perspective, she's become John's right-hand man. We've become close to his family and went to his wife's surprise birthday party last weekend.

I finally made senior partner. I'm now head of a new full-service M&A division for our firm. The division I lead brought in forty percent of our firm's overall revenue last year. So, hell, yeah. Check. That. Box.

Anna has supported me every step of the way. If I have to work late or on weekends, she never complains. She'll go into her home office or hang out on the couch and work away herself. Sometimes she paints, sometimes she works on her computer with campaigns. Our home is filled with her art, and I wouldn't have it any other way.

Before Anna, work was my life. Anna stepped in, and didn't take me away from work, but she added everything that matters to my life. Each day, I push myself to get home to her. Even if I have to bring work home, I'd rather work beside her, near her. Yes, being named senior partner is a great milestone. But my life wouldn't have meaning without Anna in it.

Yesterday, I discovered an EPT box below her bathroom sink when I was hunting for a Band-Aid. It could have been from ages ago, or it could be an unused box from when Olivia had a scare. She still has an IUD, so I doubt that EPT box is for her. Regardless, the box shone like a neon sign flashing a message. *It's time. Put a ring on it.*

Total formality. We're already committed. She is my forever. If she's pregnant, my traditional side wants us to be married. Even if she's not, it's time. I want to believe Anna's ready. My stomach is as unsettled as it used to be before a high school lacrosse game.

I've thought of a million different ways to propose. I mean, I've had this ring for over a year. Finally, though, I decided my proposal should be at home. Our home where we've selected every single piece of furniture together, where the photographs on the walls and the paintings are hers. Our home—the place that holds so many of my favorite memories of us.

I've consulted with Delilah and Olivia, and to a lesser degree, Bobby. And to an even lesser degree, Chase.

The whole apartment is lit with candles. I bought a gourmet dinner from Zagar's and set the oven to warm the food, placing everything in pans for my version of a homecooked meal.

She unlocks the door to our apartment, pushes it open, and immediately stops.

"What's going on?" she asks as Chewie bounces out to greet her mommy.

I take her coat, close the heavy door, and plant a soft kiss on her neck then her lips. "Can't I surprise you with a little romance?" I hold my hand out to Chu and say, "Place." She trots off like the well-trained dog she is to her doggie bed.

Anna tilts her head with a suspicious grin on her face. Then her arms wrap around my neck, and she pulls me down for a slow, passionate kiss. A kiss that makes me forget my entire plan. I've waited for over two years. Six years, if you want to go back to our first date. But suddenly, I can't wait anymore.

I drop to one knee, right by our apartment door. We're in the entry hall, and most of the candles I set up are at the end of the hall in the living area. But I need to do it now. Right now.

Her eyes widen. I fear she might step back, but she doesn't. Those golden-brown eyes start to glisten. This is it.

"Anna, you've been my partner for years now. You make me whole. You make me a better man. I'm committed to you for the rest of my life. Will you make it official? Will you marry me?"

She gasps a little. She can't really be surprised, can she? I mean, it was a matter of when, not if.

She gets down on her knees, so she is my equal. She places both hands on my cheeks and pulls me in for a kiss. A soft kiss at first, and then as it starts to deepen, I break away.

"So, is that a yes?"

A few tears escape down her cheeks. "Yes." She sniffles. "Of course, it's a yes."

I slip the ring on her finger, and she holds out her hand then grins. "I've been wondering when you'd think the timing was right."

"Are you kidding me?" I suppress the urge to tickle her until she can't breathe.

She bites her lip, fighting back a smile. "I found the ring ages ago. I've just been waiting." She wiggles her ring hand and squints as she studies it. "I wasn't sure why you were waiting. But I knew it would all work out."

"How'd you know?"

Her cheeks blush. My girl doesn't blush as often anymore. I squeeze her hip in a silent question. She hesitates, then tells me, "Moments before you moved into 82nd Street, a white pigeon flew around. Al said it was a sign. I didn't think much of it. On the day we moved out, Al pulled me aside. Reminded me of the pigeon. Said a white pigeon is a sign of big change, an impending engagement. Said you and I, we're meant to be."

"A pigeon? That's our sign?" She's the creative. I'll go with it if she wants.

"Nah. Not really. How I feel when you hold me? When you enter the room? That's our sign."

———

Grad student Olivia's life changes forever when she meets charismatic billionaire Sam Duke, and he pulls her into a world fraught with unexpected dangers. He'll do anything to keep her safe--and to make her his.

Read on in Trust Me.

notes & gratitude

When this book released in January of 2020 under the title "When the Stars Align," the title had as much to do about where I was in life as anything. I didn't know if I'd ever write another book or if I'd sell more than two copies of this one.

Five years later, I've published over twenty books and I'm revisiting this first series on the advice of "experts" to bring the series more in line with the Isabel Jolie brand and to arrive at a more uniform naming system and cover design.

When I started, I was all over the place— exploring, really. But this series remains close to my heart because it's my first and it takes place in the city where I spent my twenties and early thirties...my wonder years.

This book, now titled Blurred Lines, covers a heavy topic - sexual harassment. The kind of thing that happens to Anna happens to women all the time. Maybe not as aggressively, but to degrees. I was at a gathering of parent council mothers, and we were chatting about life in corporate America, and almost every single woman standing in the circle had a story to share. One of my early readers asked why Anna just didn't go to HR, as if that was the easy answer. It's not. I'd say it's not even advisable to go to HR unless one absolutely must. There are so many reasons to not go to HR. One of the women in that circle was in HR and she agreed, saying that while she always is supportive and plays a friendly role (along the lines of 'Call me Maggie'), HR is looking out for the company and has to launch a full investigation. They have to hear both sides. They can't just choose one version over another. It works out for Anna because she wasn't the only one and she had a witness. But without a doubt, going to HR is the equivalent of rolling dice. Not everyone has the Instagram following to add the #metoo and see the desired result.

There are self-defense groups that empower women by giving them defense moves should they ever be pinned against a wall. They aren't full proof, but they are helpful. One group I am familiar with is SASS www.sassdefense.com. Self-defense training is a good idea for all women.

This book wouldn't exist without my husband. When I first told him I wanted to try this - this being writing - he never laughed at me or told me I was out of my mind. He's always been my biggest supporter. Admittedly, he loves this particular adventure and at first, he told his friends I was writing porn. I had to explain it's not really porn, it's called romance. So, he's not perfect. But he is proud and supportive.

Along those same lines, I have a group of women friends. The sexy six. They were my first friends I "came out to" with this little endeavor of mine. These gals also never told me I was crazy. They've been supportive and I am forever thankful to have such a great group of amazing friends looking out for each other.

Ada and Jenn, the two of you are my first beta readers ever, and I'm so grateful to you both for your insight and feedback for this book and others along the way. It was super hard, for me, to let someone else read this and both of you made that first experience positive. And we romance writers know how important our firsts are.

Lori Whitwam took my unpolished draft, fixed all my errors, pointed out overused words and not only edited the piece but taught me so much. I'm looking forward to working with her in the future as I work to improve and grow as a writer.

And, of course, thank you to S.K., my neighbor growing up, (and also a bridesmaid!), for our text exchanges on books, suggestions for authors to read, and your ongoing encouragement. So thankful for our friendship.

And thank you to my readers! Five years ago, I wasn't sure anyone would read...and I'm so grateful to those who do. THANK YOU!

also by isabel jolie

Arrow Tactical Security Series

Better to See You (Wolf and Alexandria)

Sure of One (Jack and Ava)

Cloak of Red (Sophia and Fisher)

Stolen Beauty (Knox and Sage)

Savage Beauty (Max and Sloane) - Releasing June 6th

Sinful Beauty (Tristan and Lucia) - Releasing September 12th

Gilded Saint (Sam and Willow) - Releasing December 5th

The Twisted Vines Series

Crushed (Erik and Vivi)

Breathe (Kairi and David)

Savor (Trevor and Stella)

Haven Island Series

Rogue Wave (Tate and Luna)

Adrift (Gabe and Poppy)

First Light (Logan and Cali)

The West Side Series

When the Stars Align (Jackson and Anna)

Trust Me (Sam Duke and Olivia)

Walk the Dog (Delilah and Mason)

Lost on the Way (Jason and Maggie)

Chasing Frost (Chase and Sadie)

Misplaced Mistletoe (Ashton aka Dr. Bobby and Nora)

Standalone Romances

How to Survive a Holiday Fling (Oliver Duke and Kate)

Always Sunny (Ian Duke and Sandra)

The Romantics (Harrison and Zuri)

about the author

Isabel Jolie, aka Izzy, lives on a lake, loves dogs of all stripes, and if she's not working, she can be found reading, often with a glass of wine. In prior lives, Izzy worked in marketing and advertising, in a variety of industries, such as financial services, entertainment, and technology. In this life, she loves daydreaming and writing contemporary romances with real, flawed characters with inner strength.

Sign-up for Izzy's newsletter to keep up-to-date on new releases, promotions and giveaways. (**Pro-tip** - She offers a free book on her home page…just scroll down after arriving at her site.)

Buy ebooks and signed paperbacks direct from Isabel at www.isabeljoliebooks.com

Want to say hi? Email her through her website or reply to her newsletter…she loves to hear from readers.